PRAISE FOR MINDY KLASKY

Girl's Guide to Witchcraft

"Mindy Klasky's newest work, Girl's Guide to Witchcraft, joins a love story with urban fantasy and just a bit of humor…. Throw in family troubles, a good friend who bakes Triple-Chocolate Madness, a familiar who prefers an alternative lifestyle plus a disturbingly good-looking mentor and you have one very interesting read." *SF Revu*

Sorcery and the Single Girl

"Klasky emphasizes the importance of being true to yourself and having faith in friends and family in her bewitching second romance…. Readers who identify with Jane's remembered high school social angst will cheer her all the way." *Publishers Weekly*

Magic and the Modern Girl

"Filled with magic—both of the witch world and the romance world—complicated family relationships and a heavy dose of chick-lit humor, this story is the perfect ending to the series." *RT Book Reviews*

Single Witch's Survival Guide

Book Four of the Jane Madison Series

Mindy Klasky

Book View Café
Cedar Crest, New Mexico

Book View Café
P.O. Box 1624
Cedar Crest, NM 87008-1624

Publisher's Note: This is a work of fiction. Names, characters, places, and incidents are a product of the author's imagination. Locales and public names are sometimes used for atmospheric purposes. Any resemblance to actual people, living or dead, or to businesses, companies, events, institutions, or locales is completely coincidental.

Book Layout ©2013 BookDesignTemplates.com
Cover by Reece Notley

Ordering Information:
Quantity sales. Special discounts are available on quantity purchases by corporations, associations, and others. For details, contact the "Special Sales Department" at the address above.

Single Witch's Survival Guide/Mindy Klasky – 1st ed.
ISBN 978-1-61138-303-4

Single Witch's Survival Guide

Also By Mindy Klasky

The Jane Madison Series
Girl's Guide to Witchcraft
Sorcery and the Single Girl
Magic and the Modern Girl
Single Witch's Survival Guide
Joy of Witchcraft

Capitol Magic
Fright Court

The As You Wish Series
Act One, Wish One
Wishing in the Wings
Wish Upon a Star

The Diamond Brides Series
Perfect Pitch
Catching Hell
Reaching First
Second Thoughts
Third Degree
Stopping Short
From Left Field
Center Stage
Always Right

The Glasswrights Series
The Glasswrights' Apprentice
The Glasswrights' Progress
The Glasswrights' Journeyman
The Glasswrights' Test
The Glasswrights' Master

Season of Sacrifice

To Mark –
who helps me find what follows "happily ever after" every day

Chapter 1

THIS IS A story about what follows "happily ever after." After the girl gets the guy, after she outgrows a job she loved, after she figures out who she is and who she wants to be.

Because, really? It doesn't take long for things to go sideways. Sometimes, you don't even realize the entire world is fracturing around you, because on the surface everything seems happy and easy and perfect. Spoiler alert: those are the times you really need to open your eyes. Otherwise, it just might be too late.

"Earth to Jane! Paging Jane Madison!"

I shook my head as I looked up from the smooth orb of rose quartz I balanced on my palm. The stone was supposed to represent love and peace and happiness, but I wasn't getting a hint of spiritual warmth. I was just trying to find a good place to store a rock in the message-carrying that surrounded me. "I'm sorry, Neko," I said. "I wasn't listening."

"Obviously." My familiar clicked his tongue in disapproval. "What I said was, 'What are you doing with *this* garbage?'" He sighed in theatrical disgust as he pinched a slender paperback book between his dainty thumb and fore-finger. His disdain harkened back to his feline roots—Neko might present as a human male now, but he'd begun life as a giant onyx statue of a cat. Many days, I was tempted to send him back to that form.

I cringed as I glanced at the book he was holding. *Better Spellcasting in Seven Days.* The title was picked out in a lurid swirl of purple and pink. Neko started to read from the back cover. "Are your spells low energy? Is your astral focus flagging? Looking for a lift in your magical life?" My familiar raised one leering eyebrow. "I didn't realize you spent good money on magic porn."

"I didn't buy that! They just sent it to me. I've been on some mailing list ever since I registered the magicarium with Hecate's Court."

The magicarium. It had sounded so glamorous when I first came up with the idea: A school for witches. An exclusive institution of higher learning devoted to teaching the extraordinary witch how to access her inner powers. The Jane Madison Academy.

I'd actually shivered the first time I said the name to myself. Problem was, it was a lot easier to complete the Court's registration paperwork than it was to get the academic ball actually rolling. Eight months had gone by, and I was still settling into my new home, the farmhouse owned by my warder and boyfriend, David Montrose.

(Boyfriend! That sounded like I was fifteen years old. But "beau" belonged in a historical romance, and "lover" left too little to the imagination. "Significant other" might appear on some government form. "Steady," "sugar," "flame"… Yeah. Right. My mother called David her sin-in-law, but that didn't exactly help *me*. I'd grit my teeth and live with "boyfriend.")

In any case, the magicarium had been slow getting out of the gate. Here in the Maryland countryside, an hour from Washington DC, I was still unpacking boxes. Still organizing books and crystals and herbs. Still trying to figure out what I'd do if I ever enrolled an actual student. Or hired an actual teacher. Or, really, did anything substantive to make the magicarium more than a figment of my overactive imagination.

David was losing patience with me. *I* was losing patience with me. And that was why I'd vowed on the first day of June that I would have the entire basement organized by the end of the month. Two hours a day. That should have been more than enough to bring order to my magical life.

I didn't need to look at a calendar to know there was only a single weekend left between me and defeat. No problem. I could pull an all-nighter tonight, and Saturday, too. I could stay down here, working without interruption. Without distraction. Without—

"Come and get it!" David's voice rang down the stairs.

Fine. I'd start my marathon after dinner. I needed sustenance to work through the night. Neko followed me up the stairs to the kitchen, and I swore I could hear him smirking with every step.

David was honing a butcher knife against a steel, all of his attention focused on the precise angle of the blade. The overhead light danced off the silver at his temples, mellowing his black hair. His dark brown eyes glinted as he concentrated, relaxed but alert.

A pottery serving platter rested on the center island, cradling a massive grilled steak. Ears of corn nestled in a pottery bowl, their husks perfectly charred, hinting at the roasted kernels inside. Another bowl held thick rings of sweet onion and strips of Anaheim pepper, all speckled with black, testifying to the time they'd spent kissed by fire. A bottle of pinot noir was breathing nearby.

The food was perfect, as much a symphony for my eyes as my nose. Neko clearly thought so as well; a small whine escaped the back of his throat. The sound was matched perfectly by Spot, the oversized black Lab who watched longingly from his plaid bed in the corner of the kitchen.

David laughed. "You," he said to the dog, "have already had your dinner. And you," he nodded toward Neko, "can take down a plate and join us."

Neko sighed dramatically. "I can't. Jacques and I are going to a party." Nevertheless, he leaned in as David made the first cut into the porterhouse, and he stole the end slice with nimble fingers. Moaning in culinary ecstasy, he began to angle for another piece.

"Back, thief!" David said, angling the knife in a mock threat.

Neko pouted, but he edged away. "You could always save us a bite or two…" he bargained.

"You could always grill your own steak," David countered evenly. "One that *you* purchased, using your *own* money, during your *own* trip to the grocery store."

The grandfather clock in the hallway began to toll, and Neko looked shocked at the time. He gulped, "Jacques is waiting for me in the city. We have a birthday party to go to, and our costumes aren't even close to finished."

I felt a little guilty; he'd kept me company all afternoon,

and I didn't have any significant magicarium progress to show. I tried to make up for the wasted time by issuing a witchy command: "*Go!*" I pushed a little power into the word, astral energy that Neko immediately caught up and spun to his best advantage. Without so much as a shimmer, he disappeared from the kitchen. I could give him a magical command to return him to the apartment the guys kept in town, but on the costume front, he was on his own.

I sighed as I retrieved a couple of wine glasses from the cupboard. I really *had* started the day with the best of intentions. I'd imagined I would make it through half the boxes down there, organizing the books, finding appropriate shelves for all the crystals, my runes, and a handful of rowan wands.

Discouraged, I poured the pinot with a generous hand and began to serve up our feast. While I alternated slices of ruby steak with onions and peppers, David shucked the roasted corn. He made short work of it, slicing off the stem end with his sharp blade, then slipping the ear free from silk and husk at the same time.

"Don't burn yourself!" I said.

He grinned. "We're a good month into corn season. I'm an expert by now."

Conceding David's point with a smile, I carried our plates to our cozy kitchen table. *Our* plates. *Our* table. I could hardly believe how easily those words came to me. A lot had changed in the three years since David first appeared as my warder. The first night I met him, I'd thought he was as headstrong and obnoxiously proud as Jane Eyre's Mr. Rochester. To this day, I'd never quite summoned the courage to ask what he'd thought of me on that literally dark and stormy night.

In the intervening years, we'd had a few bumps in the road—failed romances (mine), misapplied witchcraft (mine), dysfunctional family follies (mine). Okay. *I'd* had a few bumps in the road. But David had always been there for me, patient and understanding. And when he'd invited me to move in, I hadn't hesitated a heartbeat.

"What?" he asked, settling his napkin in his lap.

"What what?"

"You were smiling."

I glanced down at my plate, suddenly shy. I *had* been smiling. But that didn't mean I was going to tell him precisely what I'd been thinking. There was no reason to inflate his self-esteem that much. I cut a bite of steak, taking care to add the perfect accent of charred onion. Before I could figure out a reply I was willing to share, the phone rang.

"Saved by the bell," David said wryly.

I glanced over my shoulder and squinted at the Caller ID. CLARA SMYTHE. My mother was the last person I wanted to interrupt our dinner. I'd prefer a million relationship conversations with David over five minutes of Clara's craziness. "Let it go," I said.

"She'll just call you on your cell."

"And I'll let that one go to voicemail too! Stop! Your dinner will get cold!"

"Steak's good at any temperature," David said as he snatched the phone from its receiver on the last ring. I knew he'd grab it. He had to. David was my mother's warder, as much as he was mine.

"Clara!" His voice was soft with a smile. "What a pleasure to hear from you. No, no, we aren't doing anything at all."

I gesticulated toward our plates of food. We *were* doing something. David only shrugged, obviously amused by my mother's so-called offbeat charm. I grimaced.

"Of course," he said. "She's right here. Just a moment." After he passed the phone to me, I covered the receiver.

"You could have told her we were eating dinner!"

"And then she would have called back later. When you didn't have an excuse to get off the phone so quickly."

Well, when he put it like that... I made a quick vow to follow his lead, to be more accommodating, more accepting of the woman who had given birth to me. "Mother!" I said, forcing myself to smile as I spoke.

"Jeanette!"

So much for smiling. I reminded her tersely: "Jane." My mother was the only person in the world who called me Jeanette—the name she'd bestowed on me right before she handed me off to my grandmother and walked out of my life for over two decades. Yielding to Gran's fierce determination over the past few years, Clara and I had reached a sort of detente, a necessary compromise because all three of us held witchy powers. Those powers, though, apparently did not extend to my own mother remembering my preferred name for longer than twenty-seven seconds.

"I hope it's not too late to call, Jeanette." Clara had a casual relationship with time zones. On one call, she was likely to think our Maryland home was six hours ahead of her Arizona retreat. The next time, she'd count in the wrong direction, calculating that we were three hours behind.

"Of course not," I said. "In fact, we were just eating dinner." I shot David a dirty look as he took an enthusiastic bite of steak. He didn't even bother to look abashed while he chewed and swallowed.

"Ah…" Clara sighed with obvious distress, as if I'd just told her about some wicked man who spent his days kicking kittens. I could picture her as she exhaled—flyaway hair more red than my own, bright hazel eyes glinting beneath an oil slick of dramatic gold eyeshadow. She certainly wore one of her caftans, its long silk panels carefully chosen to complement her current aura. Or to counter the energy of the Vortex being out of balance. Or whatever crazy idea she was playing with in Sedona that day. "I thought you might be doing a working. Something for the Academy."

"Not tonight," I said, squelching another flicker of annoyance at the unsubtle prod. If she truly believed I might be in the middle of a magical project, then why was she interrupting?

"Hmmm," Clara said. "I take it my present hasn't arrived yet."

"Present?" I had no idea what she was talking about. I raised an eyebrow toward David, but he only shrugged.

"Your *birthday* present," Clara said, as if that made perfect sense.

"Birthday?" I was starting to feel pretty stupid here.

"Your natal anniversary, Jeanette. The one you use as the basis for all of your astrological readings."

I wanted to remind my mother that I didn't *do* astrological readings. Spells, yes. Runes, sure. Drawing on the powers of plants and crystals, of the entire natural world, those were all parts of my magic. But I'd never given credence to the supposed magic of the stars, even though—maybe *because*—astrology was high on Clara's personal list of witchy pursuits.

"Jane," I corrected her again. "And, um, my birthday was in January."

David was obviously following enough of our conversation to be amused. He reached for the wine bottle and added a bit to his glass. He filled mine as well—I wasn't aware that I'd emptied it. I flashed him a grateful smile as Clara tsked.

"Well, of *course* your birthday was in January. What kind of mother would I be if I didn't know that?" What kind, indeed? "I've sent you a gift for this *coming* January. Two gifts, actually. To make up for missing this past year."

I used my free hand to snag a few curls at my nape, tugging hard as a reminder to keep my temper. "You didn't need to do that."

"I know, Jeanette. But sometimes you find the perfect thing, and you just can't help but send it along."

I could hardly imagine what would count as "perfect" in Clara's book, but the doorbell rang before I could select the words for an appropriate lie. Its chime was deep and sonorous, and I leaped to my feet as if I were late for church. "Whoops!" I said into the phone. "There's someone at the door. I have to run."

"Happy, happy birthday, Jeanette." Clara sounded so satisfied, I actually forgot to correct her about my name. Instead, I hung up the phone and looked across at David.

"Expecting anyone?" I asked.

He scowled, all of his good humor about Clara evaporating. "Absolutely not." He pushed himself back from the table with a muttered curse.

"Steak's good at any temperature," I reminded helpfully as I followed him down the hall. Spot padded beside me, a casual watchdog.

David peered out the window in the top half of the door. Through the rippled glass, I could just distinguish a vague shape in the darkness. *Two* vague shapes, I corrected after David palmed on the porch light. He opened the door with a tight smile. "May I help you?"

A blast of humid summer air rolled over the threshold. The two women on our porch looked rather the worse for wear.

The taller one was dressed all in black, a peasant skirt with a handkerchief hem and a clingy top that left absolutely nothing to the imagination. Her hair was dyed to match her attire—long black waves that tumbled to her waist, with a single streak of purple flashing above her right eyebrow. Her makeup was pasted on to emphasize her cheekbones, and her lips were slicked with enough gloss to last me for an entire year. Half a dozen silver rings twined around her fingers and thumbs, and a matching pendant glinted in the hollow between her ample breasts.

She looked like a refugee from a Seventies party, by way of a pagan convention. Despite all that vintage attire, though, she extended a smartphone toward us, obviously using the device to film our encounter. She backed up half a step as I came to David's side, and she nodded at the image on her screen before extending her free hand in the universal sign for "stop." "Just a moment," she said, still not taking her eyes from the camera. She gestured toward me impatiently. "You. Turn off the light behind you, the one in the hallway. It's giving a silhouette effect, and I really want to get this greeting right."

She spoke with the supreme confidence of Orson Welles or Alfred Hitchcock, obviously positive she would be obeyed.

In fact, her certainty was so complete that I found myself responding without thinking. My fingers were halfway to the light switch before I realized how absurd her demand was. David reacted more promptly than I; he extended a hand to block her filming.

Clearly annoyed, the woman clicked her tongue and touched something on the phone's screen. Lowering the camera, she shook her head and struck an indignant pose, jutting hip and all.

I blinked hard, half expecting her to disappear like the figment she seemed to be. She didn't, though, so I turned my attention to her companion. The second woman was dressed almost like a normal person—khaki shorts and a matching shirt. She looked a bit like she was going on safari, and I wondered if she had a pith helmet slung across her back.

In the meantime, Camera Girl was looking David up and down, her eyes flashing appreciatively. Without making a conscious decision to act, I settled a proprietary hand on David's biceps. Camera Girl smiled knowingly as she raised her gaze to mine and asked, "Jane Madison?"

"Um, yes," I replied, even as David stiffened. He didn't like strangers talking to me. Especially strangers who knew my name when I—when *we*—didn't have the first idea who they were.

"And this is the Jane Madison Academy?"

My throat went dry. "Yes," I said, without any conviction at all.

She extended her hand. "I'm Raven Willowsong. And this is my sister, Emma."

"Emma Newton," the blond woman said, apparently discovering her voice. Her very formal, very British voice, completely out of keeping with her sister's flat midwestern tones.

David still blocked the doorway. He obviously didn't trust these women.

And Emma, at least, was sensitive enough to recognize that. "Oh bother," she said. "This is a bit of a sticky wicket, isn't it? We should have been here hours ago, but we missed a turning in DC and the roadworks were awful getting out of town. A crash on the motorway held us up for ages."

I followed her vague gesture toward the driveway. A burgundy minivan was clearly visible in the light of the full moon. Its engine ticked as it cooled down.

I waited for David to say something, but he was taking his time, studying our visitors. His gaze was less obvious than Raven's camera had been, but I was certain he was recording every detail: The necklace—a pentacle, I could see now—that nestled perilously close to Raven's cleavage. The earrings that pierced her lobes—matching figurines of cats. The collection of silver rings that decorated each of her fingers and one thumb, moonstones competing with images of the sun, the green man, stars, and the moon. By contrast, Emma wore only a watch. A gold one, with a Burberry band.

"I'm sorry," I said. "No one told us you were arriving."

"But Clara said—" At least Raven had the good sense to cut off her words at my sharp intake of breath.

Of course. I should have put two and two together faster. My mother was responsible for this. "What exactly did Clara say?" I asked warily.

Raven recited, "We're perfect for the Madison Academy. She said our auras make us an exact match for the classes you're going to teach."

"And you *believed* her?" My voice ratcheted up an octave. I couldn't help myself. Even if these women were witches, even if they had some actually affinity for magic, I could hardly welcome them into my not-quite-existent magicarium if they were naive enough to believe Clara's claptrap about auras.

Emma cleared her throat before she said, "This *is* a clanger. But Clara Smythe said we'd fit right in here. She even offered to pay tuition for our first year of classes."

So, that was my birthday present. Two new students, with tuition all paid up. Except, in classic Clara fashion, she hadn't actually sent along the money. She probably never would. I started to issue a tart explanation, but Emma cut me off.

"I can see you weren't expecting us, and I'm truly sorry about that. But you have to understand. We're desperate. We've nowhere else to go."

She made the statement without any melodrama, but I could taste the anguish behind her proper British accent. There was need there, and fear, all marinated in confusion.

And, in a flash, I understood. Emma's magical powers, and Raven's, too, had not come easily. Magic had brought the women no joy. Emma's face was grave as she confirmed, "We both have powers. Skills, anyway. Some...affinity for witchcraft."

"But why come all the way out here? There have to be covens in Sedona. Or wherever you two are from."

"Sedona," Emma confirmed, nodding. The name of the southwestern city sounded strange on her tongue.

"The Oak Canyon Coven has jurisdiction there." David's voice was low, challenging. He might have been willing to give me the lead in speaking to these women, but he wasn't about to stand down entirely.

Emma's face clouded, but Raven threw up her arms in exasperation. "Oak Canyon didn't have the first idea what to do with us."

"Why not?" No one could have mistaken David's inquiry for a casual conversational gambit. Cold steel sliced beneath his question.

Raven re-jutted a hip and tossed her mane over her shoulder. The gesture made her skin-tight shirt ride up high on her belly, and she looked like the cover model for every terrible urban fantasy novel ever written (and a few really good ones, too). I wondered how long I'd be in traction if I attempted the same pose. She pouted as she said, "The Oak Canyon Coven isn't open to new ideas."

David might have been blind, for all the attention he paid to Raven's posturing. "Susan Parsons is usually quite reasonable."

"We don't know any Susan Parsons," Raven snapped, raising her chin defiantly.

Emma responded more calmly. "The Oak Canyon Coven Mother is Maria Hernandez." Her precise British enunciation left no doubt that she understood she had just been tested.

So. David had not quite believed that these women were from Sedona. Maria's name, though, was apparently correct, because he released a tiny fraction of his tension. A casual viewer would not see a change in his jaw or his stance, but I knew.

"Maria Hernandez has always welcomed new witches in

the past," David said evenly. Certainly, he would know. He'd attended coven meetings with my mother, supporting the more conventional aspects of her witchcraft.

Raven apparently took my warder's statement as a challenge. She raised her camera and started filming again, launching a somber narration: "Maria Hernandez has strict rules for her witches. All electronic devices are banned from gatherings of the Oak Canyon Coven. What is the Madison Academy's policy on modern communication?"

I hadn't exactly put the finishing touches on my student handbook. But I knew I wasn't happy with a camera shoved in my face. And I certainly didn't like the way Raven swooped forward to press her point.

"You *do* realize," she insisted, "that modern witches need to find a balance with contemporary electronics, don't you?"

"I—" I stammered, but I wasn't sure how to finish the sentence. Of course I believed in balance—essential fairness and equity were central to my powers. But those powers were based on the natural world. How did a camera fit in?

"Ms. Madison," Raven continued, sounding precisely like she was interviewing me for some gotcha reality show. "My sister and I were under the impression that the Madison Academy is on the leading edge of magicaria. We were assured that our instruction would be provided by witches who understand exactly what it means to live in the real world. The *modern* world."

"It will be!" I said. "It is!" My heart pounded as I fought to reassure her, and myself as well. I started to run my fingers through my hair, but I stopped, fully aware that the gesture would make me seem weak to Raven's viewers. A trickle of sweat slipped down my spine.

Raven pounced. "Where are those instructors, Ms. Madison?"

"They…" I trailed off, resisting the urge to turn to David. I didn't want to admit I was the only instructor, at least for now.

The quaver in my voice only poured new energy into Raven's inquisition. She thrust her camera closer with a vehemence that actually made me take a step back. "Our viewers are waiting, Ms. Madison. We *are* on the grounds of the Jane Madison Academy, aren't we?"

"Well, yes, but—"

"What was that? Speak up for the camera!"

I was still trying to summon a coherent answer when David interrupted, closing his fingers over the phone and twisting sharply. Raven yelped as if he had flung boiling water on her bare flesh. At the same time, she clutched the device to her chest, cradling it against her pentacle pendant. Her motion was violent, rough enough that she had to take a couple of steps back to steady herself. Her left heel teetered on the edge of the wooden stairs, and her head snapped back.

I started to cry out, but David took the necessary action, grabbing her arm tightly and hauling her forward so both her feet were firmly on the porch. His gesture was harsh, but it was brutally effective.

Even so, Raven cried out in a mixture of surprise and pain. She yanked her arm free, swearing loudly and succinctly, even as she thrust the camera toward her sister. "Record that, Emma! I'm going to have bruises in the morning, and I want everyone to know where they came from."

David growled deep in his throat, snatching the smartphone out of Raven's hand before Emma could decide whether to join the recording party. I was certain he was going to fling it to the floorboards and grind it into electronic dust beneath his heel. Raven must have thought so, too, because she screamed. Her wail was high and wordless, a banshee's screech that raised the hairs on the back of my neck. She launched herself at David, clawing at his hands and face, clearly desperate to regain her phone.

Emma shouted her sister's name. Spot chimed in, hulking close to the floorboards and voicing a low, constant growl. His lips were pulled back over his teeth, and his eyes followed Raven as if she were a particularly toothsome rabbit.

I was helpless to do anything. Even in his fury, David had juxtaposed his body between Raven and me. He was protecting me, keeping me safe. He was my warder first and foremost.

But Raven was a witch as well. Raven had a warder, too.

In the scuffle on the porch, none of us had heard the side door of the burgundy minivan slide open. But we couldn't ignore the sudden sword in our midst, gleaming like silver in the liquid moonlight. It carved out a perfect arc of protection for the wide-eyed, panting Raven.

The man who held the weapon planted his feet in a determined warrior's stance. His chest heaved beneath his white T-shirt as his baritone challenge rang out: "Halt! This witch is under my protection. Draw back or I will slay you all, in the name of Hecate and all her daughters!"

Chapter 2

THE WARDER'S CHALLENGE echoed off the light blue paint on the porch ceiling.

Rage bloomed on David's face, a stark fury that would have made me cringe if it were directed at me. It wasn't directed at me, though. Instead, it was focused on the other warder. On the other warder and on himself.

I could read David's thoughts as clearly as if he spoke aloud: He never should have allowed himself to be caught without a weapon. He never should have ignored the possibility of a warder in the minivan. He never should have let me slip into danger.

But the other warder wasn't wasting time with useless emotions like anger. Instead, his entire body vibrated with *focus*. He watched David and me and Spot as well, clearly evaluating the threat all three of us represented. I caught the barest flicker of energy he spared for his witch, for Raven. He was attuned to her, angled toward her just enough to assess the full extent of her injury.

And Raven milked the attention for all it was worth. She

rolled her hips with the ease of a bellydancer, tossing her wild hair over her shoulder. I could measure the precise instant she remembered that her wrist was supposed to be injured because she slipped the contested phone into her cleavage and folded her fingers around her purported bruise.

Emma caught the motion as well. The blond woman's face tightened in frustration. Disappointment, too. But mostly, I read resignation across her features, heard it in the exasperated gasp she barely swallowed.

This was clearly not the first time Raven's games had precipitated chaos. Raven's performance was forcing her warder to escalate his role; even now, the man was shifting his balance. David had no choice but to react, to brace himself for a true fight.

But I could bring the curtain down. Now. Without injury to anyone involved.

Carefully, precisely, I took a step back, toward the front door of the house. My motion brought my right heel to rest on a marble slab embedded in the porch, the centerstone for our home. As my foot made contact, a shimmer of energy rippled up my spine. I was tied in to the power I'd invested in the marble every time I entered the house, every time I brushed my fingers against the doorjamb and muttered a quick spell of protection. The astral energy spread beneath me like a moonlit pond.

Raven's warder was moving now, using his sword to sweep clear the space in front of him. David glided forward to grab the only available shield—an impossibly flimsy rattan table. Spot's hindquarters tightened; he was ready to launch at the invader whenever he was given the command.

Raven added sound to her own performance, keening as

if her arm were broken. Her wails only grew louder when Emma barked out orders for her sister to step back, to show her wrist, to calm down. Raven's warder shifted his weight, moving from a defensive posture to one of attack. The marble shimmered beneath me, humming with its reservoir of magical potential. I brushed my fingertips against my forehead and offered up the power of my mind. I touched my throat to commit the power of my speech. I settled my hand against my chest for a single instant to summon the power of my heart. The magical sequence awoke energy deep inside me, and I drew a steadying breath against the sudden, yawning core of astral force.

My surge of power provoked an automatic response in Raven. She raised both arms high above her head, apparently forgetting that her wrist was supposed to be horribly injured. Potential surged within her, and shimmering waves crashed against my own magic. Without thinking, I drained the reservoir of the marble centerstone, absorbing its prodigious strength into my own. Acting to preserve my home, my life, I shouted the single Word of a stasis spell: "*Hold!*"

One syllable, crackling with all the power at my command. One syllable, and there was a bolt of nothingness, a flash like a photographic negative of the world around us. One syllable, and we slipped outside the stream of the universe, shimmering and shivering and disappearing to the physical eye.

Then reality jolted the world back into being.

Everyone on the porch was frozen in place—the new witches and Raven's warder and David and Spot, too. Everyone was locked into position but me.

My ears rang. My throat was scraped raw on the single

word I'd shouted. Every inch of my body felt compressed and pounded, but now was not the time to hesitate, not the time to think. I couldn't give anyone else a chance to recover, to devise any counterspell. Instead, I stepped forward and held out my hand toward David. "Give me that thing."

He glared, but he was not yet able to move of his own accord, even to speak the angry words that so obviously pushed against the back of his teeth. Pretending confidence, I set my hand on one leg of the table, pushing a little of my energy through the rattan. The tendril of power was enough to release my warder, to let him resume his protective stance beside me. I extended freedom to Spot as well, confident that the animal would follow David's immediate hand signal to lie down.

As my warder recovered, I returned the furniture to its place beside the glider. I told myself I was simply restoring order, but the truth was, I didn't want to look at David's face. I didn't want to face the censure I was certain to find in his eyes.

My Word of Power had been extreme, completely immobilizing so many people, removing all of their volition. And the spell had cost me. My arm actually trembled with the effort of setting down the lightweight table. I caught a quick breath against the back of my throat. The roof of my mouth tingled. I was light-headed, and it seemed like the entire porch was swaying in a strong wind. I could barely keep my balance.

If our unexpected visitors didn't do me in, David might, now that he knew how much my spell had cost me.

But all that energy would be wasted if I didn't press my advantage now. "You," I said, pointing to the new warder.

"I'll release you if you pledge to sheath your sword." I pulled back my control over his vocal cords.

He glared at me, refusing to respond. Exasperated, I snapped, "Raven!" I allowed her to speak.

The other witch swallowed hard and licked her lips, fighting to say something, anything. I wondered if she'd ever heard a Word of Power before. Perhaps my spell had inadvertently shattered something within her own magic, some fragile ability she'd been mustering just as I cast.

Concerned for her well-being, I further loosened the hold around her face and throat. "Tony," she said after swallowing hard a few times. The name was scarcely louder than a whisper.

Her warder forced a reply past his set teeth. "You have my word."

I inclined my head in acceptance of his pledge. Anything more, and I was afraid my knees might actually buckle. Bracing myself, I pulled on the strands of my magic, freeing up another tendril that had bound the warder. I let him return his sword to its sheath, but then I immediately locked down the weapon.

Perhaps foolishly, I had hoped that unraveling the warder's bonds would restore some energy to me. Alas, breaking my spell only drained me further. The energy I had invested in my Word of Power was cast adrift into the universe, shredded into the muggy summer night without any hope of retrieval.

At least Raven's warder seemed blind to my exhaustion. He did not test my limits, either on the physical or the astral plane. Rather, he swore under his breath as I allowed him to move out of his fighting crouch, to stand upright. There.

More of my power floated away, cast off into the darkness.

I stiffened my spine, thoroughly chagrined. I had no choice, though, but to make things look normal. I had to seem in control.

I let Tony use his newly recovered freedom of motion to take a full stride closer to Raven, but I drew the line after he settled his hands on his hips. Who knew what other weapons—astral or mundane—he might have at his disposal? I knew David kept a silver dagger in a sheath at his ankle. I had to believe other warders maintained similar stealthy arsenals.

Wondering how much longer I could hide my physical distress, I tested my voice inside my head. It was almost steady. Almost calm. I gulped a deep breath and then turned to the woman who had started all this madness. "Raven," I said, simultaneously relaxing the magical bonds around her arms. I locked my knees to keep from swaying as more of my power drifted away. "Give me your phone."

"I—" she started to argue.

"Now!" I extended my hand and waited, praying to Hecate that she responded quickly.

As it was, she wasted a moment looking from me to Tony and back again. Finally, though, she fished the device out of her too-tight T-shirt. She slapped it onto my palm hard enough to sting, and I forced myself not to react as I shoved the damned thing into the pocket of my shorts.

At the same time, I slipped my bonds from Emma. After all, *she* hadn't done anything wrong. As soon as she was able, she darted a glance to the foot of the stairs. When I followed her gaze, I almost swore.

Three men stood there.

They were frozen, watching me warily, as if they half-expected me to burst into flame. Or maybe turn them into newts.

No wonder the Word of Power had drained me so dramatically. I had snagged even more people than I expected in the clutch of my command.

I resisted the urge to shake my head as I realized how truly dangerous my position had been. Three of Raven's allies had stood at the foot of the steps—and I hadn't been consciously aware of their presence. David had been, I was· sure. That was his job. That was the way his mind always worked.

But I had been so wrapped up in Raven's little drama that I had not even registered the additional newcomers. I was certain to hear about that little oversight as soon as David and I were alone. And, truth be told, he'd be right when he read me the riot act.

At least it wasn't hard to figure out the trio's roles in our little tableau. The bluff blond guy who looked like a farmhand and wore a Diamondbacks baseball cap had to be Emma's warder. The slumping one in the grey track outfit appeared to be her familiar; at least, he had his hand on Baseball Boy's shoulder, as if he were lending a base for magical support. That left the last man, the one with the spray of freckles across his face and a crest of over-gelled red hair, to be Raven's familiar.

No weapons in sight on any of them. No shimmer of magical power arrested by my own spell.

Nevertheless, I couldn't see any reason to tip the odds, to make it four against one by setting all of them free at once. I settled for clearing my throat, masking another quick survey of my fitness. I could still speak without showing the strain, at least to those who didn't know me well. I had to admit, I was gratified by how quickly I got everyone's full attention.

"We seem to have gotten off on the wrong foot here," I said. "Let me clarify a few policies for the Madison Academy." Policies. As if I'd already formulated anything quite that grandiose for my fledgling magicarium. I put steel into my voice. "Rule number one. No recording anyone without explicit permission."

Raven obviously wanted to protest. At least, she wanted to wriggle seductively and toss her hair in disbelief at my unfairness. At the barest minimum, she wanted to roll her eyes like the world's most exasperated teenager. But she wasn't a complete idiot. Her lips pursed around the words, but she said, "Fine. No recording."

"Rule number two." I continued, tightening my focus. I needed to wrap this up now, or I was going to lose all face by falling flat on my own. "Warders introduce themselves before they set foot on the property of my safehold."

Tony barely inclined his head, accepting my demand. "Anthony Morella," he said, his tone flat. "Warder to Raven Willowsong."

"Welcome, Anthony. In Hecate's name, be welcome in my house."

"In Hecate's name, I thank thee," he responded to the old formula, even though he looked as if he'd rather drink pure vinegar.

That left me scrambling for rule number three. Or, rather, scrambling to determine if I *needed* a rule number three. Yet. A single glance at Raven and Tony made me pretty sure I'd be needing rules three, four, five, and six, possibly by midnight.

But I also had to make the Madison Academy a welcoming place for promising new witches. And strangers or not, Raven and Emma *had* been sent by my mother.

Clara might drive me mad. She might infuriate me with her blasé attitude and her crazy take on the occult. But in her heart, she knew me, the magical me, the witch I'd become over the past three years. We had successfully worked spells together, under pressure, with all the odds against us. If Clara said Raven and Emma should be students at the Madison Academy, I had to believe she was right.

"Enough," I said, including everyone with the gesture that dispersed the last ripples of control from my Word of Power. "We can discuss other Academy rules later, after some dinner. Let's go inside, where it's cool."

Our visitors sorted themselves out quickly. Tony leaped to Raven's side and made a show of studying her wrist as the red-headed familiar looked on in purse-lipped concern.

"Caleb Weston," Emma's warder introduced himself as he stepped onto the porch. I welcomed him in Hecate's name, then nodded as the familiars offered up their own greetings. The man in grey was Kopek. The red-haired man was Hani.

Formulaic responses given and received, I led the way into the house, automatically brushing my fingers against the doorjamb. I didn't whisper any spell to the marble stone, though. I wasn't ready to spill a drop of power—not without a bit of grounding first, some food and drink to restore the prodigious amount of energy I'd spent.

David's concern was tangible as I passed in front of him, even though he didn't say anything. Subtly, he brushed his palm against the small of my back, lending a touch of physical support before he stepped back to let our guests follow me inside.

Spot stayed between me and the newcomers, as if he were under specific orders from David. No matter how he might have begged for a meaty second supper earlier in the evening, he was on full alert now. He was my protector, my guardian. He provided a service as important as any offered by my warder.

I leaned against my loyal canine companion as I opened the cupboards. It took more concentration than I was willing to admit to count out additional plates. I jumped when Emma whispered up to my side and said, "Well, that went a bit pear-shaped, didn't it? May I help?"

Before I could answer, she handed off the dishes to Caleb. "Here," she said to him. "Lend a hand." There was a smile behind her clipped words.

I pointed Emma toward the silverware, on my way to retrieving wine- and water glasses. We were definitely going to need more than the single bottle of pinot noir. In fact, we might want to break out the hard stuff, to restore everyone's shattered nerves. Right. As if David would let a sip of alcohol mar his reflexes now, with strangers in the house.

I couldn't help but notice that half those strangers—Raven, her warder, and her familiar—were hanging back in the doorway to the kitchen. Their unease was infectious. Spot eyed them warily from his place by my side, and I felt more than heard the growl deep in his throat.

"Spot," I warned, reluctantly pointing toward his bed. He obeyed, but only after glancing at David for confirmation. Canine traitor! So much for my believing I had any actual power over the beast.

It turned out that the dog was smarter than I was. I actually swayed without his support against my knees. I needed food. Food, and something to drink. And a chair. A chair would be wonderful. A chair would be heaven on earth.

I stared across the chasm of the kitchen, trying to calculate whether I could reach the table without fainting. I needed David *now*.

He reacted as if I'd shouted, taking three quick strides into the kitchen and pushing past Caleb as if the husky man were nothing more than a cardboard cutout. Darkness surged along the edges of my vision, roiling, pulling me down.

Before I could fall, though, the back door crashed open, and I was assaulted by a new wave of sultry summer heat. I knew I should clutch at the tattered strands of my powers. I should brace myself against this new threat. I had to react, had to work some spell.

But somehow my subconscious brain managed to process the actual scene before me.

Spot was leaping from his bed, his entire body wagging in joyous greeting. David was looking relieved at my side. Our six guests were caught in various stages of astonishment, shock, and disbelief.

Silhouetted against the moonlit night was a dressmaker's dummy, clad in pantaloons and a fur-lined robe, with padded shoulders and a fake breastplate large enough to fill the entire door. Henry VIII, my mind stuttered. King of England, Ireland, and France. I'd recognize the clothes from the Holbein portrait anywhere.

Clutching the costume, needle and thread ostentatiously

in hand, was a shadowy figure. Anne Boleyn, if I had to guess. Almond eyes. Hair slicked back beneath a lace head-dress. A floor-length crimson dress, cut absurdly low and showing way too much flesh for historical realism. Way too much *waxed* flesh. Way too much waxed, male flesh, belonging to none other than Neko.

My familiar looked up, took in the astonished audience in the kitchen, and promptly belted out, "'E's 'Enery the Eighth, 'e is", in the worst parody of a cockney accent I'd ever heard. As we all gaped, Neko glided across the kitchen to drop into a curtsey before me. He took my hand with the same laughable formality, pretending to kiss some royal ring.

As our flesh met, Neko shoved a burst of mental energy into me. The power felt like an electric shock, brilliant and searing and pure. I stood a little straighter and breathed a little deeper before I said, "You seem to have forgotten someone."

Neko shrugged. "Jacques was in the other room when David called."

So David has issued the astral summons that had carried my familiar across the miles. My familiar's boyfriend was probably standing in the middle of their DC apartment at this very moment, blinking and wondering where Neko had gone. I attempted to sound nonchalant as I said, "Nice costumes."

Neko flushed with pleasure. "The fur's a bit much for summer, but Jacques insisted. I think buttons make a much better decoration this time of year. Don't you agree?" He took my fingers and forced them to the row of pearls that framed his chest.

Another blast of astral energy cascaded through my palm

and up my arm, suffusing my body. I could have soaked it up for hours, but Neko pulled back in poorly-acted surprise. "Oh! I didn't know you were *entertaining!*" Then he whispered in a *voce* that wasn't anywhere near as *sotto* as he apparently believed. "Jane! I thought we'd talked about 'summer casual.'" He glared at my shorts and T-shirt. "And that hair! What *were* you thinking?"

Self-consciously, my fingers flew toward my unruly hair. Neko reached out at the same time, encircling my wrist and pouring a third burst of magical energy into me. Finally, my own power kickstarted, leaping steady and bright inside my chest. With the ease of long practice, Neko reflected that energy back at me as if he were made of a million mirrors.

"Thanks," I breathed.

"Don't mention it," he said.

David finally seemed to realize this would be the perfect time to distract our company. He barked out a few commands, barely disguising them as invitations. "There are two leaves for the dining room table in the hall closet. Grab those chairs from the kitchen table. No, let's move the dining room chairs back so there's enough room."

Who would have thought it would take three warders, two witches, and two familiars to prepare an impromptu dinner party? David played his role well, though. No one even thought to watch as Neko kept his fingers wrapped around my wrist for another minute, monitoring my steadiness, calculating my returning strength. Only when he was completely satisfied that I was restored did he say, "It looks like we're going to have quite a party."

"Can Jacques spare you?"

"He already has."

Against his will, I thought. And not for the first time. "Won't he need his costume?"

A momentary scowl marred Anne Boleyn's high brow. "He'll find something else to wear, I'm sure. And someone else to wear it with."

"Neko! If you need to go—

He shook his head and gestured at his gown. "This was a calculated risk. It was fifty/fifty whether Jacques was going to shout 'Off with his head' by the end of the party. And don't get your hopes up. That isn't code for some new bedroom game."

"Neko—

"Forget about it."

His dismissive wave was charming, but I saw through it like a lace mantilla. I clutched his hands between both of mine. "Thank you."

He nodded once. And then, he tore off his fancy headdress. The scarlet gown was equipped with Velcro strips for a hasty getaway, and I steadily forbade myself from speculating about Ms. Boleyn's intended disrobing during or after the evening's now-canceled festivities.

Neko wore his usual attire beneath the dress—a sleek black T-shirt and matching jeans that left nothing to the imagination. He draped his Tudor costume over the dressmaker's dummy and stowed both in the corner. Dusting his hands together decisively, he stepped up to survey the food on the center island. His resulting sigh was gusty enough to shake the rafters of a lesser home. "You're going to need a *lot* more than that," he said.

"Oh, will we?" David asked as he returned from the dining room. His voice was resignedly dry.

"Bread," Neko ordered. "That loaf over there. And a green salad—you have all the makings in the back of the fridge. I saw everything at lunch. Don't forget cheese either—the Saga Blue will be nice. And bring out the Irish butter, while you're at it."

Spot came to stand beside my familiar, whining as if he understood the feast that was being composed. Neko stopped just short of snapping his fingers as he issued his commands. Under any other circumstances, David would have told him exactly what he could do with his Irish butter.

But now David pulled the salad and cheese and butter from the fridge. And then he filled one of his handblown Riedel goblets with the whole milk we kept on hand solely to satisfy Neko's cravings. "Thank you," David said.

"My pleasure." Neko's reply was automatic. But then he noticed our newcomers were quieting down again, paying too much attention to our little gathering in the kitchen.

Neko took the glass with a flair before he whirled into the dining room to explain to Raven that she absolutely, positively could *not* sit beneath the painting on the far wall—the art would clash with the purple stripe in her hair. Even Tony was bemused as his witch was made to switch seats not once, not twice, but three times.

David shook his head as he met my eyes. "You're all right?" he asked, keeping his voice low enough not to steal attention back from Neko.

"I'm fine."

"That was dangerous."

"I couldn't have my magicarium getting off on the wrong foot! Not when Clara worked so hard to get my first students out here in the first place. I haven't even had a chance to find out what my witches are capable of."

David's smile was tight as he nodded toward Raven. "*That* one is capable of a lot of trouble."

I shrugged. "Everyone's trouble," I said. "One way or another."

Before David could respond, Neko called out from the dining room. "David? We're really going to need the camembert, to round out this meal. And the cheddar wouldn't be a bad addition, either."

My warder rolled his eyes. "Yes," he said to me as he turned toward the refrigerator. "Everyone *is* trouble."

I could tell he wanted to say more. He wanted to extract a promise from me, a pledge not to use any Word of Power ever again, at least not without proper arcane support. He wanted to protect me and keep me safe from any possible hint of danger in the future.

Instead, he settled for brushing his hand down my arm before he turned to do Neko's bidding.

Chapter 3

I HOPED EVERYTHING would somehow be perfect in the morning. I would awake with a flawless understanding of my role as magistrix of the Madison Academy. A perfect class schedule would have appeared out of thin air, transcribing itself on my calendar. My witches and I would thrum with energy, ready to work all sorts of powerful spells in dedication to the glory of Hecate.

Alas, I spent a restless night jerking awake from an endless series of bad dreams. Three separate times, I startled David out of a sound sleep, and it took him longer to settle back each time. When I finally crawled out of bed at dawn, my boyfriend had abandoned me. I had a crick in my neck, a fog over my thoughts, and a nasty taste in my mouth.

At least toothpaste solved the last problem.

I tried to convince myself that a long shower would banish my other woes, but I started sweating even as I tried to towel myself dry. The farmhouse's air conditioning simply could not compete with the heavy blanket of June humidity.

When I opened the bedroom door, Spot was lying in the

hallway. He raised his massive head from his front paws and pounded his tail against the floor. I assured him he was a good boy, and he pranced as he accompanied me down the stairs. Leading the way into the kitchen, he kept himself between me and the witches who were seated at the table.

Raven had exchanged her tight blouse for an even more body-skimming black T. Her skinny jeans made me wonder if she actually had room inside her body for all her organs. She'd wrapped a deep purple scarf around her waist, and the fabric matched the streak in her long, wavy hair. She looked more like a sexy pirate queen than an up-and-coming student of witchcraft.

Emma, on the other hand, looked cool and composed and utterly, completely ordinary in denim shorts and a loose-fitting pink blouse. The guys—both warders and familiars—were lounging around the living room, keeping conversation down to a dull roar. Neko was nowhere to be seen. He must have spent the night in his apartment above the garage.

Raven lifted her phone as soon as I set foot in the kitchen. "Okay if I film?" She was already moving her fingers across the screen.

"Absolutely not." I needed caffeine in my bloodstream before I could even consider being ready for my close-up. I could just make out the ghosts of bruises around Raven's wrists, evidence of where David had gripped her the night before.

As my cinematographer pouted, Emma spoke up. "We helped ourselves to brekkie. David said you'd want a cuppa."

And that explained Spot's watchful presence upstairs.

The dog must have been under strict orders to guard me. After all, it was decidedly un-warderlike for David to leave me alone, sleeping, while half a dozen visitors took over the downstairs of our home.

Emma pressed a mug into my hand. "He said to remind you he had some sort of confab in the village? A meeting with an estate agent?"

I ran a rapid English-to-American translator over her words. David was meeting with a realtor in Parkersville? First I'd heard of it. A twist of anxiety rippled through my gut.

To disguise my concern, I took a sip of tea. Emma had brewed it to her English standards—strong enough to melt a spoon. I stumbled to the refrigerator and fished out the cream. Or, rather, I excavated an empty cardboard carton. I dropped it into the trash, silently cursing Neko.

"Oh," Raven said, looking up from her own mug of some delectable ecru beverage. "I guess we finished off the cream."

I cast a silent apology toward my familiar and fortified myself with a slug of bitter tea. When I looked up, Raven and Emma were staring at me with curious eyes. I tried to put myself in their shoes. They'd traveled halfway across the country on Clara's word that they'd find a magicarium waiting for them in Maryland. Whether they were paying their own tuition or not, they'd made sacrifices to be here. At the very least, they'd left behind their home. Probably family. Friends.

And it was up to me to make sure their journey was worthwhile. What sort of impostor was I, pretending to be a magistrix?

The sort of impostor who had learned a thing or two in her first career, as a librarian. In my last professional job at the Peabridge Library, I'd regularly conducted "reference interviews," asking my patrons a series of questions so I could track down the information they *actually* wanted, instead of what they initially asked for. It was time to use the same skills in the service of my magicarium.

I took a deep breath and jumped in. A few easy questions, to break the ice… "How long ago did you awaken your familiars?"

Emma answered promptly. "Seven years ago, this past May."

"And they're bound directly to you?" Some familiars were tied to specific witchy resources. Technically, Neko was bound to the Osgood collection in my basement, not to me.

Emma nodded, casting a fond glance toward the living room. The familiars and warders had broken out a deck of cards. It looked like Kopek was in the hole by three stacks of pennies.

I didn't want to ignore Raven. I asked her directly, "And Hani? What was he before you woke him?"

"A rooster," she said. As soon as the words were out of her mouth, I could see the animal roots—the red hair bright as a coxcomb, the bustling way he collected cards to deal the next hand.

I glanced at Emma. She said, "Basset hound." I could imagine her holding the figurine of her familiar, running her fingers down its flanks before she spoke the spell to bring it to life. While many witches might have asked for a more dynamic partner, Emma seemed content with Kopek.

As moon-bound familiars, neither Hani nor Kopek

would be quite as…challenging as Neko. They wouldn't be quite as interesting, either. But that was no fault of the familiars or their witches.

"And your warders? You haven't been teamed with anyone else?"

Emma shook her head. Raven, though, looked distinctly uneasy. "How many?" I asked her.

"Counting Tony?"

I braced myself as I nodded. I'd seen witches who had burned through multiple warders before, and there was always some tangle of drama involved.

"Four."

Four. I tried to believe there was a benign explanation, but she certainly didn't volunteer any exculpatory facts. I decided not to press her. Not now. Not when I was trying to build some essential rapport. Instead, I turned my attention back to Emma. "What do you want from the Madison Academy?"

"Well, I… We…" She turned to Raven, but I cut her short.

"No, I'll ask your sister in a moment. I want to know why *you* came here."

"I always fancied going back to uni. Getting another degree."

There. A general answer, just waiting for the fine tuning of a reference interview. "But if that were true, then any magicarium would do. There are plenty of coven schools, most a lot closer to Sedona. Why did you come to mine?"

"Your mum said you had different ideas about witchcraft. You weren't all bound up in the whys and wherefores of a *proper* magicarium."

A proper—I bit the inside of my cheek. I needed Emma to continue working with me, and ranting about Clara's word choice wasn't going to earn me any trust. I kept my voice perfectly level as I asked, "What different ideas appeal to you?"

Emma fiddled with her mug of tea, running her fingers over the handle. "The local coven were put out with me in short order. Said I needed sorting, needed to master a dozen different spells for lighting a candle. Took me months, that did. A couple of years. I still think one spell should be enough, if it's worked properly."

I nodded. Oak Canyon would follow the Rota, the traditional education system for young witches. In ordinary magicaria, students worked through a series of standardized spells, practicing each one dozens, hundreds, thousands of times, until she could complete it perfectly under all conditions. Once a single task—lighting a candle, to take Emma's example—was perfected with one spell, the novice witch learned an alternative incantation. Or two. Or three dozen. The process was deliberately mind-numbing, forcing the novice to submit over and over again to the authority of her coven.

My training had been a lot less conventional: David had taught me how to channel my power, drawing on the books in my basement. That haphazard education had crazed the conservative Washington Coven, but it had left me with virtually unequalled powers.

"We certainly won't be working the Rota." I was rewarded by Emma's quick, grateful smile. I turned to Raven before I could lose my momentum. "And you? What do you want from the Madison Academy?"

"Emma wanted to come. I couldn't let her go alone."

"Actually," I pointed out, "You could. She'd have Caleb and Kopek. What did *you* want to accomplish by coming out here?"

Raven fiddled with the rings on her left hand, twisting each a full circle. Her fingertips went to the pendant that hung between her breasts. Reflexively, she counted off all five points on the pentacle. I waited with pretended patience, knowing she had to find the wherewithal to answer my question. I couldn't offer it up for her. I could, though, prompt a little. "Or maybe you were trying to leave something behind?"

"I didn't make friends in Oak Canyon," she said at last. She met my eyes, defiance blazing as bright as the violet stripe in her hair.

"What kept you from bonding with them?" My voice was steady, non-judgmental. Hecate knew I'd had my own conflicts with my supposed coven sisters before I'd found the strength to walk away from them forever.

Raven shrugged, as if she were trying to buck off a bad memory. "Derek Gleason." Her jaw set defiantly, even as Emma snorted out half a laugh. "Alex Wilcox. Ryan Bard."

I held up a hand. "Those are warders, I take it?"

She twitched a shoulder by way of answering.

"They were sworn to Oak Canyon witches?"

"Sworn to me, eventually," she said. "When things didn't work out, Derek and Alex stayed with Oak Canyon. Ryan left the job."

I pushed. "And you left Oak Canyon too, after Ryan. But why did you come *here*? What do you want to learn from me, Raven? What can I teach you?"

She stared into the living room, letting her eyes lose focus as Tony raked in a pile of change. I didn't think she was conscious of taking out her phone, of turning the electronic device from edge to edge to edge. She didn't make any move to turn on the camera, so I let her keep her pacifier. And I waited. And waited. And waited.

And Raven finally yielded. "I want to learn how to focus my powers. I start a spell, and I can feel the magic well up inside me. The energy is there. The strength. But it…leaks away while I'm trying to channel the working. No one understands that. No one in Sedona, anyway."

I heard the yearning in her voice, an honesty that cut through everything—her vampish clothes, her camera, her drama queen tactics. And in that moment, I wanted to help her. I wanted to help both of them, to make my magicarium a place of perfect refuge and learning.

And the next step in doing that would be to get them settled in adequate living quarters. "Okay," I said, breaking the solemn atmosphere with an intentionally cheerful voice. I called out to the card sharks in the living room, "Guys? Can you join us for a sec?"

I was gratified that they abandoned their poker game immediately. Spot didn't seem as thrilled; he padded over from his bed and sat beside me as all four men traipsed into the kitchen. I settled my palm on the dog's neck, simultaneously taking and giving reassurance.

"First things first," I said. "We obviously weren't prepared for your arrival last night, but we're back on track now. Emma, Raven, I appreciate your willingness to share the guest room last night, but that obviously won't work on a long-term basis."

I gave my students a smile filled with more confidence than I actually felt. "I'm going to ask Neko and Jacques to move out of their apartment above the garage. The place has two bedrooms, along with a full bath."

Emma protested, "We can't chuck them out!"

"They spend most of their time at Jacques's place in the city." They *had* anyway. When I'd come up with my brilliant plan in the middle of the night, I'd conveniently forgotten the dire relationship news Neko had hinted at the night before. I resisted the urge to chew my lower lip.

Raven cast a dubious glance toward her own familiar. "Doesn't Neko need to stay close by?"

"I awakened him on the night of a full moon." I watched them absorb that little bomb. Most witches considered my action rash to the point of insanity. When I'd first bound my familiar, though, I hadn't known that the phase of the moon mattered. As a result, Neko could roam as far as he wished.

My lack of conformity to arcane norms clearly made an impression on my students. Good. That would help when we got to our first unconventional working, in about five minutes. But I still had to clarify the rest of the rooming arrangements. I turned to the warders and familiars. "Gentlemen, I appreciate your willingness to make do last night, but we obviously can't keep you sleeping on couches and the floor. There are a couple of outbuildings on the property, an old greenhouse and a barn. Both have plumbing and electricity, and there are some cots in storage. Nothing very grand, but we'll upgrade as we go along."

"We'll be fine," Caleb said, before the others could speak. His eyes looked earnest beneath the bill of his baseball cap. Hani, though, looked like he had a few complaints to

register, and Tony was gearing up as well. Caleb merely repeated in a forceful voice, "We'll be fine. All of us."

I smiled my appreciation, trying to include Emma as
well. After all, she was the one who had conditioned her
warder to such a positive outlook. Maybe she channeled
Mary Poppins with that posh British accent. Come to think
of it, where did Emma's Brit thing come from? Raven didn't
have a hint of the U.K. in her own speech.

Making a mental note to find out more later, I settled
down to the real business of the morning. My students had
to show me their basic magical capacity. I had to find out if
they were truly amenable to my unique ideas about working
group magic. I said, "I don't know how much Clara told
you, but here at the Madison Academy we function as a
community. Our goal is to provide constant mutual support
in all magical workings."

Emma and Raven nodded eagerly.

No time like the present to prove my point. I said, "Why
don't we move outside, then? Where we can be more comfortable?"

Comfortable. Not exactly. The air slapped us like a waterlogged towel the instant we stepped onto the porch. Beside me, Spot's thick fur radiated heat like an electric
blanket. I tried to nudge him away with my knee, but he
steadfastly refused to yield. Sighing, I led my little party
down the steps and into the center of the dusty lawn that
surrounded the farmhouse.

We were witches. We harnessed the powers of the natural world. Even a natural world swaddled tight in summer
heat.

I slipped off my sandals and wiggled my toes in the grass.

Watching carefully, Raven and Emma followed suit. The thirsty blades prickled. It had been weeks since we'd seen measurable rainfall, despite the constant moisture in the air.

Raven presented her phone as soon as we were arranged in an uneven triangle, but I shook my head. My magicarium, my rules. Technology had no place in the middle of a magical working. Besides, in a few moments, she wouldn't have a free hand to work the controls.

Determinedly ignoring her exasperated sigh as she tucked the device into her bra, I brushed my fingertips against my forehead, my throat, and my heart, dedicating my magic to the power of Hecate. Then, smiling with what I hoped was honest encouragement, I spoke the words of one of the simplest spells I knew:

"Word flows, power shows,
Force grows, wind blows."

I used my magic to give the slightest *push* to the air around me, and a gentle breeze wafted across the yard. Everyone—witches, warders, familiars, and Spot—relaxed at the cooling touch. I watched Raven and Emma settle more comfortably on their bare feet.

The breath of fresh air drifted away, and we were left sweltering beneath the leaden sky. I smiled at both my charges. "Simple, right?"

Emma nodded, but her eyebrows knit. She clearly didn't understand why I had just demonstrated one of the most elementary spells in the entire witchy arsenal. Raven swallowed a sigh, tossing her hair over her shoulders, flashing the violet stripe like a warning. She was already bored with the Madison Academy.

I was going to enjoy the next stage of my little demonstration.

Before I could extend my hands for theirs to start our communal working, Neko wandered over from the garage. His hair was set in immaculate little spikes, and his T-shirt and jeans were a perfect match for Raven's body-skimming garments. My tiny spell had summoned him, as I'd known it would. Spot whuffed and shifted a few steps away.

I smiled. "We're just getting started." Neko nodded and glided to my side, standing close enough that I could feel the heat from his body, distinct from the oppressive air. I gestured to Emma and Raven. "Come on. Bring your familiars into the circle."

Kopek lurched to Emma's side and put a blunt-fingered hand on her shoulder. When Hani strutted over to Raven, he expanded his chest, as if he were crowing about all his grand accomplishments. Tony and Caleb watched from the sidelines, clearly uncertain about the demands I was making of their witches. Neither seemed inclined to intervene—yet—but I wondered how long a leash they would grant me.

Of course, I knew we weren't doing anything dangerous. Nothing that would require warders' protection. This demonstration was just a simple group wind-summoning, nothing that would exercise even David's over-developed sense of protectiveness.

I nodded at my students. "Make your offerings."

They complied, focusing on their breathing and yielding up their minds and voices and hearts. Emma shifted her weight to lean more heavily on Kopek. Raven fluttered her fingers over her bra, reaching reflexively for her camera. When I gave a tight shake of my head, though, she sighed and settled her fingertips against my proffered palm. I closed the physical loop with her sister.

Neko hovered at the back of my thoughts, bolstering my magical presence with the mirror of his craft. Kopek and Hani were more difficult to sense, but they flickered at the edges of my arcane awareness, each offering energy to his own witch.

I took a calming breath and exhaled slowly, willing my students to follow my example. I breathed again and tightened my focus. One more time for complete centering. And then I made my voice steady and firm as I spoke the beginning of the spell: "*Word—*"

My students' power manifested around mine, taking a form that seemed nearly physical. Nervous, they both fed too much energy into our connection. I was braced against the competing pushes of their magic, but the intensity of their combined drive made me stagger. Neko leaned in so I could draw stability from him. His presence let me focus on the witches beside me.

In one quick glimpse, I could see what had truly driven Raven from the Oak Canyon Coven. Not her dalliances with multiple warders. Rather, her magical energy manifested as a blatant contradiction. At first glance, her powers seemed like a granite monolith. That surface, though, was actually like pumice, riddled with channels. The more I peered, the more I made out a network of intricate passageways that offered virtually unbounded magical capacity. A coven, however, would see the countless cracks as deformities, faults that should be ground down and destroyed forever.

Even as I discovered the truth, I backed off, determined not to undermine my first student before I could teach her how to use her strength to her best advantage. Instead, I turned to Emma. And there, I found a magic that could not have been more different. If Raven was fine-carved stone, Emma was a placid pool—unfathomable, uncharted water. Her powers drove to the core of the earth, glowing with the placid silver of liquid moonlight. I could only imagine how frustrated she had been by whatever baby steps the Oak Canyon Coven had offered her.

Stone and water. Intricate lacework and bottomless potential. Violet and silver. The sisters were radically different from each other, and from myself as well. I could never lead us in the sort of easy, united working that had become second nature between myself, my mother, and my grandmother. Making the attempt would be like juggling a brick, a plush toy, and a scoop of melting ice cream.

I was surprised to discover I'd closed my eyes, the better to sense their power. The better to avoid their questioning eyes, the vulnerability of witches standing before a new Coven Mother. No. Not a Coven Mother. A magistrix. A teacher.

I blinked hard. This should be easy. At the very least, I should be able to bring up a windy gust on my own. I should be able to show the others how it was done.

I couldn't, though. My energy was too wrapped up in theirs. My force snagged on the intricate channels of Raven's stone; it drowned in the depths of Emma's water. I couldn't find my place with these witches. I couldn't strike the necessary balance.

I tried a dozen times. I made us change positions, taking different points on our triangle. I had Emma start the spell, with Raven joining in, then me. I had us trade off individual words. I ordered us to chant together.

Throughout it all, Tony and Caleb watched over our working. At first, they stood on high alert, ready to protect all three of us from whatever magical forces we raised on the farmhouse lawn. As our repeated attempts proved fruitless, though, both men relaxed. They settled on their heels, no longer twitching every time we shifted position. Spot finally sighed and retreated to the shade on the porch.

I hoped our guardians' standing down would help me to concentrate. Yeah. Not so much. The mere fact that warders waited nearby sapped my concentration, keeping me aware that there was a dangerous potential in our working, in any working.

Or maybe I was only making excuses.

When I finally accepted that I wasn't going to synchronize our witchy powers through the words of the spell alone, I tried another tactic. I teamed Neko with Emma. I sent Kopek over to Raven, and I took Hani for myself. But when I dove deeper into my powers, the red-headed familiar skimmed the surface. When I rose to work with him, he pushed for a more complete connection. I shuffled the familiars again, but had no better luck working with Kopek.

Finally, I shook my head and stepped back from our poor trodden circle. "Let's take a break," I said. Everyone was polite enough to pretend they didn't hear my voice shaking. Or maybe they were simply too tired to care.

I couldn't let our first attempt at communal spellcraft end this way.

I didn't have a choice.

I raised my chin and said, "This afternoon, the two of you should try working together, without my powers in the mix." There. That sounded authoritative. I'd given my students their first assignment. "For now, let's focus on getting the rest of our lives settled. When you're not practicing this afternoon, go ahead and move into your new rooms. Unpack. Explore the farm. Make yourselves at home."

Home. I winced at the belated reminder that I hadn't yet told Neko about the housing situation. Damn. "Um," I said to my familiar. "May I talk to you for a moment?"

My heart pounded as I led him toward the chopping block, a work-smoothed tree stump that David used for splitting endless cords of wood. On this summer day, the axe was nowhere in sight. That was probably just as well.

I swallowed hard and spoke to the ancient stump's heartwood, my words running together in a single stream. "I-sort-of-told-the-witches-they-could-live-in-your-apartment-I-hope-you-don't-mind-too-much-but-I-couldn't-figure-out-what-else-to-do."

Neko's voice was colder than the breeze we'd just failed to summon. "Excuse me? Did you just say you're throwing me out of my home?"

"I'm not! You and Jacques have been living in the city!"

"I slept above the garage last night," Neko said. Last night. When my need had summoned him from his boyfriend's side. When I had interrupted their plans for a party. When Neko had as much as told me that his relationship was on the rocks.

"I should have asked first, I know that. But I panicked. Clara sent those two without giving me any warning. If you're going to be angry with anyone, you should be angry with her."

"*Clara* didn't give me an eviction notice. Oh, wait! You

didn't bother with that either."

I'd never heard Neko this angry. But he had to realize that the Academy meant... He had to understand... No. He didn't. He didn't need to turn his life upside down just because I wanted him to.

And then I glimpsed the coward's way out of this disaster. "Will you do me a favor, just for now? Help the guys get settled in the greenhouse and the barn. You're so much better at that type of thing than I am."

He gave me a withering look. "Do not *even* start with the flattery, Jane."

"But you *are* better at it." I braced myself and brought out the big guns. "I know it'll take money to make things livable. We're going to need all new bed linens." I threw caution to the wind. "I'll give you my credit card!"

"Sheets and blankets won't be enough," Neko pointed out, and I could have laughed in relief. I had won. It would cost me, but I had won. Neko went on. "They'll need towels. And throw rugs. And a lamp or two, at the very least. And *window treatments*. We can't forget window treatments."

I gulped and sternly reminded myself that poverty was the lesser of two evils. I *had* acted entirely out of line. And we *did* need to convert the barn and greenhouse into dorms.

Neko was just getting geared up. "Maybe if I picked up some new things for the place in D.C... Jacques has his eye on some dishes. And we saw some *stunning* napkins just the other day."

I swallowed hard. In for a penny, in for an entire savings account. I might as well cement my familiar's forgiveness. "I'm sure you'll be exhausted after all that shopping. Maybe if you treat Jacques to dinner at that new oyster bar on Connecticut Avenue, you'll recover faster." Oysters. Like I needed to coach Neko on aphrodisiacs of any type.

He knew a good deal when he heard it. As he extended his hand for my card, I knew I would regret this. Probably with interest payments for months. But a magistrix does what a magistrix has to do. I just hoped I wouldn't be forced to declare bankruptcy before the Madison Academy had ever truly begun.

Chapter 4

SOMEHOW, I MANAGED to feed lunch to the invading hordes—there was a loaf of bread in the freezer and plenty of peanut butter and jelly—but I couldn't avoid the all-too-obvious truth. I had to make a major run to the grocery store—sooner, rather than later. Clara's tuition money couldn't arrive quickly enough.

David pulled into the driveway as I finished dishing up the last of the sandwiches. Instead of coming into the house, though, he strode across the lawn. He paused at the circle of our abortive working before he headed toward the treeline behind the garage.

I frowned and wiped my hands on a towel. "Okay everyone. You have your marching orders. Neko should be over shortly, to help you all get settled in your new rooms." I called Spot from his hopeful post beside the table and ducked out of the kitchen before anyone could ask questions.

At least the walk through the woods was soothing. My feet knew the trail without my providing any conscious thought. Oak trees arched overhead, the tips of their branches meeting like the vault of a cathedral ceiling. I barely registered the presence of squirrels and birds, the constant scurry of forest life at the edges of my sight and hearing. Sunlight dappled the ground, painting an ever-changing canvas beneath my feet.

Spot took point as often as he lagged behind. It was apparently hard work, keeping track of all the smells in the forest, but he made a valiant effort. Likewise, he embraced his duty of marking half the trees along the path.

Even though I knew the way, I was still surprised by the panorama as I stepped out of the sheltering forest. A lake stretched to the horizon, its still water mirroring the overcast sky above. A spray of sand arched around the shoreline, testament to some long-ago property owner who had dreamed of a true waterside retreat. A ramshackle boating shed nestled on the edge of the beach. I knew from past experience that it held a canoe and a couple of kayaks, life preservers, and a handful of beach chairs in varying stages of collapse.

I loved this lake. The water was perfectly still until a fish broke the surface, telegraphing its coded message in a flow of concentric rings. Reeds whispered on the shore, first as lush springtime grass, then as summer-dried stalks. Animals drank from the water and left their tracks in the wet sand, and ospreys nested in the lightning-shocked oak closest to the shore, calling to each other with their high-pitched cries.

The lake brought together all the elemental aspects of my power—the earth of the shoreline, the air of the sky above, the fire of sunlight reflecting off cool, clear water. The lake made me whole.

A dock was anchored on the sandy shore, and its weathered boards marched out over the water. David sat on the edge of the platform, staring out at the peaceful scene, look-ing like a painting by Edward Hopper.

He turned to watch as Spot ran along the shore, finding the perfect place to drink his fill from the lake. When the Lab shook his head to clean his muzzle, water droplets turned into rainbows. Spot made a visual survey of the entire beach before he turned three times and sank onto the end of the dock. Settling his jowls on his front paws, he began the serious business of an afternoon nap.

I stepped over the dog and walked out to David. He shifted to his left as I approached, making room for me. I sank down beside him, leaning my head on his shoulder as his arm circled my waist. I closed my eyes against the sun-light sparkling off the water, realizing how deeply tired I was, how little I'd slept the night before.

I forced myself to complete a long exhale, trying my best to get rid of all of my frustration and fear. "I hope your morning went better than mine."

He grunted, a response that could have meant anything at all, and then he asked, "What happened?"

I gave him the five-minute summary of our failed work-ing, wrapping up with my decisions about the new accom-modations. We both winced over the slight matter of impending financial doom at the hands of Neko's decorating binge. "How about you?" I asked. "Did you really have a meeting? Or were you just trying to get away from *Candid Camera* and *BBC Presents?*"

"The meeting was real." His voice stayed mild, but I felt him pull away from me, even though he didn't move a mus-cle.

I was the one who leaned back. "What's going on?"

He ran a hand through his hair, a rare gesture of unease. "Your mother's generous, er, gift is making me act a little faster than I'd planned. The magicarium will take a lot of money to run."

Of course a magicarium would take money. We'd need real housing for one thing—for students, their warders, and familiars. Camping out in the farm's outbuildings was a temporary solution at best. And while many of our classes would take place out of doors, we should have real rooms dedicated to study—sturdy tables, reliable chairs. Indoor study space would be especially important after the summer, when the weather changed and open air study became impractical.

And magical goods didn't come cheap, either. I could share the Osgood collection; that was part of my impetus in setting up the Academy in the first place. But my students would need their own textbooks and runes, crystals and herbs. Obtaining enough precious stones for everyone to work at once could drive us over a fiscal cliff in a single semester.

I reminded David, "I'm responsible for raising the money we need."

"*We're* responsible," he corrected. "We work together on this."

I was torn. His words were an immediate comfort, a balm that eased all my fear and frustration from the morning's failed working. But I was the one who had set us on this path. I had walked away from a perfectly good job, in a perfectly good library, solely because I'd come up with a crazy idea about opening a magicarium. I said, "I can't ask you to—"

"You aren't asking. I'm volunteering."

Volunteering.

As my warder, David wasn't required to raise money for me. But as my boyfriend... His calm acceptance of the financial situation doubled down on our personal relationship. I had to admit, I was thrilled by his words. And I was more than a little terrified.

"I can go through the collection in the basement to see what I can sell," I said. "The Washington Coven would love to get their hands on some of those books."

I didn't want to have anything to do with the coven, ever again. But if a sacrifice now—even a painful one—could guarantee full autonomy in the future? It was worth it. One hundred percent worth it.

David shook his head. "You'd be taking away one of the main reasons students have for coming to you in the first place." He took a deep breath. "I'm going to sell the lake."

"What?" My shout was loud enough to startle a red-winged blackbird from a branch at the edge of the forest. As if in sympathy, one of the ospreys shrieked a mournful cry across the water.

"It makes sense," he said. "We'll be able to finance the magicarium now, and for the foreseeable future."

Any other day, I would have trembled in excitement at the notion that David was thinking about our foreseeable future. Now, I had to demand, "How many houses are you talking about?"

"Not many. No more than the land can bear."

I wasn't asking about the land. I was asking about David. About the farm that had been in his family for decades. About the home he loved. "How many?" I pushed.

"The deal isn't even final yet."

"How many?"

"Thirty, to start with. Jonathan says this is a prime spot for one of those mixed communities—some condos and townhouses, along with single-family homes."

I couldn't believe he tossed off the words so easily. He sounded like he was quoting some slick, full-color, real estate brochure. Which, I realized, he probably was. Or Jonathan had been. "You can't be serious! Developers will build roads right through the woods. They'll need access from the highway. They'll dig wells and septic tanks—they'll ruin everything!"

"Not everything." He didn't quite manage to push conviction into his words.

"Near enough. You love this lake!"

And he did. I *knew* he did. He came out here when he was upset, when he needed a chance to think. He relaxed by the water, spinning out the tension that otherwise clung like fog on a London night. He let down his guard when he sat on this dock. For whatever short time he spent on the lake, he wasn't a warder, wasn't responsible for anyone or anything. He was himself.

And he was talking about giving up all of that for me.

"I can't let you do it," I said.

"We don't have any other choice." Frustration sparked beneath his words.

We, he'd said. This was a problem for us to solve together, not as witch and warder, where I had absolute say about magical goals, where he could issue fiats about my safety. *We* needed to work together to make the magicarium a success. *We* needed to function as a couple.

"There are always other choices." Frantic, I tried to come up with one of them. "What about the southern part of the property? The land closest to Parkersville."

"What about it?"

"If we have to sell something, why not sell it instead of the lake? Proximity to town should make it valuable."

"Not as valuable as waterfront."

"But there's more of it!" The force of my argument was growing. "We could sell more acres. We could harvest timber first, then put the property up for sale. Townhouses, condos—your Jonathan could build an entire planned community there!"

I knew I should feel a kinship for all the land. There were trees on the southern point—some massive oaks. Animals made their homes in the forest, birds and a whole host of mammals—foxes, raccoon, a lot of deer. There was power in the woods.

But there was also an old logging road that cut between the main property and the southern portion. And there was a deep ravine, too, the bed of a creek that ran dry every summer. The southern woods were beautiful, but they were already cut off from the land we called home.

Desperate times. Desperate measures. And if sacrificing those acres could save the lake's delicate ecosystem, it would all be worthwhile.

I could feel David turning over the idea inside his head. He'd already steeled himself to forfeit something he loved. He clearly hadn't considered that there might be another path, another way. "We'd have to give up at least twenty acres," he said. "Maybe more, depending on the value of the timber."

I nodded. "And we can look at the magicarium too. Figure out ways to scale back before we enroll a full class."

"You're not going to limit yourself there," David warned.

"Not limit," I said. "But *structure*. I don't have to accept every student who finds her way to our doorstep. I can have standards. I have to." I sounded so determined I knew I would have fooled any other person in the world. But David knew me better than that.

"Isn't it pretty to think so?" he asked, but there was a smile behind the words as he delivered the bittersweet Hemingway quote.

"I know you don't believe me now," I countered. "And it doesn't seem like having too many students is something we'll ever have to worry about. But I'm planning for the future. At least Clara is paying for Raven and Emma."

David looked at me as if he feared I'd suddenly gone insane.

"I know," I laughed. "Betting on Clara isn't a good idea. But I'm going to make her follow through this time. She cared enough to send Raven and Emma in the first place!"

"She's probably already forgotten they're here."

That's right. David knew my mother. He was fully aware how irresponsible she could be. I dug my elbow into his side. "You can make her pay up. You're her warder after all."

"Right," David said dryly. "Like I can demand anything from one of my witches."

I blushed. Clara was just as headstrong as I. David's warder magic would never turn my mother into a responsible, attentive woman, just as his unique astral skills had never tamed my own personal brand of insanity. "You've got a point there," I conceded.

He laughed, clearly relishing the victory. I leaned in close, pleased to realize he was relaxed again. Comfortable. Hopeful for the lake's future.

The lake that was distinctly lower than usual, if the water markings on the dock indicated anything. Or maybe I just didn't know how to read the signs. I'd never spent a summer out here at the farm. "What's up with the water level?" I asked.

"Drought. Three years running now. There should be four creeks feeding in, but one is already dry. Two more will go by the middle of July, and the last will be pretty much mud by August."

A fish jumped, as if to defy the bad news. Ripples made their slow way toward us. "It doesn't seem that bad."

"Not yet. But when the water level drops, the whole lake heats up. Plants die off and algae blooms. It's a mess."

The osprey called again from the edge of its nest, and its mate answered from somewhere on the edge of the shoreline. "But they'll be okay?" I nodded toward the raptor I could see.

"The parents should be. The chicks..." He shrugged. "Only twenty percent live in a good year."

But I had seen *these* chicks. I had watched the parents feeding *this* trio of young. The strongest fledgling was going to try flying any day now.

As if I'd spoken aloud, David grimaced and said, "I should do more to protect them."

"Climate change is above your pay grade."

There was that grunt again, the one that meant everything and nothing at all. He didn't accept my pronouncement, but he wasn't going to challenge me outright. I pulled his hand into my lap and traced the length of his fingers with my own.

I longed to have the power to fix the lake. It would take some incredibly complicated workings, interweaving earth and air, fire and water. There were countless living creatures to take into account. A real coven harnessing the power of dozens of witches *might* be able to work the necessary changes over a period of years. But me? Standing alone, outside every tradition of witchcraft? Who was I fooling? I couldn't even harness a simple wind spell with a couple of students.

I swallowed galling disappointment as I looked out at the southern end of the lake. If David sold the timber on that land, the ecological problems would only be compounded. Without the tree canopy, animals would suffer. There'd be erosion. More earth running into the lake, decreasing its depth, raising its temperature.

All for a magicarium that had no guarantee of success. No real *hope* for success if the morning's working was any sign.

"Don't even think it," David said. He kept his voice low, but his note of warning was very real.

"Think what?" I pretended innocence.

"You're not giving up on the Academy now. Not before you've even begun."

"I wasn't—"

He laughed and bent down to kiss me. The touch of his lips was easy, gentle, as if we had all the time in the world to stay together. "Don't lie to me, witch. I'm your warder. I always know."

I settled my palm against his chest. "And I know things, too. I know you don't want to sell the lake. We can find another way. Promise me you won't do anything right away."

His fingertips were warm against my throat, settling over the pulse point just below my ear. He kissed me again, harder this time.

My belly flipped at the unspoken urgency in his touch, but I wriggled away. "I'm serious, David." And I was, even though my breath caught in my throat. "Promise."

"Hmmm," he murmured while his nimble fingers did distracting things with the buttons on my blouse.

"David," I whispered, and his name was half a moan.

"I promise," he breathed against my lips.

And then I heard it—a single sharp bark. I knew the tone—Spot was demanding our immediate attention. David froze around me, his arms hardening into a protective cage. I slipped my hands down to my sides, twisting around to see what had upset the dog.

And I nearly laughed out loud. Our unexpected visitor looked as if he'd reported from Central Casting, responding to some imperious director's demand for "Accounting Dweeb." He wore trousers from a rumpled brown suit and a short-sleeve dress shirt with—honest to Hecate—a pocket protector. Aside from a few wisps of hair combed sidewise across the dome of his head, he was bald. His overbite made him look like a rabbit, an impression that was reinforced by the nervous glances he cast at Spot. He carried a beat-up briefcase, the russet leather worn almost bare on the corners.

David ordered Spot to lie down, and then he climbed to his own feet, never taking his eyes off the newcomer. He reached down and helped me up, keeping a palm on my elbow, as if he didn't trust me to find my balance. I took advantage of his interposing body to button my compromised blouse before I followed him to the end of the dock.

"Jane," David said when we stood beside our softly growling dog. "I'd like you to meet Norville Pitt."

My blood froze. Not because "Norville Pitt" meant anything to me—it didn't. Not because there was anything remotely threatening about the awkward man who licked his lips and darted his gaze to the bristling Spot.

I panicked because David Montrose was quite clearly afraid of the man at the end of our dock.

Chapter 5

OVER THE PAST four years, I had watched my warder face down physical threats without a second's hesitation. He had escorted me past men armed with swords. He had confronted policemen and Secret Service agents. I had witnessed his unequaled skill at verbal fencing; he'd traded barbs with witches and warders alike. I had relied on him to put me back together after disastrous encounters with my mother, after terrifying medical emergencies for Gran, after failed romances.

Through it all, David had never hesitated. But now my warder seemed lost. For the first time in my life, I realized it was a curse to know someone well enough to tell exactly what he was thinking. Especially when he was thinking he'd rather be anywhere but here.

To give him a moment to collect himself, I extended a hand in greeting. "Mr. Pitt."

"No relation to Brad," our visitor quipped, shaking with a sweaty palm.

Um, yeah. No possibility of confusion there.

Spot whined, loudly enough that David spoke his name in warning. The dog's attention was stapled to our visitor. David issued a tight hand command, insisting that Spot maintain his prone posture.

Attending to the dog finally allowed David to recover enough composure to take some action. He tugged open the door of the ramshackle boat shed and dug around inside for a few plastic chairs. After taking a couple of swipes at the sturdiest one, he gestured toward our guest. "Please, Norville. Have a seat."

Pitt's shoulders hunched as he perched on the edge of the chair. His glasses slid down his nose, sped on their way by a sheen of sweat. He pushed them back into place with an automatic gesture that told me they slipped a thousand times a day, sweat or no.

This was this man who put fear in David's heart?

My warder flicked his hand to indicate I should take another one of the chairs. I automatically left room for him to sit between Pitt and me. Spot's whine ratcheted another notch toward desperate, and David took pity on the poor animal, allowing him to cross the beach, to fold himself across my feet.

Pitt swallowed noisily before he began to speak. "Miss Madison. I am here today in my capacity as Head Clerk of Hecate's Court."

David stiffened beside me.

"Yes, Montrose," Pitt said, and he actually chortled. "You're one of the first to hear about my promotion. It will be announced officially at Lughnasadh."

I glanced from Pitt to David, trying to fathom the importance of the promotion. Hecate's Court, of course, was the bureaucracy that managed all the witches in the world. I'd sent them the registration papers for my magicarium a couple of months back. Now, I tried to swallow, but my throat was too dry. It took me three tries to choke out, "I'm always happy to serve the Court, Mr. Pitt."

The Head Clerk beamed as he released the clasps on his briefcase. The spring-loaded fittings sounded like pistol shots. I jumped despite my best intentions, and David leaped halfway out of his chair to save me from a nonexistent danger. Spot was on his haunches.

Even as David sat and ordered the Lab to do the same, Pitt reached inside the case. As he took his time, digging deep for some supposed treasure, my mind flashed over possibilities, cataloging things that could warrant David's jagged emotion.

Pitt might have a magical stone in there, a chunk of jasper that would drain my powers, leaving me helpless and exposed. He might have a rowan wand, a tool to bolster some deadly spell a witch had packaged for his use. He might have fresh-harvested bay leaves and rue, powerful herbs that would disrupt the balance of my own magic, render me as helpless as a child. He might have a gun.

Pitt cleared his throat as he extracted a sheaf of papers.

The pages were covered in small type. A column of numbers ran down the left margin, counting off rows of text. Some words were printed in bold; others appeared entirely in capital letters. A copper grommet bound the document together, and a red ribbon was threaded through the ring.

David collapsed back in his chair. "All these cloak and dagger games to deliver a *charter*?"

Pitt's smile was different now. He'd gone from unctuous to carnivorous. "I assure you, Montrose. This is not a game."

David reached for the papers.

"Ah, ah, ah! These pages aren't for warders' eyes. We have *rules*, Montrose. You used to know that."

"I still do," David snapped. Good. His temper was rising. I'd rather see him angry than afraid.

"Then show a little respect. I busted you back to apprentice when you reported to me seven years ago. I hardly need to remind you the Court doesn't offer *third* chances. One more Class A violation, and you're through with warding forever."

Seven years ago. I knew the whole story. David had warded a Washington Coven witch, a woman named Haylee James. They'd had a series of fiery disagreements about proper uses of magic, about the roles of witches and warders. Ultimately, David had been cast out from the coven, sent back to Hecate's Court. He'd only been allowed to ward me after years of rehabilitation. Even then, the Court had only sent him my way because I was an upstart. An unknown. Someone who couldn't possibly be important in the long run.

And now, I understood what I should have recognized the instant our unwelcome visitor materialized on the beach. Norville Pitt wasn't some hapless accounting clerk, running errands for Hecate's Court. He was an *enforcer*. Pitt held the power of arcane life and death, the ability to terminate David's career. And mine too, in all likelihood.

I cleared my throat. "Excuse me, Mr. Pitt. I'm afraid I don't know what's in that packet of papers."

"Forgive me, Miss Madison." I'd been wrong when I'd

thought the man was a shy rabbit. He was more like a snake, hypnotizing me with his bulging eyes. "May I present the Madison Academy charter?"

He handed over the beribboned papers with a greasy flourish. I glanced at the front page, taking care to hold the document at an angle so David could read along with me.

"WHEREAS, Hecate's Court has been charged for time immemorial with the management and training of all Witches in the Eastern Empire, and

"WHEREAS, Jane Madison has founded the Madison Academy as a magicarium for the training of Witches and established herself as the magistrix thereof, and

"WHEREAS, Jane Madison wishes that all graduates of the Madison Academy be recognized as official Witches within the boundaries of the Eastern Empire..."

There were a dozen more statements like that, all formalizing the background of my Academy, all stating what I had supposedly thought through and done before I launched the magicarium. I thumbed past the rest of the whereases until I got to a statement printed in bold: "NOW, THEREFORE, Hecate's Court and Jane Madison are agreed that this document shall control all interactions between them with respect to the Madison Academy."

Okay... I turned the page to a lengthy collection of DEFINITIONS.

"Magicarium shall mean a school for training Witches in the use of Witchcraft.

"Affiliated Institution" shall mean any Coven, Magicarium, or Court that offers formal or informal support to a magicarium, including but not limited to support in the form of instruction, financial aid, material goods, or astral energy.

"Witchcraft shall mean the casting of spells, the reading of runes, and/or any magical use whatsoever of crystals, herbs, or other elements of the natural world."

All right. I couldn't offer much argument there. I flipped past another few pages.

One lengthy paragraph was labeled MILESTONES. I skimmed over the words, trying to force them to make sense. "All students enrolled in the Madison Academy shall be tested at regular intervals to determine their achievement of the Milestones set forth in this document." A series of benchmarks was defined: Awakening a familiar, lighting a candle, changing the appearance of a substance, converting an item from one substance to another.

The list of accomplishments went on and on. Some of the achievements were laughably simple; I'd mastered them on my own before I'd even learned that Hecate's Court existed. Others, though, were substantially more involved. At the bottom of the list, I found one that had given me nearly endless grief: Awakening an anima.

Right. Like I'd be teaching *that* to any of my students.

The document went on in the same legalistic vein, page after page. I understood all the magical concepts, but some of the formal language left my head spinning. It seemed unnecessary both to "attest and aver." And I was pretty sure I didn't want to "assert, verify, and proclaim" that I was entirely in charge of my students' magical workings whether those undertakings were conducted on the premises of the Madison Academy or elsewhere. I was absolutely positive I didn't want to indemnify the Court for any loss, pecuniary or magical, that they perceived to have accrued to the possessions of Hecate's Court, in their sole evaluation and at their sole determination.

And then, I found the real kicker. It was a few pages from the end, buried in a collection of paragraphs about how we parties could notify each other about changes in our address, about how we couldn't assign our rights to anyone else, etc.

"MAJOR WORKING: In the event the Madison Academy fails to complete one (1) Major Working by the conclusion of its first semester of operation, all magical materials belonging to Jane Madison and the Madison Academy shall be forfeit to Hecate's Court without any compensation or recourse for future return."

I tossed the agreement onto Pitt's briefcase. "I won't sign this."

He simply turned to my warder. "Montrose? Perhaps you can explain to Miss Madison why it's in her best interest to sign?"

David was clutching the arms of his chair. "I'm not doing your dirty work! I've seen hundreds of charters before, and not one had a clause like that."

Pitt licked his liver-colored lips. "You saw those charters when you worked as my *clerk*. A rather headstrong clerk, as I recall too well. A rather headstrong clerk, with entirely inappropriate ideas about how the Court should and should not conduct its business."

"That's between you and me, Norville. You can't punish the Madison Academy because you didn't like the way I filed papers."

"Can't I?" Pitt clambered to his feet and pointed a pudgy finger toward the center of David's chest. I automatically dropped a hand to Spot's muscled neck, and I could feel the animal trembling to intervene. If David hadn't flashed an immediate silent command, there might have been blood spilled on the sand.

"Let me tell you something, Montrose. When this little document came up to the Front Desk, no one was particularly inclined to bring it out here. No one wanted to leave the cool, comfortable hallways of the Court to travel in the sweltering Maryland summer."

Pitt took a step closer. His feet shifted in the sand, and the tip of his index finger touched David's shirt. Spot began to growl, low and steady. "But I realized they were all being short-sighted." *Poke.* The growl rose in pitch. "I realized this was quite an opportunity." *Poke.* Spot's lips curled back over his teeth. "I realized I was finally going to see David Montrose bound by the very rules and regulations he claims to hold so dear." One more *poke*, and this time Pitt did not pull his hand back. Spot's growl became an uninterrupted snarl. "The Court issued the charter, Montrose. Get your witch to sign it, or suffer the consequences."

David's fingers curled into fists. If I'd been Norville Pitt, I would have stumbled backward across the sand, doing my best to get away from a warder's unrestrained anger, not to mention the increasingly distraught Cujo who was slavering for release. I had no idea what the true stakes were between these men, but I knew I had to intervene. "Mr. Pitt?" I asked. "Could you give us a moment?"

He finally took a step back and ran a hand over his trio of hairs. "Of course, Miss Madison. After all, *you're* the magistrix. For now."

I snatched up the pages and waited for the repulsive man to excuse himself, to head across the beach so David and I could have a little privacy. Fat chance. Instead, David snapped his fingers to command Spot's attention, and then he led us both onto the dock. David kept one eye on Pitt as I turned my back on the clerk. "What the hell happened between the two of you?" I asked.

"You heard him. He was my boss, when I was sent back to the Court."

"That doesn't explain *that* level of animosity."

David pointed out, "We don't have time for this now."

"Fine." At least the remnants of his fear were gone, completely replaced by anger. I'd get the truth from him later. "I can't sign this, David. I can't bet everything on a single ritual. Not when I can't even raise a simple wind spell with my students."

"I don't know how he talked them into this. All those charters I filed, and not a single hint of a Major Workings clause before."

"What happens if I don't sign?"

"You'll be declared rogue. The Court will send a letter demanding you shut down operations. If you don't comply in a week, they'll send a Termination Team."

"That doesn't sound good."

"It isn't. They'll bring a dozen warders to guarantee I won't be a factor. An equal number of witches to restrain you. They'll carry off the Osgood books, and whatever you've collected on your own. And Neko, too, of course."

Of course. I'd lost Neko before. I never wanted to live through that nightmare again. I glared at the charter. "I'll take my chances against their Team. I'm stronger than they think I am."

"You're not listening. This is the *Court*. They make the Washington Coven look like Matchbox cars test-driving the

Indy 500. If a dozen witches aren't enough to restrain you, they'll bring two dozen. A hundred. They have unlimited resources, and they'll do whatever it takes."

"And there's no way for me to appeal?"

"The Eastern Empire doesn't have any jurisdiction here. So long as you're a witch in good standing, Hecate's Court is the ultimate arbiter."

"What's a Major Working, anyway? How major is Major?"

David shrugged. "I don't know. I suspect they don't either. You'll have to choose something big enough that there can't be any doubt."

Great. Maybe I could negotiate peace in the Middle East while I was at it.

But what choice did I have? If I went rogue, Neko was automatically forfeit. If I signed the damned charter, at least I had a fighting chance to keep him. And I meant to fight. A lot.

I turned on my heel and stalked back to the beach, Spot on my left side, and David on my right. Thrusting the charter in Pitt's face, I asked, "What do I do? Sign it in blood?"

"Ink should suffice." He smiled as if he'd just told the best joke in the world. As I fumed, he extracted a Bic from his well-protected pocket. My stomach turned when I saw the cap had been chewed to a pulp.

He flipped to a page in the middle of the Agreement. "I am required to point out that you have a deadline here." He tapped the paper. "Please initial where it says you have until Samhain to complete your Major Working."

"Samhain!" That was Halloween. A mere four months from now. The Madison Academy semester didn't end until

December; we should have had until Yule to prove our-selves. But Samhain marked the traditional end and begin-ning of a witch's year.

I clenched my jaw and initialed the deadline.

Then, I signed the last page of the charter, taking great care to make my name legible. Pitt added his own signature on behalf of the Court before he passed the sheaf of papers to David. "If you'll bear appropriate witness?" he asked with oily politeness.

David nearly tore the paper as he crossed the "t" in Montrose.

"Excellent," Pitt declared, snorting with adenoidal glee. I half expected him to start rubbing his palms together like Snidely Whiplash. "We'll make copies back at the home of-fice and deliver one to you, post-haste. Did you have any questions, Miss Madison?"

"Just one. Do you actually like your job, screwing with honest witches who only want to make the world a better place?"

He blinked, as if my words did not compute in whatever feeble machine passed for his mind. "I don't understand, Miss—"

"Let me show you the path back to the house, Norville," David said. He shot me a glance, clearly warning that the Court's eternal blacklist might be only one more insult away.

"I'll find it myself, thank you." Pitt looked like he didn't want to spend a second alone with David, and he wasn't all that fond of Spot either—confirmation, if I'd needed it, that he wasn't as foolish as he looked.

We watched Norville Pitt waddle across the beach. He swung his briefcase at his side, all the while slipping and sliding on the sand. I waited until he'd disappeared behind the treeline before I asked, "What do we do now?"

David collapsed into one of the deck chairs. He buried his hands in the thick fur around Spot's neck. "Good boy," he murmured, and the dog's tail started a steady tattoo. It took ages for him to raise his gaze to me. "I'm sorry," he said at last.

"About what?"

"About dragging you into all of this. If you had another warder, Pitt wouldn't have gotten involved."

"If I had another warder, I'd never have gotten this far."

"Jane—

"I'm not listening," I sang, stopping just short of putting my fingers in my ears. I waited until David slumped back into the chair. "Hey," I said, reaching out with my foot to shove at his calf. "The Court is doing this because they want to get the Osgood collection. It's not you. It's me."

He managed a wan smile. "Great. What every man longs to hear."

"Seriously," I said. "I'm sorry Pitt came after you like that. It wasn't fair for him to use either of us to get at the other. But he did, and the Court did, and now we don't have a lot of options. Let's get back home so I can share the good news with my students."

I could tell he didn't believe me. He still blamed himself. But he clasped my hand tightly the entire way back to the house. Spot stayed close every step of the way, on high canine alert.

We found Raven and Emma lounging in the living room, tall glasses of iced tea sweating on nearby coasters. Raven immediately raised her phone, pushing the button to activate the camera.

"Forget it," I snapped. And then, I told them about the charter. I explained that my entire witchcraft collection was on the line, Neko included. Their reactions actually made me like them more than I thought possible—each sucked in her breath as if she'd taken a blow to the gut.

"So that's it," I concluded. "We have until Samhain."

Emma's voice was very soft as she shook her head. "That won't be a doddle. What do you want us to do, then? What's our Major Working?"

I looked at David. Ordinarily, I would consult with him about something this important. We might spend days, weeks even, bandying about possibilities, considering pros and cons, measuring out costs and benefits.

But we didn't have the time. And I *was* the magistrix, after all.

I looked at Emma and saw how she fought to be patient. I watched Raven's fingers twitch as she started to reach for her phone out of habit. And then I said, "We're going to restore the health of the lake here on the farm. We're going to reverse the effects of the drought and make it thrive once again."

My students merely nodded. I wondered if they knew enough to comprehend how substantial a working I had just announced.

But David wasn't a student. He understood before the words were out of my mouth. "Jane," he said. And I watched him struggle for his next words. He obviously didn't want to undermine me in front of Raven and Emma. He didn't want to say that my suggestion was patently absurd— a weather working on that scale was more than any trained magistrix could manage, with dozens of enrolled students.

I raised my chin. "There can't be any question," I said. "There can't be any doubt that our working is sufficient. After we repair the lake, no one on the Court can possibly argue that we failed to do a Major Working. I refuse to let them win."

Chapter 6

THE FOLLOWING MORNING, I tried not to worry about the Major Working as I fortified myself with a sourdough waffle. And orange butter. And pure maple syrup—the type that came from real trees in frosty northern forests. I was deep in the middle of brunch with my grandmother and Clara, a tradition that Gran had instituted a few years back. She thought shared meals would bring all three of us closer together.

She was right—at least in the literal sense. Ever since Clara had retreated to Sedona, we had relied on David to transport her to our monthly gatherings, using his warder's magic. This morning had been no exception; he had spirited Clara from her perch by the Vortex, dropping her off at Teaism in Washington, DC, a mere stone's throw from the National Archives and a few other government buildings that all looked like Greek temples.

Gran swallowed a hefty bite of French toast and reached across the bamboo table to pat my hand. "Well, dear, I think you were incredibly brave. I don't know what I would have done, if that horrible man had showed up in my living room."

Despite my anxiety, I smiled. Gran made Norville Pitt sound like some sort of insect pest that could be taken care of by an exterminator. "I'm sure you would have come up with something."

"It's not right," Gran said. "If our David antagonized that man, there has to be a reason. The Court should be *rewarding* David, not antagonizing him like that." She stared morosely at her side order of tea-cured salmon. Or maybe she was studying her chicken sausage. It was hard to tell with the array of dishes on her side of the table. "If your mother and I had any real powers, we'd take a stand on his behalf. The three of us together, we could make the Court see reason."

"You *do* have powers," I said loyally. Although, truth be told, my grandmother's abilities were rather limited. Clara on the other hand… Her magic ebbed and flowed, but she usually managed to tap into her strong potential.

As if on cue, my mother stopped pushing her fork around on her plate of scrambled tempeh. Kale, tomato, and cilantro gave the dish plenty of color, but Clara eyed Gran's sausage with longing. "I think we should consult with Sister Moonsilver. See what the spirit world has to say about this Norville Pitt."

I forced my lips to curve into a smile as I tried to phrase a non-incendiary response. I needed to *sound* like I thought my mother's suggestion could possibly have merit. In some other world where astrology was actually real magic. "Sister Moonsilver isn't really a psychic, Clara. Her only magical ability is using enough vague words to lure her patrons into completing her sentences." *She's a fraud*, I wanted to add, but Gran had long-since forbidden the F-word.

Clara drew herself up very straight. "Sister Moonsilver correctly predicted my power animal. If she isn't a psychic, how did she know I'd dream of a mountain lion the first night I slept in her tent?"

Maybe because she fed you copious amounts of a very suspicious tea before you fell asleep. And because she never stopped talking about mountain lions, even while you were dreaming.

But this was Mother-Daughter Brunch. There was nothing to be gained by challenging Clara on some of her most closely held beliefs. Instead, I took a generous bite of apple gingerbread and watched the koi swim in the stone-lined pond that filled the center of the dining room. I had almost achieved perfect Zen peace when Gran launched a new, supposedly-safe topic of conversation. "Tell us, dear. How are your students settling in?"

"Raven and Emma?" I took a sip of Golden Monkey tea as I considered my answer. "Fine, I guess. Things were a little chaotic when they showed up Friday night, but I think David and I covered pretty well."

Gran buttered a ginger scone and smeared it with marmalade. "I'm sure you're getting excellent advice from Neko. This must be right up his alley, the social aspects of welcoming students to your magicarium."

I leaned back in my chair. "Actually," I said to the oversized goldfish, "he's barely talking to me."

Gran was shocked enough that she put down her scone without taking a bite. "What have you done now, Jane?"

What had I done? Why did she assume I had done anything? Oh. Maybe because I had.

"This all happened so fast! David and I never expected witches to appear on our doorstep, along with warders and familiars!"

Gran pressed: "What did you do to Neko?"

And so I told them about asking my familiar to give up his apartment to Raven and Emma. They listened to my justifications without interrupting, even when my voice rose to a notably shriller register. "Under the circumstances," I concluded defensively, "it was the best thing for everyone."

"The best thing for you, perhaps," Clara said, looking up from her plate, where she was adding thick slices of sausage to her tempeh.

Gran added, "But it certainly sounds as if Neko might have felt blindsided."

"I didn't—" But there was no use finishing the sentence. "You both know if I had to choose between Neko and my students, I'd choose Neko in a heartbeat! I never wanted to hurt his feelings." I shifted my mug from hand to hand. "Between the three of us—and seriously! This goes no further!—I'm not even sure I *like* my students. Emma's love of all things British wears thin after about a minute, and Raven... She can be a bit much to take."

Of course, Gran was ready with an immediate answer. "I see one possible solution. Have Raven and Emma live in the main house, with you and David."

Hadn't she listened to a single word I'd said? "I want to spend *less* time with them. Not more."

Gran patted my hand. "Sometimes, we don't understand what we really need."

"There isn't room! We only have one guest room."

Clara said helpfully, "You can always move things around. In fact, I've been worried about the feng shui in David's office. The energy is terrible in there right now." She'd given up on her tempeh completely, and now she was scraping her fork against the empty plate that had once held two plump chicken sausages. That didn't keep her from launching into a detailed explanation of polarity and the cardinal directions. I was totally lost by the time she got to the Blue Dragon and the Red Phoenix.

Clara's interior decorating plans aside, it wasn't actually impossible to bring my students into the house. And David's office *was* the logical room to commandeer. It was upstairs, and it was about the same size as the existing guest room. All we'd have to do was move in a bed, and a dresser. A nightstand. Maybe a small desk.

But it was David's office. I'd already gotten into trouble making one person move for my magicarium housing. As Clara finally ran down, I said, "It wouldn't be fair to David."

Gran turned her head to the side, looking exactly like a curious bird. "But it was fair to make Neko move?" She had a point, of course. She was Gran. She *always* had a point.

"I've already paid for my mistake with Neko." I held up one hand to forestall a protest from Clara and Gran, my familiar's two greatest fans. "I mean literally paid—I gave him my credit card, so he could outfit all the new rooms."

"Ouch," Clara said, immediately recognizing the cost of my quest for absolution.

"Ouch, indeed. Speaking of which," I braced myself with another sip of tea, "we could really use the tuition money you promised."

Clara smiled serenely. "I'll have it for you shortly. The

new moon is July 8."

"The new moon?" I asked, puzzled. "What does that have to do with anything?"

"I have a new ritual I'm trying out. I'm going to fill my cauldron with rainwater and put a pure silver coin in the very center. I'll light a green candle and a white candle just as the first rays of moonlight strike the water, and I'll say, 'Silver, silver come to me, fill my purse now, three times three.' I'll send you the tuition money as soon as the spell works."

I swallowed my immediate words of skepticism. But when Clara continued to look me with great satisfaction, I said, "We were really hoping for something a little more...immediate."

"Well, Jeanette, I don't see any way that 'immediate' is going to happen. I've just bought new robes for the Oak Canyon Coven."

I bridled when Clara called me the wrong name, a clear sign that she'd stopped listening to me, stopped paying attention to who I really was. Gran jumped in before I could say something I'd regret. "So, dear. Tell us a little more about the magicarium. Are you teaching your students how to work the way the three of us do? All unified? All together?"

Good old Gran. She was determined to remind me that I shared a common heritage with both her and Clara. I was so amused by her blatant deflection that I almost didn't mind admitting, "I tried that yesterday. But we couldn't find the balance. Couldn't even raise a gust of wind."

Gran frowned, but her loyalty was undiluted. "I'm sure that with a little practice..."

"We don't have time for that," I said. "It's all I've been

thinking about since Norville Pitt left. If I only have four months to complete a massive weather working, I'm going to have to use traditional teaching methods to get us ready."

Clara looked skeptical. "Can you do that, Jeanette?"

"Jane," I reminded her through grinding teeth. "And I don't know. But at least I can build on whatever training they've already had. I can focus on each individual element of our working, making sure we have a solid foundation before moving on to the next thing. Walk before we can run, and all that jazz."

Gran beamed. "It sounds as if you've thought this all out, dear!"

Thought it out, yes. But I was a long way from being confident about implementing the results. Dissatisfaction with traditional training was exactly what had driven Emma and Raven from Sedona into my arms. Would they even stick around if I tried to force them into a traditional education?

At least Gran's enthusiasm temporarily dispersed my cloud of self-doubt. I had to laugh as she leaned forward and whispered conspiratorially, "Now, how about dessert? I hear this place is known for their salty oat cookies!"

No amount of magic would ever explain how Gran managed to pack away so much food. But who was I, to pass up a salty oat cookie?

I only felt a little like a traitor as I approached my best friend's bakery, Cake Walk, an hour and a half later. Sure, I had indulged in a hearty brunch. And I'd done my best to keep pace with Gran when it came to dessert. I had no business even *looking* at another baked good. But I wanted to see

Melissa in person. I only got down to DC once or twice a month.

"Walk on in!" said the cheery sign in the window, and the bell over the door jangled to announce me. No one was sitting at the tables in front. In fact, Melissa was nowhere to be seen, but I could hear her.

"No, Mother, I am *not* telling Aunt Agnes to wear beige and shut up. That's the mother of the groom." Pause. "No, I'm not telling Rob's mother to wear beige either." Pause. "I'm not telling anyone to shut up!"

I shook my head in sympathy. Melissa and her boyfriend had announced their engagement a month ago. At the time, it had made perfect sense to choose a wedding date more than a year away—Rob's sister would be home from her stint in the army, and Melissa's recently-expanded catering business would be on sturdier footing. As a practical matter, though, the long lead time had only given Melissa's relatives a chance to dig in their heels about a million details the happy couple could not care less about.

"Mother—" Melissa said three times, but she was apparently unable to wedge more than that single word into the tirade streaming over the phone line.

Melissa and Rob had originally planned on a simple morning service with a light brunch for guests—baked goods from Cake Walk, a couple of urns of coffee. Yielding to familial demands, though, the happy couple had been convinced to switch to an evening ceremony, complete with a full dinner reception and a twelve-piece band. Melissa's grandmother had insisted on a rehearsal dinner to feed every guest traveling to the wedding. Great-Aunt Sarah had campaigned for a morning-after brunch. Melissa's father had plotted a golf outing the weekend before the blessed event, and Uncle Joe had upped the ante with an evening smoker at his favorite cigar shop.

And there were still twelve months to go. Plenty of events to add. Maybe the boys would go to a strip club. Or we girls would. And there was ample opportunity to schedule a few bridal showers. By the time Melissa's family was through harnessing the might of the wedding-industrial complex, I was pretty sure the overall cost for the White-Peterson nuptials would be greater than the GDP of several small countries, combined.

"No, Mother," Melissa finally bulled her way through the barrage on the other end of the phone line. "I'm sorry I hurt your feelings. That's not what I meant to do. Look, I've got to go. There are seven people waiting at the counter. I can't keep talking right now. Whoops, bye!"

The phone crashed into its cradle and then there was a suspiciously long silence, while I imagined Melissa running her hands over her face. When she finally stepped out of the back room, I was waiting for her with as strong a smile as I could muster. "I'm not seven people. But I can buy seven different things, if that would help."

She came around the counter to give me a hug. Her slight frame seemed to have shrunk since the last time I'd seen her. Perhaps for the first time in memory, her perfect honey-colored hair was in disarray, standing on end as if she'd spent the last half hour combing it with frustrated fingers. Which she probably had. "Nothing will help," she mourned. "Nothing at all. I was insane to get engaged."

"Don't be ridiculous. I've never seen you happier than the night Rob proposed. What's on the Greatest Wedding

Hits list today?"

"Aunt Agnes wants us to order roses tattooed with our initials. Little Ms and Rs burned onto every petal. Apparently
they're all the rage at her country club." She picked up a rag
and began scrubbing at the perfectly clean countertop. "Am
I a terrible person, for wishing we'd never invited Aunt Agnes?"

I grinned and quoted, "Thy marriage, sooner than thy
wickedness."

She laughed. "*All's Well That Ends Well?*"

"Good. For a minute, I thought you'd been too traumatized to recognize a perfectly apt quotation."

"I'm traumatized enough to consider doing my Ophelia
impression. It's not a bad day for a dip in the Potomac, is it?
'There's rosemary, that's for remembrance.'" I laughed as
she did her best imitation of a madwoman. She took a shuddering breath before saying, "Okay. What can I get you?"

I wanted to say "Mojito Therapy," so we could shut
down the bakery, take lime and mint from her perfect kitch-
en, and retreat upstairs to her oven of an apartment. We
could drink the night away, bemoaning demanding aunts
and controlling Head Clerks of Hecate's Court, and everything else that was wrong with our lives.

But I couldn't do that. I had to drive home eventually,
and rum would not mix well with David's Lexus. Besides, it
was barely after noon.

"Yoo-hoo!" Melissa said, saluting me with a glass of ice.

I forced my attention back to the beverages at hand.
"Mango Mamba, please."

Melissa complied, and then she put a couple of Sugar
Suns on a plate. Sure, I'd had a feast at Teaism, but I

couldn't hurt my best friend's feelings, could I? I nibbled on one of the iced lemon cookies. Wow. Absence really did make the heart grow fonder.

"So," I said with the curiosity of a small child poking a bruise. "I have one wedding-related question. Why do you put up with this stuff?"

"You're my maid of honor, and you have to ask?"

"Humor me."

"I'm the only girl on both sides of my family. Everyone's been planning for this since the day I was born."

"But if you're not happy…"

Before I could continue, the bakery door opened and a pair of women rushed in. They wore shorts and T-shirts, with sweatbands cinching their foreheads and wrists. From the expensive tennis rackets in their hands, it was clear they'd just come from the courts. Melissa dished up everything they ordered, a couple of Cinnamon Smiles, three Lemon Grenades, and a handful of giant Ginger-Butterscotch Dreams in a separate bag. Melissa smiled as she took their money and told them she'd see them next weekend.

"Regulars?" I asked dryly.

"Like clockwork. They insist they've each worked off 3500 calories by playing doubles tennis for half an hour. I'm afraid of the hit on my bottom line if I tell them the truth."

I waited for Melissa to get back to the real matter at hand—her struggle to declare independence in her wedding travails—but she was rescued by two more customers, a father and his adorable toddler. The little boy debated between four different treats before going back to his first choice, a Vanilla Vroom.

As they walked out the door, I said, "I miss this."

"So come around more often."

"I would, if I could. Things are getting…interesting out at the farm."

"Interesting, as in you're learning where little bitty lambs come from? Or interesting, as in you're discovering you and David can't live under the same roof?"

"Interesting, as in class is in session at the Madison Academy."

"Do tell!"

Between interruptions from customers and refills on my Mango Mamba, I caught Melissa up on all the dramatics. She laughed until I told her about Norville Pitt and the Court's demands.

"So what are you going to do?" Melissa asked.

"What *can* I do? I'm going to start official classes tomorrow morning. The next four months are going to be like final exams in college. Why sleep when I cram in one more detail about reading runes?"

"You've got plenty of time," Melissa said confidently.

I shook my head. "Maybe if I'd done this teaching thing before. I'm starting to think I bit off more than I can chew. I mean, I've completed difficult rituals on my own, and with Gran and Clara. But whatever made me think I can do something like that with absolute strangers? I should have thought things through a bit more before I registered the Academy."

"You've wanted to do this for months," Melissa reminded me.

I feel like a fraud, I wanted to say. *I'm as bad as Sister Moonsilver.* But I shoved down that nagging voice of self-doubt.

"Enough about me. I came here because I'm your maid of honor. And as your maid of honor, I'm telling you, you've got to put your foot down on some of this wedding stuff."

"Fat chance," Melissa said. As if to avoid my quirked eyebrows, she took out a pasteboard box and started to fill it with two huge squares of Almond Lust. She carefully centered a square of tissue paper on top of David's favorite treats before adding a couple of cream-filled Lemon Pillows for Neko. She tucked in a few of the peanut butter treats she kept for the canine companions of her favorite customers. Spot would be in heaven.

I let her tape up the box before I forced her back to the matter at hand. "Am I going to have to Friendship Test this?" I was pulling out the big guns. If I made her promise on a Friendship Test, she'd have no choice but to follow through. "Seriously. Talk to Rob. Find out what he thinks about tattooed roses. And if he thinks they're an abomination against nature, then tell Aunt Agnes she's out of luck."

Melissa smiled wanly. "And you'll back me up, when the Four Horsewomen of the Wedding Apocalypse come riding to my door?"

I laughed. "I don't even know who the Four Horsewomen would be."

Melissa counted them on her fingers: "Vanity. Gluttony. Avarice. And Pride."

"Not Lust?"

"Ewwww. I don't want to put Aunt Agnes and Lust in the same *conversation*. Much less the same sentence."

I laughed and reached for the box of treats. "Really, Melissa. Just do it. Stop the madness now, or the next year will be a nightmare."

A trio of kickball players tumbled through the door, already shouting out their drink orders. As Melissa set up glasses on the counter, she gave me a meaningful glance. "Go on," she said. "Hit the road. Don't you have something all important and magical to do back at the farm?"

"Friendship Test," I reminded her.

"Okay," she said.

"I mean it."

"I said okay!" But she was smiling as she waited for the athletes to place their orders for sweets.

By the time I got back to the farmhouse, David was ensconced in his office. I assumed he'd already worked his warder's magic, whisking Clara back to Sedona. I wondered if he'd mentioned tuition payments. Maybe he'd made better headway than I had.

I stood in the doorway, watching my warder work. A stack of papers was centered on his desk, each sheaf fastened by a grommet and threaded with ribbon, just like the contract Pitt had made me sign. A sleek fountain pen rested beside the documents, and I could just make out a column of numbers on the nearby pad of legal paper. An adding machine purred at the edge of the desk, its spool of paper curling onto the floor.

"I know you're there," David said quietly. Of course he did. I smiled and stepped into the room as he rose to greet me.

"I stopped by Cake Walk on my way back from brunch." I held out the pasteboard box. "Lust?"

"Always," he murmured, and a smile twitched across his lips. As he took the box, his eyes never left my face. Somehow, he set it down on the desk without upsetting any of his official papers.

His fingers were warm through the fabric of my sundress as he pulled me close. I leaned in to kiss him, a quick brush of my lips against his, but I caught my breath when he folded me into a full embrace. Tension radiated across his back, tangible even through his shirt.

"Hey," I said. "What's all this?" I pulled back enough to gesture at the papers.

"Court records."

"Are you supposed to have them here?"

"I kept a copy of everything, toward the end." Well, that didn't really answer my question. Or, maybe, it did.

"What are you looking for?"

"I'm checking the numbers again. Making sure my accusations about Pitt were right the first time. He shouldn't have been promoted to Head Clerk. Shouldn't be working for the Court at all."

"Accusations?" I frowned at the vehemence in David's voice. "What *happened* between the two of you?"

He shook his head.

"Hey," I said, bumping him gently with my elbow. "I'm on your side. I'm your witch."

His fingers tightened on my hips for just a heartbeat before he backed away. "It's ancient history. No reason for you to worry about it."

I frowned but decided to let him have his way. "Hey," I said, brightly enough to alert him I was changing the topic. "I had an idea. I think we should bring the witches closer. Move them into the house."

"*You* think that?"

"Gran thinks that," I amended. "She says I should give the apartment back to Neko. But that would mean you'd have to move your office to the storage room in the basement, and that doesn't feel right to me. You shouldn't lose your personal space for me."

"For your students," he corrected.

That sounded better, but... "I wouldn't mind changing things around for Emma, but..." I bit my tongue to silence my uncharitable thoughts.

David's lips curled into a wry smile. "Raven's a piece of work, isn't she?"

"That's one way of putting it," I laughed. "Say what you're really thinking. She's a scheming, manipulative—

But I cut off the rest of my thought. David would never say those words out loud, not about a witch. Not so long as he was still a warder sworn to Hecate's Court.

"Hey," I said, tightening my arms to bring him closer. "Are we okay?"

"Of course," he answered. "Why wouldn't we be? I can probably get more work done downstairs, anyway."

He set about proving the fact that we were fine with a most reassuring kiss. With a knowing smile, I reached behind me and closed the office door to guarantee our privacy.

Chapter 7

WITH ONE THING and another (ahem), I didn't get to break the good news to Neko until the following morning. Everyone was gathered in the kitchen—my students, their warders, and their familiars. David had just poured himself a bracing cup of coffee when Neko sauntered in.

"Just the man I was looking for!" I said, as he crossed to the refrigerator.

Neko froze, his fingers clutching tight around a quart of cream. "I have receipts for everything. I swear!"

I'm sure he did. Not that my sobbing bank account would care. "That's not what I was worried about. I've been thinking. It makes more sense for Raven and Emma to stay in the house than out in the garage apartment. We're going to be working pretty intensely over the next four months, and we'll make more headway if we're all under one roof."

If David hadn't made a miracle catch, there would have been cream all over the kitchen floor. As it was, Neko nearly crushed me with his ecstatic embrace. "Really? I mean... You think..." He crushed me tighter. "You don't know...

It's just… Jacques and I…" I was really starting to have trouble breathing. "Thank you," he said.

And he didn't even sniff at my rumpled T-shirt, my missing makeup, or my haphazard French braid.

That utter lack of snark made me realize how upset poor Neko had truly been. He didn't even protest when I announced that he was responsible for managing the move of David's office to the basement. He just nodded a dozen times and started issuing orders to Kopek and Hani, insisting that the team of familiars could get everything taken care of by the end of the day. It took him a full fifteen minutes before he asked, "What about the shopping? Do I have to take back everything I bought yesterday?"

I shook my head. "We'll find a use for it. I'm sure."

He yelped with glee.

In light of the major residential shift, I postponed classes until the following morning. That turned out to be a wise decision. It took until after noon for the familiars to carry all of David's boxes to the basement. The warders pitched in during the afternoon. In short order, the new guest room was graced with a swiftly purchased bed, a chest of drawers salvaged from the barn, and an armoire from the flea market halfway down the road to Parkersville.

Late that afternoon, Emma stopped me in the hall. "Have you any flannels?"

Flannels. Um, those were washcloths, right? "Over there," I said with a one-shouldered gesture.

"Ah! The airing cupboard."

No, I wanted to say. The linen closet. That's what any red-blooded American witch would have called it. Instead I asked, "How long did you live in England?"

"*Live* there?" She laughed. "Cheeky monkey! I never lived in England! I spent a fortnight, though, seven years ago. I was on a coach tour."

She'd spent two lousy weeks on a bus, and now she sounded like an extra for *Masterpiece Theater*? I might have said something I would truly regret, but I noticed out of the corner of my eye that Raven was recording our conversation with her camera.

"School meeting," I said, before I'd even really decided to act. "In the kitchen. Now."

As soon as Raven and Emma were sitting at the table, faces tight with identical wary expressions, I said, "The night you arrived, you asked about my policy on modern communication, and I never got a chance to answer. Here's the policy: All photography, still or motion picture, is forbidden."

Raven clutched at her chest as if I'd just delivered a direct shot to her heart. "You can't do that!"

"I just did." Even as I issued my edict, though, I thought about how Gran had handled similar life-or-death matters when I was a teenager. More often than I'd care to admit, I'd had the same rebellious look I now saw on Raven's face. And once Gran had thought things through, she'd usually relented. Within reason.

I took a deep breath and held it for a count of five. I was the magistrix here. I was the one in control. I could afford to be a little generous. "Okay," I said. "You can use your camera in your own room. You can film things outside the Academy—personal walks through the woods, on the streets in Parkersville. But don't even think about bringing the camera to our workings. No disrupting magic classes with technology. And you aren't allowed to film David, Neko, or me any time."

Raven's face was as easily read as *A Girl's First Grimoire.* Her first reaction was anger, but she swallowed that in a few seconds. Her second thought was snide, but she set that aside as well. Her third response was fear, obvious terror at interacting with the world without the mediation of a camera lens. And then she settled on acceptance. Nodding slowly, she made a great show of turning off her phone before she slipped it into her hip pocket.

All the while, Emma watched with intense interest. Her reaction made me suspect that no one had ever successfully bridled Raven before. No one—at least in a witchy context—had ever told her what was what.

"Thank you," I said, trying to sound as if I'd known all along that Raven would comply. "Now, let's finish getting both of you settled upstairs. The Jane Madison Academy begins in earnest first thing tomorrow morning."

On Tuesday morning, breakfast was served at 7:30. Everyone was fully caffeinated and in the living room by eight. Familiars were present and accounted for. I gave warders the day off, inviting them to spend their time on other activities supporting the magicarium.

David took that as his cue, and he announced a major project down at the barn. Caleb and Tony were drafted for some renovation work, something manly and mysterious that involved multiple trips into town to retrieve lumber and drywall, carpet and paint.

My students and I settled down to the basics of witchcraft. We spent all day Tuesday focusing on lighting candles. I hadn't purposely lapsed into the traditional Rota for educating witches. I just needed to make sure my students were confident when it came to the basics. We were building a foundation for all our future work together, and I had to know they were absolutely, perfectly, one hundred percent rock solid.

At least, that was the justification I built for myself.

This was not the magicarium I had envisioned. From the first moment I'd thought of running a school for witches, I'd assumed I would do things *my* way. I'd take chances. I'd push boundaries.

But the Rota was tried and true. With the Rota, I should be able to guarantee *some* Major Working. After that, I'd be out from under the Court's thumb, and I could transform the Madison Academy back into the magicarium of my dreams.

So, Tuesday was candles. Wednesday, we trained with our rowan wands, memorizing the feel of every whorl. When I woke up Thursday morning, I pictured myself spending the rest of the day perched on the edge of the living room couch, monitoring my students' incremental discoveries about the wonders of an iron cauldron.

I just couldn't do it.

Instead, I made sure our cereal bowls were stacked in the sink as the tall case clock chimed eight. Kopek, Hani, and Neko waited for us witches on the porch. I called for Spot, and the Lab led the way into the woods. My students were cheered to be free of the house, and we all laughed as we sauntered along the trail. I remembered all the turns correctly, and we arrived at a clover meadow without incident.

The sky was burnished steel overhead. Neko and I spread out an old quilt, placing the comforter at the edge of the trees so we could take advantage of the shade, even as we worked with the green, growing things that flourished in the clearing. Spot sniffed all four corners, and then he settled in the precise center of the fabric, completing three turns to trample the imaginary grasses of his canine memory.

Emma sank cross-legged on the edge of the blanket. Her assumed British identity mercifully subsumed in silence, she studied her surroundings in detail. I suspected she was stabilizing her power, drawing on Kopek. In any case, her familiar sat close by; his knee just touched hers.

Perfect. Maybe this would work even better than I'd hoped.

But no. Raven was putting on her usual show. Sprawled across a corner of the blanket, she wore her typical black attire. Today's outfit included a gauzy top knotted high against her rib-cage, providing a perfect frame for the sweetheart bra beneath. Her shorts were even more microscopic than normal. Shifting position, she draped one leg across Hani's still form. He lay on his belly and rested his chin on his hands, as if he were studying every blade of grass at the edge of our blanket.

At least Raven's phone was out of sight.

I glanced at Neko before I launched into the day's lesson. "According to the Rota, we should begin our study of herblore with cultivated plants. We should study each one individually, memorize each in isolation. Here on the farm, though, we have a chance to explore nature in a more primal form. We can study the balance of the greenery around us, the way things grow together and apart."

Herblore was more an art than a science. It could never completely be taught; a witch either had the ability or she did not. I was a decent herbalist, but I'd never be the best. It was time to discover where my students fell on the spectrum. I had to learn how much remedial work we'd have to do at our painful Rota pace.

"Close your eyes," I told them. "Take a few deep breaths. See what plants you can identify solely through your sense of smell."

Raven inhaled noisily, mimicking a wine connoisseur slurping up a rich burgundy. Her ribcage filled so completely I thought her bra might snap open. When she exhaled, I imagined I could see her spine through the dimple of her navel. She repeated the process half a dozen times, each breath hooking her leg more tightly around Hani's body. I blushed at her frank sexuality; I felt like I was intruding on some private moment with her familiar. No wonder Raven had worked her way through so many Oak Canyon warders. If this was the way she executed her magic, no man was safe in a hundred-mile radius.

Emma, at least, was less ostentatious, settling for placing her palm on Kopek's shoulder. "Honeysuckle," she said after a moment.

"Good. What else?"

Another half a dozen breaths for each of them. "Wild chives?" Emma proposed.

"Yes. And?" She started to chew on her lower lip. "Raven?" I prompted.

"Red clover." Her voice was distant and soft, as if she were reciting the plot of a barely remembered dream. "White clover."

"Excellent. Anything else?"

"Bee balm. Lupine. Wild senna. Milkweed. Big bluestem

and little bluestem. And wild rye. I don't know if its Canadian or Virginia." She opened her eyes and sat up, stretching so thoroughly I thought she might give Neko a proper lesson in feline behavior.

Wow. If she had that sort of sensitivity to plants, then I'd put up with her acrobatic postures any day of the week. I only knew half the things she'd named because I'd researched likely candidates online the night before.

"Excellent," I said, as if I'd planned that pause all along. I eased back into my intended lesson. "The field is a mix of many plants. Some are common; they have no magical powers. But others can be incorporated into rituals. What do you know about the magical properties of the specific ones around us? Emma? What magical uses do we have for honeysuckle?"

The shrub in question grew in a large bank to our right, spilling over the remnants of a tree trunk that must have fallen years before. "It helps with memory, I think. With clarity of thought." She sounded tentative, her English accent thinned almost to nonexistence. "Maybe it increases psychic ability?"

"Anything else?"

She looked at Kopek, as if he might be harboring some secret store of information. The man shrugged so despondently that I wanted to cut some of the sweet flowers and drape him in their comforting scent. Emma patted her familiar's knee in a gesture of reassurance and said, "Sorry. I own a copy of Grayson's *Encyclopedia of Herblore*, back in Sedona, but I haven't looked at it in a long time."

"That's all right." As a librarian, I had long ago learned there was more value in knowing how to find specific information than in brute-force memorization. "Grayson's is a great resource. There's a copy in the basement, along with three other key texts—Snyder's *Herbs Through the Ages*, Hunter's *The Herbal World and You*, and Watson's *Herbalist's Handbook*. With those three, you can look up just about everything you'll ever need."

Raven nodded as I named each of the books and then she asked, "Do you have Sallon's *Compleat Hedgewitch?*"

I didn't bother to disguise my pleased surprise that she knew the obscure title. "Yes! There are only a handful of copies still in existence, but mine has the original hand-tinted plates, tipped in." I was bragging, but I couldn't help it. I was proud of my collection.

Thinking about the *Hedgewitch*, though, sent a sharp pang through my heart. It was one of the treasures the Court would take if I could not deliver a Major Working by Samhain.

I grabbed onto my emotions quickly. That rueful twist in my chest was only telling me to incorporate more herblore in our project. Herbs formed a natural inroad for combating climate change. I just wasn't sure of the specifics of how we'd use them. Yet.

I was getting ahead of myself. "Raven, what else do you know about honeysuckle?"

"You can place it around a green candle to enhance spells for prosperity. It's an herb of devotion and fidelity. If you dream while wearing a sachet over your heart, you'll see your one true love. The flower is associated with Mercury, and it's grounded in the element of Earth."

I gaped. She *was* good at this. Really, really good. I'd spent the past week misled by all her games—the sex-kitten ploys, the wannabe film-maker, and the Goth pagan play-acting. But it wasn't fair to reduce her to any of those roles. I attempted a quick recovery. "Let's go through the other herbs. What was next? Chives?"

We spent the rest of the morning going over the properties of every plant in the field. Emma did her best to recall facts, but it was Raven who had all the information at her fingertips. She recited details effortlessly—not only culinary and healing properties, but magical uses as well. Her vast store of data included the elements most associated with every plant, along with planetary associations. I didn't put a lot of stock in that last tidbit—astrology remained more my mother's witchy area of supposed expertise than my own—but the rest of Raven's knowledge pretty much floored me.

It was almost time to head back to the house for lunch, but first I sent my students out to collect samples of milkweed. As they prowled through the meadow, Neko leaned close. "You are going to wrap things up early today, aren't you?"

"Why should I?"

"Fourth of July? Marching bands? Sparklers and Roman candles and *boom*?"

Of course I knew it was Independence Day, but I had a deadline. Norville Pitt had left me no time for frivolities like Souza marches and parades.

Neko read my mind in his usual uncanny way. "Your students can't work nonstop until Samhain. You'll get more out of them if they don't burn out in their first full week of classes."

He was right, of course. The Fourth of July would have been a holiday at any other magicarium. "Fine," I said, abashed. "We'll head back now. Let me guess—you and Jacques are going down to DC for fireworks on the Mall?"

"Of course not!"

I squinted at him in disbelief. "But you love fireworks! And Parkersville canceled theirs, because of the fire ban."

Neko sighed as if he were talking to a very young child. Or a very stupid witch. Same difference. "The Parkersville Fire Department is hosting an ice cream social. I thought you and David would treat us all!"

My first response was to pity the fire department. They couldn't have any idea what they were up against—Neko had a nearly insatiable appetite for ice cream.

Oh well. Maybe David could make a sizable donation to the fireman's Widow and Orphans Fund in recompense.

When Emma and Raven returned with the milkweed, I congratulated them on their harvest and explained that we would carry the plants back to the house. We'd take a few days to drain all the milky sap into a silver ewer. Once it was harvested, we could mix it with rainwater collected on the night of a full moon, and the resulting potion would both calm the intractable and cultivate patience in the rashest soul.

I could have used a little calming tincture myself, especially when I saw how thrilled my students were about getting the afternoon off. They were positively overjoyed at getting Friday free as well. But their excitement didn't hold a candle to Neko's enthusiasm as he rushed off to the garage. I could only imagine the Independence Day outfits he and Jacques would throw together on such relatively short notice.

Back in the kitchen, I tossed a couple of dog biscuits to Spot. I was too hot to think about lunch, though. Instead, I decided to take a long, cool shower. Ice cream would make the perfect dinner.

We barely squeezed into the burgundy minivan for the short ride into town. It would have been a tight fit under any circumstances—three witches, their warders, and their familiars. But when one familiar insisted on dressing like the Statue of Liberty (complete with a six-inch tiara, and a foot-long torch), and he dragged along his French-swearing boyfriend who was dressed like Uncle Sam (yep, top hat, swallowtail coat, spats, and a full fake beard), the trip became downright unpleasant.

At least Tony sat behind the wheel. I wasn't surprised to discover that the pugnacious warder had a lead foot. I was grateful, in fact.

When we arrived in Parkersville, alas, the streets were filled with enough mundane citizens that Tony couldn't employ his warder's skills to make a parking space appear. He made two valiant attempts at parallel parking on Main Street, but the minivan wasn't as mini as the laws of physics required, at least for those tight spaces.

Muttering under his breath, Tony pulled into a loading zone across the street from the police station.

"You'll get a ticket," I warned, before we could all tumble out of purgatory.

"We've got out-of-state plates. And it's a holiday."

And you really don't want to screw up another try at parallel parking, I almost said. But I was only the magistrix, not the parking police. And Lady Liberty's torch was gouging a hole in my side.

I shrugged and led the way to the ice cream social. Not

surprisingly, Parkersville Fire Station Number One (and, um, only) was packed. Neko immediately picked up a bowl and cut through the crowd, homing in on the whipped cream like a heat-seeking missile. Jacques squawked and clapped his hat to his head, trying to follow suit.

The rest of our party split up. I chose one of the shortest lines—there just weren't enough people who understood the decadent glory that was coffee ice cream. The rugged fire-man scooping out the heavenly stuff apparently agreed; he loaded three scoops into my bowl and was going for a fourth when I held up a hand in laughing protest.

Hot fudge ladled from an aluminum vat. A sprinkle of salted peanuts. A single maraschino cherry. No whipped cream for me—Neko had surely taken any portion that was rightly mine. Just as I added a spoon, David came to my side.

"What flavor did you get?" I asked.

"Praline pecan."

"You hate praline pecan!"

"I seem to remember some bewitching woman who says coffee and praline pecan make the perfect combination."

I laughed. By the time we escaped into the open air, I needed to apply some emergency confection management, rapidly spooning up melting ice cream before it cascaded over the side of my bowl. When I had vanquished the im-mediate danger, I glanced back over my shoulder.

"Shouldn't we wait for the others?"

"Raven and Tony already left with Hani in tow—Raven wanted to film the locals. Neko isn't going to budge until the last molecule of whipped cream is gone. And Emma seems just about as stubborn."

I followed his gaze past the long line of customers waiting for their chance at dairy carnage. My student witch was standing off to one side, chatting with the handsome fireman who had been so generous with my coffee ice cream. Even as I watched, he laughed at something she said and shifted closer, brushing his fingertips against her arm. A quick glance confirmed that Caleb was keeping watch from a discreet distance, a dejected-looking Kopek at his side. Emma was chaperoned, whether she wanted to be or not.

I could empathize with my fellow witch. I turned back to David, a smile on my lips. "Time for us to escape," I said.

He led the way past laughing crowds. Some people held bowls of ice cream while others indulged in hot dogs or burgers fresh from the Rotary's grill. Norman Rockwell couldn't have painted a better Independence Day.

We ducked around the corner of the building and headed toward the relative seclusion of the car wash, which was shut down for the night. There was a bench there, meant for customers waiting for their cars. I took a seat and automatically shifted to make room for David before attending to another looming ice cream disaster.

"I feel like I've barely seen you this week," I said, between bites of coffee praline bliss.

"We're making good progress down at the barn. We decided to build out four rooms, instead of two. Not much more work, and they'll be useful down the road."

"I didn't realize you knew how to do all that."

He shrugged. "I've taken care of basic repairs around the farm since I was a kid. It turns out Caleb put himself through school working as a handyman."

"And Tony?"

"Caleb's a good partner on projects like this." David's observation was dry. I suspected Raven's bellicose warder would wear thin after a couple of hours.

"At least Tony hasn't pulled a sword on you. Again."

"Thank Hecate for small favors."

I laughed and started paying serious attention to my ice cream. David and I chatted easily enough while I ate, but as soon as I dropped my spoon into my empty bowl, he said, "Finished? Let's find everyone else and get back home."

"What's the rush?"

"I have some paperwork to finish up."

I laughed, thinking he was kidding, but he didn't join in. "What possible paperwork could you have to finish on a holiday?"

"Hecate's Court isn't bound by federal holidays," he pointed out.

I put a little space between us, so I could better see his face. "This is about Pitt, isn't it?"

"It's warders' business."

I bristled at his dismissive tone. He'd tried that before, when I'd asked about the Court documents in his office. I'd let him get away with it then, but enough was enough. "Fine. You're my warder. Your business is mine. What's going on?"

"You're not a warder. You wouldn't understand." His voice was laden with cool confidence, with the absolute certainty that he knew what was best for me.

My temper flared with a corresponding heat, and I poured that sudden rage into two concise words. "Try me."

"Stay out of this, Jane. I don't want you getting hurt."

"I've already *been* hurt! My entire magicarium is on the

line because of you!"

Ouch. Up until that instant, I hadn't realized that I blamed David for the charter, for the requirement of a Major Working. He couldn't have looked more shocked if I'd slapped his face.

"I'm sorry," I said. "I didn't mean that."

He stared at me, his eyes solid black in the moonlight. "Yes. You did."

He was right. "Okay," I said. "I meant it. But I really blame Pitt. So tell me what happened between you two. It can't be as bad as everything I'm imagining." And there were *lots* of things I was imagining. Blackmail. Seduction. Sex scandals involving the most senior members of the Court.

David set his jaw, clearly intending to carry his secret to his grave.

His stubbornness goaded me like iron spurs. I snapped out a reply before I'd fully considered the words. "I command you, as your witch. *Tell me what happened between you and Pitt.*"

He froze.

In all the years we'd worked together, I'd never played the witch card. I'd thought about it a few times. Even threatened to do it once or twice. But I had never actually spoken the words, never made my power over him so absolutely, explicitly clear.

I could rescind the command. Tell him I was joking. Release him from my order. But somehow, in a matter of seconds, the secret he was hiding had become a referendum on everything—on the viability of the Academy, on our entire relationship. I bit my lip, but I didn't take back my words.

David swallowed hard and stared into the darkness. "Pitt made an example of me for three full years. He was sending a message to all the other warders—if I could be broken, any of them could be too. When I couldn't take it any more, I forged documents to make it look like Pitt was stealing. I planted them in the Court's records. He found them before I could make them public."

David Montrose, champion of rules and regulations and every law I could think of, had framed Norville Pitt. He was a hypocrite and a liar.

"And the documents you were reading the other night?"

His eyes flashed fire. "You don't want to know about those."

He was right. I didn't. But I'd pushed things this far, and I wasn't going to back down now. "*Tell me,*" I said.

Again, he complied with the letter of my witchy command, but he refused to meet my eyes. "I know he's dirty. And I'm going to prove it to the Court, if it's the last action I take as a warder."

Last action. He accepted that his hounding Pitt might strip him of his rank forever. And he was willing to take that risk. He was willing to chance abandoning me so he could have his satisfaction against Pitt, paid in full.

I closed my eyes. My head was suddenly pounding, and my stomach reminded me that ice cream made a spectacularly lousy dinner. Especially after a skipped lunch, and a morning spent running a magicarium that was failing to meet my dreams.

I felt guilty that I'd pushed David as his witch. But more than that, I was angry that he was putting his own revenge ahead of me. The entire situation made me feel frustrated that Pitt had trapped me, had made all of this happen in the first place.

This was all too much to handle. I couldn't sort out the tornado of my feelings, here in idyllic Parkersville, surrounded by people who didn't have the first idea that witches or warders or Hecate's Court even existed. There was too much at stake. Too much to handle, without having a clear mind. I should sleep on it. We both should. We could figure out a path forward in the morning.

"Come on," I finally said. "Let's go home."

David stepped away, shoving his hands into his pockets. "Go on back to the car. I'll get another ride."

And that was when I realized the truth. I'd broken something.

By ordering David to act, by wielding my power as his witch, I had shattered a link between us. Not the magical bond we shared—that could never be so easily severed. But the other ties, the worldly ones. The ones that made him my boyfriend. My lover. Whatever.

"David—"

He shook his head and turned away, disappearing into the shadows without another word.

This couldn't be happening. Everything had been *fine* just a few minutes ago. He couldn't have… I couldn't have… We…

I waited for him to change his mind, to come back, to tell me we could talk it out. But I couldn't even imagine the shape of that conversation. And he didn't return.

Even when I waited for half an hour.

I should be crying, I thought, as I made my way back to the car. I should be sobbing, and gasping for breath, and digging out my phone to call Melissa. But I wasn't doing any of those things. I couldn't, because I was numb. I was swaddled in cotton, cut off from the world.

And I almost walked into the middle of a fight when I got to the minivan.

Tony stood by the driver's door, clutching a slip of bright yellow paper. Hani was crowing as if he'd just been told the funniest joke in the world, and Raven was filming her warder with undisguised amusement. "It'll come out of your paycheck," she said, and when Tony snarled, she tossed him a saucy air-kiss and zoomed in for a close-up.

Neko and Jacques gawked from the sidelines, as if the tableau were the finest Broadway entertainment. Apparently, my familiar was unable to resist hamming things up. Raising his Statue of Liberty torch, he strode over to Tony and proclaimed, "Give me your tired, your poor, your crumpled parking tickets, yearning to be—

Tony's snarl turned into an outright roar. He slammed his fist into the minivan, punching the side panel three times in rapid succession. Neko yelped in surprise and leaped away. Hani cut himself off, mid-cackle. Jacques stared in blank astonishment.

I waited for Raven to intervene. Any witch worth her wand would go to her warder in need. She should reach out to Tony, soothe him, ease him back from the sharp precipice of his rage. Easy for me to say, right?

Instead, Raven shoved her camera into her bra and asked, "Are we *really* doing this again?"

Without another word, she stalked around the minivan, threw open the door, and climbed into the very back seat.

Hani barely waited for a count of three before he scampered after her.

David, I thought. He could fix this. But David wasn't here. And he wasn't coming any time soon. Because *I* should have gone to *him*. I should have reached out to him, comforted him after the confession I'd forced him to make.

That left Neko to glide up to Tony's side. My familiar dropped his green torch, not even noticing when it rolled around by his feet. His fingers were straight and strong as he settled his hand on the warder's biceps.

Tony flinched, and he made a bruised fist. Neko merely leaned closer, saying something so softly that I couldn't even guess the words. He stroked Tony's arm, slowly, even tenderly. He moved his other hand to the back of the warder's neck.

Tony swallowed hard. His arms began to tremble, and I thought he was going to break down completely. I braced myself for him to bellow, to unleash the violence held so close beneath the surface.

And then Tony rolled his head back. He leaned into Neko's touch. He took a shuddering breath and stared up at the sky. Neko said something, another secret. Tony nodded slowly, painfully. And then he straightened and kissed Neko hard, full on the lips.

I was shocked. Not because I'd never seen two men kissing—plenty of movies and TV had taken care of that education well before Neko provided in-person instruction. I was stunned because I hadn't imagined Tony as anything other than a fighter, a hot-headed warrior with an all-too-ready sword.

Neko had clearly seen something else. He had read between lines I hadn't even imagined. And now, my familiar ignored Jacques's shouted protest, all the while returning Tony's kiss with enthusiasm.

Jacques thrashed like a speared eel, working his way out of his costume. By the time he ripped off his fake beard and ground it into the pavement, Neko and Tony had both come up for air. My familiar leaned in and murmured something, and Tony plunged his bruised hand into the front pocket of his jeans. He pulled out a tangle of leather and silver and gold and passed it to my familiar.

Neko looked over his shoulder. "Caleb?" he called, and I realized that the other warder had appeared at some point during the drama. Kopek and Emma were beside him. Even in the moonlight, I could see that my student's lips were swollen, and I wondered if there was still a Parkersville fireman lurking nearby.

Neko asked, "Can you drive everyone home?"

Caleb nodded once, and he caught the keys that Neko tossed.

Jacques spluttered. "*Où vas tu?*" He was obviously so shaken he forgot to translate his question.

Neko's voice was steady. "I'm going with Tony. He needs me now."

"I am zee one that needs you!" Jacques shouted.

Neko only shook his head. "I'm sorry," he said.

"Thees ees not work! You cannot say thees ees work!" Jacques was furious. "Eef you go weeth that one, we are through!"

"I'm sorry," Neko said again. And then he shifted his gaze to Caleb. "Get them out of here."

Jacques stomped off into the night. Emma's warder marshaled us into the car, pausing only to ask if we should wait for David. I shook my head, dazed.

Raven still fumed in the back seat. Emma rode shotgun. I sat on the middle seat, with Hani on one side, and Kopek on the other. We rode back to the farm in our suddenly spacious car in absolute, stunned silence.

Chapter 8

DAVID NEVER CAME home. I woke half a dozen times during the night, but the sheets were always smooth on his side of the mattress. Cool. Untouched. I considered reaching out to him, witch to warder, but the thought of using my powers that way again sickened me.

I finally woke, for real, just before noon. Spot was waiting for me in the kitchen, whining by the back door. I let him outside and watched him anoint half a dozen shrubs around the driveway. When he was back in the house, I wiped my palms on my ratty sweatpants and told myself it was far too early to panic. David would return soon enough. He had to.

Besides, I had more immediate problems to solve.

The kitchen looked like it had been blasted by a cyclone. Remnants of multiple meals were scattered across the counters. The bottom layer held remains of the sandwiches we'd eaten for dinner the night before—breadcrumbs and slivers of tomato, trimmings from cold cuts and a handful of wilted lettuce leaves, all anchored by a phalanx of condiment-smeared knives. The top level consisted of breakfast dishes—

syrup-crusted plates and a few leftover bites of frozen waffles, caps from strawberries and a rind of cheese. Someone had scrambled eggs, and the scent of bacon was still heavy on the air.

It would take an hour just to get the place neat enough to pour a bowl of cereal. At least I could manage a cup of tea without risking ptomaine poisoning. I grimaced and filled the kettle with water.

Just as the whistle blew, Emma came into the kitchen. She blinked at the chaos on the counters and said, "Blimey."

The colloquial English exclamation grated on me, but I forced myself to smile. I even offered Emma water for her own tea, and I waited for her to take a seat across from me at the kitchen table. There were lots of things we could have spoken about. My warder. Her sister's warder. My familiar. The fireman who had—I could see by the light of day—left her with a hickey.

I settled for fortifying myself with a huge sip of orange pekoe, and then I launched into a relatively safe topic. "You said you spent two weeks in England, seven years ago. That vacation certainly made quite an impression."

Emma eyed me warily over the edge of her mug. She wasn't a fool. "Quite," she said, drawing out the single syllable.

"You don't often hear the Queen's English in…where are you two from originally?"

"Chicago," Emma said, and she couldn't completely hide the flat vowels of her youth. Banishing a quick frown, she retreated to her Earl Grey, administering a slice of lemon.

I waited. I could have asked specific questions. I could have told her she was driving me nuts with the fake accent, the affected vocabulary. I could have demanded that she set aside her pseudo-British identity, just as I'd required Raven to give up her phone. But I wanted to learn more. I wanted to understand.

My patience was finally rewarded. Emma stared into her mug and said, "It started as a joke, with the friends who were on the trip. We challenged each other to see if we could the fool the assistant at the greengrocer, make him think we were British. Everyone else went back to normal as soon as we got home, but I couldn't let it go." Her index finger circled around the lip of her mug, clockwise, then counter-clockwise. "I made Mum and Da laugh. They paid attention to *me*."

Instead of to Raven. I heard those words, loud and clear, even though they weren't said aloud.

"After a while, it just became second nature. I got a summer job as a receptionist in a doctor's office, and everyone loved my accent. They smiled, and they relaxed, and it made their appointments just a little bit easier. At uni, a lot of boys thought I really was from England, and I ended up with a lot more dates than I might have had otherwise. I stopped... I don't know... translating, and this just became the way I talk. I'm happier this way."

Well, when she phrased it that way... I *wanted* my students to be happy.

But she wasn't through. She looked me straight in the eye and said, "And that lets me be a better sister to Raven. Less jealous. More supportive. We're twins, you know."

Her tone was challenging. I couldn't believe she was actually calling me out on my dislike of Raven. I stammered, "I—I didn't realize—"

"Most people don't. We're fraternal, obviously. But we did a lot of classic twin stuff while we were growing up. We had our own language, and we did our best to dress the same, even when Mum refused to buy us matching outfits. We shared a cot when we were babies, and a bedroom until the day we went to uni."

"When did you realize you had magical powers?"

"We've always known. When we were infants and the child-minder put us down for a nap, she'd wind up a mobile above our cot. After it stopped moving, we'd cast a spell together to get it going again."

She made it sound simple. But a mobile would have a mechanical engine, a structure of metal and gears. No witch would find it easy to work a device so far removed from the natural world. For two babies to generate enough power...

"That's amazing!"

"Yeah. We went through a lot of child-minders."

"Was your mother a witch?"

"If she was, she never understood her power. I tried to talk to her about it—we both did, when we were around five years old. Mum laughed and told us we had such great imaginations. Raven insisted, and she got punished for telling lies."

"But someone taught you how to use your magic."

She shrugged. "At uni, Raven majored in dance, and she took a certificate in Asian religions. She talked me into going on a retreat with her, to an abbey outside of Sedona. The leader was a witch. She's the one who told us what we are."

"So you stayed in Sedona."

Emma nodded. "It's all worked out quite well for me. I'm a bookkeeper, with a speciality for doctor's offices. I can land a job whenever I need one. Raven hasn't had it as easy."

"Where does she work?"

"Anywhere that will have her. She's been an assistant in a solicitor's firm, and a cashier at nearly every shop in town. She taught ballet to kids for a couple of months, but she kept helping the gormless ones with a bit of magic and her guv got suspicious."

"It must be hard on you, watching out for her all the time."

"She's my sister. That's what family does."

And just like that, she closed the door on the conversation. She was good at this. She'd had years to get used to dealing with Raven's drama. I accepted her decision, but I couldn't resist asking one more sly question. "So. What's the fireman's name?"

She blushed the shade of an English rose. "Rick," she said. "Rick Hanson."

"You two seemed to get along well."

She settled herself very primly on the edge of her chair. "I'm not the type to kiss and tell."

Despite myself, I laughed. "Fine," I said. "Caleb was okay with him?"

"Caleb was fine."

So Emma was safe. Parkersville's fastest-moving fireman wasn't a threat.

And that knowledge was going to have to suffice on this off-kilter Friday. It wasn't enough, of course. I still didn't know where David was. I couldn't begin to explain whatever relationship had been forged between Neko and Tony. I was no closer to figuring out the magicarium's Major Working, to restoring my original concept for the Academy's classes, to righting all the wrongs of the past couple of weeks.

But I had to move forward. And a good first step would be clearing the piles of dishes around us. "Ugh. These aren't going to wash themselves, are they?"

As I pushed to my feet, I experienced a wicked flash of déjà vu. I had stood in front of this sink before. I had stared at these dishes. And I had used magic to clean everything up.

I shook my head. That wasn't déjà vu. It was *memory*. Three years ago, when I first realized I had witchy powers, I'd tried to use my magic to dispose of an entire sink full of dishes. Alas, most of the water had ended up on me, and I still had to do the dishes by hand. But I'd learned a lot since then. I gestured toward the sink and asked, "Want to try something new?"

Emma's eyes gleamed. "What do you have in mind?"

I waved her over to stand beside me. "Pick your poison—water or plates?"

She shrugged. "Water."

"Let's try this." We caught each other's gaze. I brushed my fingertips against my forehead, my throat, and my heart, then watched as she completed her own offering. She matched the first deep breath I took. Another. A third.

I reached out to sense her power. It was there, just as it had been when we'd tried to work with Raven, that first day. Her energy was deep and mysterious, and when I closed my eyes, I could sense molten silver, drawing me closer, luring me deeper.

No. "Lure" implied that evil was involved, that Emma was somehow preying on me. This sensation was the opposite of prey. She was offering herself, opening her powers to mine.

In a heartbeat, I understood what Clara must have seen in this witch, out in Sedona. Emma was a natural for a community like the one I wanted to build. Her powers were expansive, reaching out for others. Her energy glowed like a candle flame, as if her entire magical being was a wick that took in arcane oxygen and gave off brilliant supernatural light.

Laughing, I spun out a few tendrils of my own. My energy manifested as golden glints, amber ribbons that dipped into the pool of Emma's silvery potential. The resulting arcane swell made me take a step back in surprise. Suddenly, impossibly, our joint magic defied the laws of earthly science. Our combined force was greater than its component parts.

Emma must have felt it, too, because she laughed and peeled back another layer of protection. I could access more of her strength, dive deeper into her reserve. I tossed in more streamers of my own energy and was rewarded with a rolling, rotating wall of force.

It was all well and good to discover a sympathetic energy. The true test, though, was whether we could apply it in a constructive manner.

Slowly, waiting for Emma to match my physical motions, I turned back to the sink. I watched her gather the physical water, train it with a dollop of the power we shared. Almost immediately, steam curled from the surface, clean and inviting. Emma nudged the soap dispenser with a thought, and the hot water filled with a mountain of tiny bubbles. Within my heightened senses, they tickled like champagne, and I fought to keep from giggling.

My turn was next. I mentally lifted a mustard-smeared

knife and dragged it through the sink. The gold of my power intersected with the silver of Emma's; the utensil glowed like electrum. Together, we thought away the mustard. We banished a clinging crumb of bread along the edge of the blade, and then Emma added a flourish to erase a palimpsest of fingerprints. The knife emerged from the water bone-dry, sparkling as if it had just been forged. I flicked a thought toward the appropriate drawer, and it returned home amid a sparkle of gold and silver energy.

We lost no time tackling the rest of the mess—silverware, plates, even the bacon-slick frying pan. When my powers were combined with Emma's, I didn't need to worry about the size of an item, about its weight. Washing the dishes took so little of our combined energy that nothing was a challenge. Best of all, every feat we completed together recharged the well of our mutual strength, and we ended up with more force than when we began.

As the last bowl found its way to the cupboard, I flicked a thought toward Emma, a flash of gratitude combined with a smile of victory. Slowly, reluctantly, I pulled my magical awareness back into myself.

I shivered as I separated from my fellow witch, a shudder that worked its way from the base of my skull to my toes. For one long moment, my lungs were frozen, and my entire body felt as if it were buried in a snowbank. Then a comforting rush of heat chased away the cold, and I closed my eyes to take the deepest breath I could manage. Only then did I became aware of the sound of clapping.

When I looked up, Caleb stood in the kitchen doorway, bringing his massive hands together. Kopek and Neko were behind him, craning their necks for a better view of the kitchen.

Emma took a moment longer to recover from our separation. She staggered back a few steps, until she leaned against the counter. I started to reach for her, but Caleb and Kopek were there before I could do anything. The warder took his witch's arm despite her protestation that she was fine. Kopek leaned in close to her side, obviously pouring magical strength into her.

At least, that's what Neko would have done for me, if I had needed his assistance. To the contrary, my working with Emma had left me completely invigorated. My only concern was that I had somehow harmed my student. "Are you all right?" I sounded like I was shouting in the silent kitchen.

"I'm grand," Emma said, smiling tightly.

I knew that smile. I'd offered it dozens of times, when I'd pushed myself beyond the comfortable limits of my strength. Emma was putting on a brave front, but she would pay for our working. Fatigue was the price of learning new magic.

Nevertheless she would grow as a witch. That was why she'd come to my magicarium, after all. All in all, it was a fair trade-off.

Neko piped up from the doorway. "If I'd known someone else would do the dishes, I would have left more on the counter."

"You created *more* than enough mess last night." I said. Neko inclined his head, gracefully accepting my accusation. Right on schedule, Emma swayed on her feet. "Caleb?" I said. "Can you help Emma upstairs?"

"I'm perfectly fit," she insisted. But her hands shook as she tried to push her warder away.

He accepted her objection with the same equanimity David would have shown, half-guiding and half-carrying her up the stairs. Kopek followed silently, his flat face shadowed with worry.

Neko slouched against the doorframe. "You know, these things would be a lot easier if you witches let your familiars help you with spells."

"I wasn't quite sure where I could find my familiar today."

He looked abashed for about a heartbeat before he started to examine his fingernails as if they held all the secrets of the universe.

"You can do whatever you want in your personal life, Neko. But I can't have you upsetting the magicarium."

"Nothing's upset," he said to his hands.

"Where's Tony?"

A quick grin before he met my eyes. "Asleep. In my apartment."

I sighed. Neko *could* do whatever he wanted in his personal life. And Tony, too. But I couldn't deny that things would be a lot simpler if neither of them wanted to do anything with the other. "How did you know?" I asked, honestly wondering.

"That Tony wouldn't be able to resist my animal magnetism and grace?" Oh *my*, Neko *was* pleased with himself this morning. I didn't bother answering. He shrugged and said with perfect seriousness, "High-frequency brain waves that are only visible on the gay spectrum."

I rolled my eyes. "Is his hand okay?"

"Just bruised. I made him keep it on ice."

"Has he spoken to Raven?"

"Not yet."

"Have you talked to Jacques?"

That finally broke his composure. He glanced out the window. At the refrigerator. At the stairs that led to the basement.

"Neko?"

"Jacques never understood us." At my questioning glance, he clarified, "Witches. Familiars. The whole astral world. I explained it to him, over and over. He saw you work a thousand spells. He understood that your powers are real, that magic does exist. But he couldn't accept that I had a role in it. That I had a commitment."

Those were a few dozen words more than I'd ever heard Neko use to describe a relationship. "I'm sorry," I said.

"It was time." He sighed. "I just didn't mean for it to happen that way."

I winced. "We usually don't mean for things to 'happen that way.'"

And just like that, we were through talking about Tony and Jacques. "Jane," Neko said in a voice so low I almost missed it. "Fix this."

I had no doubt he was talking about David. "Nothing's broken!"

He didn't bother contradicting me. "The magicarium needs you and your warder on the same page."

"I know that!" I snapped. And then I realized a better answer was, "We are!" My lie was only partially weakened by my needing to ask, "Where is he?"

Neko consulted whatever interior map was scrawled across his familiar's mind. "In the barn."

"Fine," I said.

"Fine," Neko agreed.

I pushed past him and headed toward the back door. Then, I had a brainstorm and slapped my hand against my side, summoning Spot to come with me. The dog might be a necessary distraction in what promised to be a challenging conversation.

I took my time walking the half-mile to the barn. I replayed every word David and I had exchanged the night before, trying to figure out when everything had leaped to DEFCON 1.

I'd asked him for the truth three separate times before issuing my command. We were both more stubborn than toddlers; I'd had no reasonable expectation that he'd ever voluntarily tell me the truth.

In fact, I wondered if I knew it, even now. My mind kept going back to the documents I'd seen in David's office the day I'd come back from brunch with Gran and Clara. He'd said they were copies. But the Court guarded all its materials jealously. They didn't keep *copies* floating around. And I'd seen the grommets and ribbons—those had to be originals.

I could understand what David was doing, even if I couldn't condone it. If he could find proof of Pitt's indiscretions in those smuggled documents, David could have the Head Clerk removed from office. David's earlier crime, creating false documents, would become moot, laundered clean by Pitt's proven multiple wrongdoings.

Still, he should have told me. As his witch, I needed to be kept in the loop. As his girlfriend, I wanted to be his ally.

But in the interest of moving forward, I could apologize for commanding David to speak. He could apologize for keeping secrets. We'd both admit we'd over-reacted, and then we'd get back to the serious business of running the

Academy.

By that point in my rumination, Spot and I were approaching the barn. It looked like a drawing out of a child's picture book—red boards, peaked roof, a hayloft that opened above the main doors. As I watched, David stepped· outside, raising one hand to shield his eyes against the afternoon glare. He wore blue jeans and a plain white T-shirt. With a pencil shoved behind one ear, he looked like a carpenter, stopping to take a mid-day break.

Spot took off like a racehorse, his body lean and low to the ground, his tail straight out behind. He pulled up just in time to shove his nose into David's loose fist, searching for a treat. David fondled the Lab's ears and patted his side with a cupped hand. Spot was in ecstasy.

When I finally caught up, I could see a spray of fine wood shavings fanned across David's chest. Sawdust was smeared on his right cheekbone, and I started to reach out to brush it away, but I stopped myself just in time. I opened and closed my fingers, as if I were working out a cramp, and I forced myself to meet his eyes as I stated the obvious. "You didn't come home last night."

"I slept down here."

"You belong in your own house. In your own bed."

"I'm a warder. Warders sleep in the barn."

Not all *warders. Tony didn't sleep in the barn last night.* But Tony was a distraction, a tangent I desperately wanted to follow so I didn't have to continue this difficult conversation. I made myself push ahead. "It's not that simple, and you know it."

"From where I'm standing, it's very simple. You commanded me, witch to warder. I told you what I did to Pitt, and what I plan on doing. What else do you want from me, Jane?

"I *want* you to treat me like your partner! I want you to trust me!"

He frowned, as if he were having trouble diagramming my sentence structure. "Partners don't issue unilateral orders."

"And I'm sorry I did that. I'm sorry I blamed the Major Working on you. I'm sorry we ever went to Parkersville for the Fourth of July, that we ever had the entire stupid, screwed up conversation!"

He waited politely before he asked, "Anything else?"

"Anything—? Aren't you going to respond to what I just said?"

"I don't have any possible response. I'm your warder until the day you release me from service. As my witch, you have an absolute right to command me. Without apology or regret."

No. I *did* regret. I'd figured this whole thing out on my walk to the barn: I apologized, he forgave, and we moved forward together. But he wasn't reading the same script.

My perfect solution had overlooked one massive problem: David Montrose was the proudest man I'd ever met. Sure, he was couching all of this in terms of our astral relationship: Witches, warders, who was allowed to do what. But the fact was, I'd battered his pride by issuing my command. And that wasn't all. I'd cut him to the quick when I said my magicarium was suffering because of him.

He *lived* for the Madison Academy. He lived for *me*. And because of that, I had nothing else I could say.

"That's it, then?" I asked. "We're through?"

At least he didn't pretend to misunderstand me. He offered a half shrug. "We could call it a break."

"I don't *want* to call it a break! I don't want it to *be* a break."

He ignored my second sentence. "Then let's not call it anything. Let's focus on the magicarium for now. We'll see where we stand after Samhain."

On one level, his proposal made perfect sense. My hands were full with the Academy—between Emma and Tony and Neko, there were more than enough complications. If David and I stripped our relationship down to its simplest confines, the magicarium could only be better off.

But I didn't want simplicity. I wanted the give and take, the confusing tangle that was my full life with David.

Which was all well and good, but he had to want it, too. And right now, smarting from my accusation and my witchy ultimatum, he didn't. And there wasn't a thing I could do to change that.

I swallowed hard. "Do you need help moving your things out here?"

"The guys will do it."

And that was all. I didn't have any other questions. I couldn't make any more apologies. I couldn't change what had happened. So I called Spot to my side and began the long walk back to the farmhouse.

Chapter 9

OF COURSE, DAVID proved as good as his word. He moved out of our bedroom without my assistance, relying on Caleb and Tony to do the literal heavy lifting. I made a point of being out of the house while they worked, taking a walk under the leaden summer sky. While I told myself a stroll through the woods would help me focus on what was important, it only succeeded in making me see how dusty and dry everything had become.

My long, unhappy ramblings gave me a chance to realize one important thing. The entire magicarium needed to buckle down if we were going to complete our Major Working by Samhain. No more trips into town for unnecessary diversions. No more ice cream socials. Nothing but work.

I divided each day into morning and afternoon sessions, and come Monday, my students and I dug in with a vengeance. We alternated wildly between herbs and crystals, between casting spells and focusing on magical wards. I took inspiration from everything around us—a clump of wild blackberries required a full day to dissect their arcane significance. A glint of pink quartz on the path near the garage functioned as an entire encyclopedia on crystals. Every session demanded our utmost concentration, and I refused to accept any type of distraction as an excuse.

My classes were like the Rota on steroids—all the single-minded concentration, and four times the subject matter.

As a consequence, everyone started blowing off a lot of steam in their free time—what little of that there was. Raven announced that she was undertaking a seven-day cleanse. She swore off all meat, gluten, dairy, and sugar, along with anything that contained unpronounceable chemical compounds. She fully expected all of us to join her, and when we didn't, she invested a lot of time and energy explaining how we were poisoning ourselves. When she wasn't policing our food, she worked at her impromptu video editing studio in the living room, fiddling with film clips she'd created around the farm and in Parkersville. Hani waited on her, fetching her bowls of farro and toasted kale chips, offering advice on her cinematic masterpieces.

Emma was having her own wild time. In a matter of days, she and Rick became inseparable. He stayed overnight when he wasn't on shift at the firehouse, joining us for awkward "brekkies" in the morning. I wasn't sure how much Emma had told him about her magical life. Having walked that line with mundane boyfriends before, I understood how hard it could be to find a proper balance.

Of course, we needed to look no farther than Neko to see just how challenging mixed magic/mundane relationships could be. But Neko wasn't fighting that particular battle at the moment, not with Tony. Certainly, the guys *could* have discussed magic in a way Emma and Rick could never do.

But I got the distinct impression they weren't doing a lot of talking when they were alone together. At least Neko implied as much, as he yawned his way through our classes. We both pretended not to notice when he nodded off as I demonstrated a particularly delicate crystal purification spell. I was especially leery of throwing around any ultimatums, witch to familiar.

Whatever was going on in the apartment above the garage, it certainly seemed to mellow Tony. He completely abandoned his combative stance, on everything from the proper way to cast a protective circle to who was responsible for washing dishes. If I didn't know better, I would have said that aliens had replaced the belligerent warder. But I *did* know better, and I was willing to let the relationship continue, so long as my familiar did not get hurt.

Caleb divided his time between the television in the living room (which carried more baseball games than I'd ever dreamed possible), construction work at the barn (including cabinet-making—the man seemed to have unlimited skills with power tools), and keeping a watchful eye on Emma, whenever she would tolerate his chaperoning services. Kopek followed him around like a moon in an irregular orbit.

And David… Well, David was the one person I barely saw. He remained the model warder, present for every working that raised any significant level of power. He even acted as a consultant, advising me on teaching methods, suggesting avenues of study with regard to runes and crystals and herbs. Occasionally, he worked downstairs in his office, but he spent most of his free time away from the house.

After one stilted conversation, we'd agreed he should take Spot down to the barn. The dog had been David's long be-

fore I'd ever moved into the house. I missed them both—
more, with each day that passed.

More than once, I regretted taking Gran's advice. I
wished I'd never moved Raven and Emma into the house.
There was always someone underfoot when I most needed a
moment of peace and quiet. I spent a lot of time in the
basement, reading up on whatever topic we intended to cover in the next day's class.

I refused to admit I was keeping an eye on David's office,
basking in the glow of his overhead light when he actually
worked there. Mourning his absence when he was gone.

After three weeks of the most intense study I'd ever imagined, I had to do something to change things up. The Court
had set its Samhain deadline because that was the magical
new year. But another key date in the witch's year, Lughnasadh, fell on August 1. It was the first harvest festival of
the year.

I decided to use the power inherent in that date. I would
harness the sabbat to my own magical cause. Come Lughnasadh, everything about the Madison Academy was going
to change.

August 1st arrived, heavy and hot before the sun had even
cleared the horizon. I climbed out of bed early, consciously
looking past the smooth sheets where David should have
slept. Downstairs in the dark kitchen, I was startled to find
Neko sitting at the center island, perched on the edge of a
barstool. He sighed explosively as he stared into his giant
mug of milk.

"Long night?" I asked.

"I don't want to talk about it."

I shrugged and shambled toward the refrigerator.

Before I could decide between a peach and a plum, Neko said, "He snores." I started to offer sympathy, but Neko interrupted. "No. I don't want to talk about it."

I settled for a wordless sound and returned my attention to the fridge.

"It wouldn't be such a big deal," Neko said, "if he'd just roll over when I poke his side."

"You—"

"I said, I don't want to talk about it!"

I gritted my teeth and retrieved a container of organic yogurt from the top shelf of the fridge. I peeled back the foil cover and started to stir up the sweet raspberry sauce from the bottom.

Neko sighed. "Raspberry… Tony loves raspberries."

I put my spoon on the counter. "If Tony—"

"Why is this so hard to understand, Jane? I don't want to talk about it! This is very private. Between Tony and me. I only pushed him out of bed because he woke me up six separate times. I didn't mean for him to *leave*. It never crossed my mind he'd walk all the way back to his old room in the middle of the night. And it's really not my fault he found the one stand of poison ivy between my apartment and the barn."

"Really," I said. "And we're not talking about this? I have some Benadryl upstairs."

"Go ahead, Jane, just like you always do. Make everything about you!" Neko crashed his mug down on the counter with enough force that I feared the pottery would shatter. Before I could decide whether to offer an undeserved apology, my familiar flung himself across the room.

"Neko!" I called, just before the door slammed shut. I

whispered to the empty kitchen, "Don't forget our working. Tonight. At dusk."

And Neko proved to be the most stable person in the household that morning.

By noon, Raven was snarling because she'd accidentally deleted several hours of footage from her documentary-in-progress. Hani was sulking because she wouldn't listen to his suggestions for rebuilding the file. Caleb was in a funk because the Diamondbacks had carried a no-hitter into the eighth, only to lose by an astonishing five runs.

Raven gave Kopek the evil eye when the familiar carried a liverwurst sandwich into the living room. "You are *poisoning* yourself with that so-called meat," she sniffed.

"Better than starving to death on shoots and leaves," Kopek said morosely.

"Does my sister know you eat that disgusting stuff?"

Kopek hung his head like a puppy caught chewing on a shoe. As smelly as the sandwich was, I felt sorry for him. He was a grown man, and he deserved to eat what he wanted. I chimed in to cut off Raven's inevitable next barb. "Where's Emma?"

Raven shrugged one shoulder, allowing her T-shirt to slip free and reveal a silken violet bra-strap. "Still upstairs with loverboy."

"Fine," I said, even though I was annoyed. "Just make sure she's at the lake by eight."

I left then. My own belly was flipping beneath my ribcage, from nerves about the working we were going to undertake that night. I drove into town to pick up the last few things we needed, repeatedly telling myself the ritual would be fine.

Parkersville was quiet. The air was heavy, the heat oppressive. The few people who had to be outside moved slowly, as if they were trying to preserve their energy. I wasn't tempted to linger beneath the dusty elm trees lining Main Street.

Back at the house, I headed directly up to my bedroom. I opened my closet door and reached to the very back. A few garments hung there, gowns, robes, things I would never wear out on the street. Some had come with Hannah Osgood's books, and I'd found others in the past few years.

The dress I took out was one of the latter. It was a deep crimson silk, a shade that caught the darkest highlights in my hair. Its hidden side zipper, sweetheart neckline, and ruched pleats all combined to make me feel like a princess. No. I felt like a *queen*—strong and powerful, in control of my fate and the destiny of those around me.

I freed my hair from its high ponytail and brushed a dozen strokes. Rummaging in the bottom of my closet, I found a pair of flat sandals, and then I collected a basket from the top of the bureau. I'd been placing items in it for the past couple of weeks, things we would need for the evening's ritual.

When I headed back downstairs, the house was quiet. Refusing to worry about whether everyone was preparing properly for the working, I collected the bags I'd procured in town and headed down to the lake.

Walking through the woods, I was preternaturally aware of my dress brushing against my legs. The touch awakened me to living things in the forest around me. Yes, the forest was dry. Animals were scarce. But hope was buried deep around me. There was a possibility for change.

The lake was still when I emerged from the woods, looking like melted iron beneath the heavy sky. If anything, the air had grown thicker since I'd been in town. The constant summer haze had condensed into lowering thunderheads.

I kicked off my shoes and walked out on the dock, relishing the warmth of the wood beneath my feet. My calves flexed as I stood on the very edge of the platform.

Alas, David had made an accurate prediction about the quality of the water. The summer's unabated heat had pushed the lake out of balance. Without rain to churn the surface, the water had grown stagnant, and there was a faint scent of rot in the air. A mat of duckweed floated on the surface, and a slick of oily yellow spread across the water.

I looked across to the far shore. Several trees had succumbed to the poor conditions, leaving nothing but skeletal branches to scratch against the sky. I could just make out a raft of brown grass floating near the distant edge, yet another product of decay.

No matter. After our working, all would be changed.

A flurry of wings interrupted my study, and I looked up in time to see the male osprey returning to his nest. As he settled on the edge of the loose array of twigs, he dropped a fish from his talons and opened his beak to offer a sharp victory cry.

A trio of miniature ospreys tumbled from nearby branches. The fledglings were awkward; they flapped their wings too hard, and they barely managed to make it back to the nest. They wasted no time feeding, though, tearing apart their father's offering with sharp beaks.

The male hadn't pulled his prey from our lake; I'd seen no ripples. He must have flown farther afield, forced to hunt elsewhere because of the stagnant water.

I took a steadying breath and walked back to the sandy beach to prepare for our working. Reaching into my basket, I extracted four thick candles, each the rich red of new-harvested apples. I breathed in the scent of their beeswax, centering myself, pushing my awareness toward the cardinal points.

There. East. I placed the first candle carefully, taking care that it was level on the sand. I paced a quarter circle to my right, measuring out a space that was a few yards across, large enough for three witches to work with their familiars. Our warders would stand outside our sacred circle, protecting us from any interference. At the southernmost point, I planted another candle. When I was satisfied with its placement, I walked the circle to the west, then to the north.

In the center of the space defined by the four candles, I spread a woven cloth, also taken from my basket. I had no idea how Hannah Osgood had used the fabric, but it was perfect for this working, with its crimson and orange threads, all bound together with a sparkle of gold. The fabric would symbolize our altar; it would indicate a space specifically dedicated to Lughnasadh.

When I was satisfied that I had centered the cloth perfectly, I dipped into the bag from Parkersville. The loaf of bread I pulled out was nearly as big as my head. I'd chosen it because it had half a dozen whole grains baked into its sourdough crust. For a proper ritual, I should have baked my own bread, but I knew any loaf *I* attempted was certain to be flat and misshapen, burned on at least one side. Better to support the bakery in town. Far better.

I reached into my basket one last time to extract a vermilion cloth sack. When I loosened its drawstrings and peered inside, I was heartened to see the dried kernels of corn I'd procured weeks ago. Our own corn harvest was in serious jeopardy, the stalks stunted and sere, but the symbolism of our ritual would remain intact. I centered the bag on the altar cloth.

As I straightened, my companions began to make their way from the woods onto the beach. I wasn't surprised to see Raven leading the group and David bringing up the rear.

The men were clothed in black robes, simple garments that hung in straight lines from their shoulders to their feet. Like me, Emma had dressed for the occasion—she wore a stunning gown of tangerine silk shot through with a lemon ribbon that echoed the glint of her hair. Raven, alas, seemed to have missed the memo. Like the men, she wore a black robe. Its nubby fabric stole the luster from her hair, making even the violet streak seem drab.

I sighed. I hadn't told my students what to wear when I outlined our ritual. I had no right to be disappointed that Raven had not read my mind.

"Greetings," I called, but I kept my voice low, tamped down by the steely sky above us. As if in reply, a peal of thunder rumbled in the distance. My heart leaped. Approaching rain was a good omen for our working.

The others offered up their greetings. They found their places without my prompting—the witches and their familiars standing inside the circle I'd defined with my candles, the warders taking up protective stances outside.

I told myself not to look at David. As my warder, he was ready for his role in this working, an island of calm and reason. As my boyfriend... No. That thought was meaningless tonight.

I licked my lips and swallowed hard. This first ritual of the Madison Academy was going to be everything I'd planned for. Everything I'd dreamed. Well, not precisely everything. I wasn't going to attempt true communal magic with my students. We weren't going to share powers the way I had with Emma, washing dishes in the kitchen, or with Clara and Gran, in the past. We were following the more traditional route dictated by our shortened semester.

Despite straying from my original goal for the Academy, I was heartened by the sabbat energy gathering around us. Power pulsed through the air even though we had yet to speak a single arcane word. The tiny hairs on my arms were charged as if I had bathed in electricity. I drew a deep breath to steady myself, and then I said, "To the greater glory of Hecate. Let us begin."

I inclined my head toward David. Now I couldn't help but see that his face was gaunt, as if he were not sleeping well in the barn. Nevertheless, he produced a silver sword from the folds of his robe, and he strode to the first candle, to East, to Air. I met him at the border of the circle, ready to speak my words of Calling even as he traced an etheric circle to bind us all safely.

Neko leaned in close to my side. Alas, I could tell he was still out of sorts. His fingers rubbed against his thumbs, and he flinched to duck away from a buzzing fly. I raised my eyebrows, but he only huffed and shifted his feet on the sand.

I fought against a frown and turned my attention to David. I could work the Calling without Neko's assistance.

Once we had cast our circle, my familiar should be more focused on magic, more removed from the mundane world.

I nodded, and David raised his sword, managing to look in my general direction without ever meeting my gaze. Pushing down annoyance at his impeccable distance, I knelt before the candle and raised my palms in polite invitation to the spirits of the Quarter. "Blessings of the East upon us, Guardians of Air. Bring us perfect love and perfect trust."

I cupped my hands on the far side of the candle and gathered together magical energy. "Guardians of Air, light our way," I breathed, and the fresh wick kindled. I collected the light with my hands, bringing it up to my eyes as a gesture of respect for all the natural world. Even as my fingertips touched my forehead, I felt the slightest of breezes, the presence of the Elementals of Air.

After I stood, David glided to the next candle, the southern one, tracing the tip of his sword just above the ground. As I matched him, pace for pace, a golden fire trailed from his weapon. Power sizzled into the sand, bubbling up to form an arched wall above my head.

Caleb waited at the southern point, his own sword held ready. Emma came to stand opposite her warder. Kopek hovered a few steps behind her, as if he were embarrassed and had no idea where else to stand. I made a mental note to address his lack of confidence at our next classroom session.

Emma raised her hands above the candle and recited, "Blessings of the South upon us, Guardians of Fire." She stumbled on that last word, on *fire*. In fact, her cheeks kindled, brighter than any flame. It didn't take a lot of conjecture to realize she was thinking of Rick, of her own personal fireman.

I considered stopping the ritual, then and there. But my students—and I—needed to learn how to work past distractions. Emma cleared her throat and continued: "Bring us perfect love and perfect trust." She cupped her hands behind the candle and lit the wick, flushing prettily as she said, "Guardians of Fire, light our way."

I tried to calm my pounding heart as the six of us— witches, warders, and familiars—walked another quarter turn around the circle. Caleb's sword traced fire in the sand, taking on a silver tint that rippled where it met David's gold. Half the arc was set above our heads when we reached Raven.

Tony stepped up outside the circle, baring his own sword and taking over the lead from the other warders. He wore white gloves, the better to hide poison ivy blisters, I assumed. His face was flushed.

Emma and I assumed our positions on either side of Raven, embracing our role as handmaidens to the magic she was about to summon. The dark-haired witch lifted her arms high above her head, and in perfect choreography, the sash of her robe fell open. The garment slipped from her shoulders and pooled at her feet. Hani leaped forward to collect it from the ground; he was already folding it into a rough square when Raven jutted out her hip in an all-too-familiar gesture.

Except, this time, she was stark naked.

I fought to shut down my surprise. After all, Emma didn't look astonished. Caleb, either. Tony and Hani obviously expected to find their witch without a stitch of clothing. Neko arched a single eyebrow. David's face was carved from stone; he was concentrating on the weapon in his hands, on the protection he offered all of us.

Apparently, I was the only person discomfited by the naked witch. Raven met my gaze with a little smile. "If you've never worked skyclad, you really should try it."

I reminded myself that I was the magistrix of the Jane Madison Academy, and I gestured to the third candle, inviting Raven to cast the western quadrant. "Blessings of the West upon us," she said. "Guardians of Water." The candle lit without a problem.

All three of us witches spoke the words for the North together, inviting the Guardians of Earth. I felt the shudder of the circle joining together. The warders closed off their protective cordon, matching three sword-tips as one.

In the end, everything looked right. Four candles burned, their wicks straight and tall inside the shelter of our circle. A shimmering arc of colorless energy crackled above us. The heavy pressure of the brewing storm was held at bay.

I reminded myself not to be overly critical. I was looking for perfection, and we were a group of witches working together for the first time. I needed to trust myself, trust my magicarium. This was Lughnasadh, after all. The great power of the sabbat grew out of twilight, out of the transition between day and night, between summer and autumn, between growth and harvest.

I stepped to the center of the circle and raised my hands overhead. The fabric of my dress was heated to body temperature now. It slipped over my skin like warm bathwater. Trying to hold that image in my head—water—I touched my forehead, my throat, and my heart before beginning my spell.

"Witches gather, joined in union, one strong voice as darkness falls,
Freed from worldly cares and toils, safe in nature's world sans
walls."

I drew out the last word, waiting for Emma to join in. She was supposed to build on the foundation I had set. After a lifetime of hesitation, she finally spoke the next words:

"Here beneath—"

She cut herself off, realizing she'd used the wrong word. Intent meant more than any vocabulary choice, but there would be time enough to teach her when we resumed normal classes in the morning. Emma shook her head and started again. Her voice trembled as she recited:

"Here beside the oaken forest, here upon the lakeside shore,
Let the storm clouds roll in closer, let the raindrops start to pour."

She was supposed to call for *rain* clouds, not storm clouds. Moreover, her emphasis upon correcting her first mistake torqued all the energy raised by her couplet. Nevertheless, I could still turn this into a teaching moment for our next class.

During the few moments I hesitated, Emma poured more strength into our fledgling working. In fact, she transferred astral energy with an alarming efficiency, pumping out power from her vast reserves. In a dozen heartbeats, I felt as if I were walking along a mountain ridge in a fierce windstorm. Setting my teeth with determination, I leaned into one gust of wind, only to be sent reeling when another rose from a different direction. I was pushed, twisted, spun around until I nearly lost my footing.

I tossed my head, trying to cast out all the interfering thoughts. I was a witch. I was a channel. I was a vessel for the powers of the natural world around me.

I had almost accommodated Emma's modifications to the spell when Raven began her part of our working. Her voice rolled forward with the force of a gale, brutal winds pushing word after word, line after line.

"Increase rainfall at our summons, rise up to our desperate need,
Fall upon the lake and forest, nurture all that grows from seed."

They were simple words, a spell we'd all discussed. But I was astonished by the power of Raven's working. I'd sensed the intricacies of her strength before, the stony framework, the countless interstices where arcane energy could spark and multiply. I had never imagined, though, the sheer volume of that amplification, the rushing, rolling torrent that would crash over us as she spoke.

Even as I fought to find my proper balance, desperate to keep my literal and figurative feet, Raven embraced the energy that Hani offered as her familiar. Somehow, impossibly, her power doubled.

We three witches were wildly out of sync. We had summoned a prodigious amount of energy, and every breath we took threatened to spin us off our physical and astral axes.

I clutched at the lifeline Neko tossed me, the guy-wire he cast across the buffeting gulf. There wasn't time to defuse the excess power. I could not possibly siphon off the energy safely, feed it to the gathered Elementals of Earth and Air, Fire and Water.

I had no choice but to plunge ahead, to lead us off the cliff, into the chasm, into the heart of the burgeoning storm.

Lightning flashed, brighter than any noon-day sun. At the exact same instant, deafening thunder shattered above us. The earth rose up beneath our feet, shaking hard enough to throw us all to our knees. Our protective dome shattered, nowhere near the equal of the energy we had raised. All the air around us was sucked away, and for a terrifying eternity I couldn't see, couldn't hear, couldn't breathe.

"Jane!"

That word had no meaning.

"Jane! Dammit!"

The voice was pushing on me, beating against me.

"Neko, over here. No, kneel beside her!"

Beating against *me*. I was separate from the void.

"Jane, I need you to focus. Take her hand, Neko. Feed her power—now!"

White heat surged into me. Burning. Searing.

"Too much!"

The heat pulled back. Returned, more gently.

"A little more. That's it. More."

The heat crept into my wrist. I had a *wrist*. I had a wrist, and a *body* and *lungs* that were desperate to breathe. I gasped, gulping air, choking, flailing.

"Easy," the voice said, and I discovered that it had a hand, too. It had hands, and arms, and a steady, solid chest. It folded around me, cradling me, sheltering me. It surrounded me, protected me, and I could sink into it and be safe forever.

"Hush," it said, and I realized I was sobbing. "You're fine, now," it said. "Breathe. You're safe. Breathe." It crooned words to me, easy words, simple words, endless words of comfort. I could float on whatever that voice said. I could slip back into the void. I could drift away, far away, forever.

"Jane," the voice whispered. No. Not the voice. *David*.

I opened my eyes.

David was sitting on the sand in the center of the circle we had cast. He cradled me in his arms. My crimson dress was sandy and torn. The silk was drenched. My hair was dripping, and so was his.

I tried to take in everyone else—Raven and Emma, clutching each other as if they shared one soul. Nervous warders, darting protective glances into the woods, across the lake. Familiars, hovering near their witches, helpless, unsteady.

"What…" I meant to speak. I meant to ask the questions that loomed out of the fog inside my head. My throat was raw, though, as if I had screamed for a thousand lifetimes. I tried to swallow, but I was too parched to complete the motion.

David shook his head. "Your power was too great. Too unbalanced."

"Rain?" I managed, trying to put an entire cavalcade of questions into the word.

He nodded. "A hurricane. All of it—rain and wind, thunder and lightning. The power passed through you, over all of us. It was gone before we knew it had struck."

I understood each individual word, but together they made no sense. I could never have survived such a storm.

I looked past him, to the tallest oak on the shoreline. To the osprey's nest, where barely an hour ago the male had fed his three chicks.

Or, rather, I looked to where the osprey's nest had been.

Now, there was nothing. Now, the oak was split in two, its massive trunk halved into a pair of curling strips. The sprawling nest, the majestic birds—gone.

I didn't realize I was sobbing again until David pulled my

head against his chest. He said something to the others, issued orders. Someone retrieved the quenched candles. Other hands gathered up the altar cloth. The bag of corn, the sodden lump that had been a loaf of bread, all of it was collected. Someone—Neko, it was Neko—slipped my sandals onto my feet.

And then we were walking through the forest, David clutching me close. It was too far for him to carry me. The ground was too rough, especially with the channels that had been carved by the instant, deadly downpour.

I leaned into him. I melted against his side. He matched his steps to mine, and a century later, we finally made it back to the farmhouse. I was nearly asleep as he swept me into his arms, as he carried me over the threshold, like some travesty of an eager groom welcoming his bride. I felt him put one foot on the stairs that led to our bedroom. And then I knew nothing more.

Chapter 10

THE OSPREYS WERE attacking me. The male tangled his feet in my hair, closing his talons and raking my scalp. The female slashed at my face with her beak, as if she were peeling strips of flesh to feed her chicks. I screamed as she tore my cheek, as she gouged a trough beside my eye.

"Jane." David spoke my name and drove off the raptors. His voice was calm and certain. "Look at me, Jane."

I couldn't look at him. I had to protect myself. I had to brace for the next attack. Shadows writhed in the corner of our room. The three fledglings hid there, waiting to strike at me.

"Jane. Look at me."

I found his gaze. In the gloomy light, I couldn't make out the color of his eyes, but I knew they were brown, a deep and steady chestnut. His eyes conveyed the essence of his patience, his calm. He was absolutely certain I was safe. Only then did I realize the ospreys had been a nightmare.

David ran his hands down my trembling sides, and I braced myself, a part of my scrambled brain still believing he would recoil at the stickiness of my blood. But there was no blood. There was only the soft cotton of my nightshirt.

My ruined Lughnasadh gown was pooled in the corner where David had discarded it the night before. In the grey light of almost-dawn, I couldn't tell that the dress was the color of blood. But in my heart, I knew it was.

David blinked, and I was finally free to move. I was safe from the ospreys. Safe from the nightmare. But there was nothing David could do to rescue me from memories of the magic I had unleashed by the lake. The ospreys—the real ones—had been struck by lightning. They had been devoured by the storm, their nest shattered into a million fiery pieces.

David's hands were firm as he pressed me back on the bed. I tried to protest. I could not stay here. I did not want the luxury of my pillow, the forgiveness of the mattress. I struggled to sit up, but David touched my forehead with his index finger. "Sleep," he said. The low thrum of warder's magic echoed through my body, and I slipped into oblivion.

I awoke sobbing, gasping, desperate for freedom from my tangled sheets. Sunlight striped the edges of the bedroom shades, too bright, too strong to ever gaze on directly. I fought to break away from the grasping bed. I struggled to escape.

And David was there. He released my trapped arms, worked the twisted bed linens from my thrashing legs. I choked for air, heaving like a sprinter at the end of a heat.

David took me onto his lap. He eased my head against his shoulder. He rubbed my back, gently, calmly, and he rocked me until my sobs drifted away.

My third awakening was easier. I swam up from a sleep deeper than any dreams could penetrate. I was groggy from the depths; I'd lost my words, lost all but the vaguest shell of my thoughts.

David helped me into a seated position, swinging my legs over the side of the bed. He told me to hold on to the edge of the mattress. He needed to repeat himself twice, but some part of my lizard-brain finally understood.

He took a washcloth from somewhere, a soft one, and he dipped it into a basin of warm water. He bathed my face slowly, carefully. He traced my eyebrows, the line of my nose, my chin. He went over my hands, holding each one lightly between his own. He smoothed my fingers, wiped the length of my arms. When I shivered, he dried me with a towel, taking care to remove every hint of moisture.

I was still cold, though, frozen to the core. My teeth started to chatter, and when I set my jaw, my entire body shook.

David eased me back onto the bed, swinging my legs around. He covered me with the sheet, the cotton blanket, the feather blanket we'd stored in the top of his closet months earlier. He stretched out beside me, and his arm was heavy across my chest as he anchored me to the bed. He cradled my swaddled body against his until I slept again.

I wasn't sure what I sensed first—the hum of the electric clock on my nightstand or the sun that shone scarlet through my eyelids. I lay as still as I could, listening for David's breath beside me.

The working had been a nightmare. So much power, and I'd lost control of all of it. I had put myself and my students directly in harm's way. The storm alone could have devastated us—torrential rain, lightning strikes. And that was before I began to calculate the magical backlash...

Nevertheless, David had been there for me. All the tension of the preceding weeks, all the distance and uncertainty... I had felt his arms around me, and I had known I would be safe. He would never let me be harmed. I had trusted him in a way I'd never been able to trust any other person.

Remembering the velvet iron of his body around mine, I sighed and stretched my legs beneath the sheets. I reached out one hand, seeking his chest—or maybe some more interesting part of his anatomy. With any luck, we could spend the entire morning here in our bedroom. Finish things off with a shared shower before heading into town for lunch at the café. I moaned a little in the back of my throat, imagining the decadence of it all.

"Jane, dear!"

That wasn't David's voice. My eyes flew open.

Gran was sitting in a ladder-back chair beside the window. She wore an orange cotton sweater set and a faded denim skirt. White socks protected her feet from her navy blue Keds. She had crossed her legs at her ankles, and the position made her sit up straight in her chair. She looked prim and proper, the polar opposite of the lascivious home movie I'd started to play inside my head.

"What are you doing here?" I meant to shout the question, but my words faded into a rasp after the "what." I swallowed hard, suddenly realizing how parched my throat was.

"Here, sweetheart. Have a sip of water." Gran helped me sit up. I felt ridiculous leaning against her, but my hands were trembling so hard I needed both of them to hold the plastic cup she gave me. It took three tries to close my lips around the drinking straw. The water was so cool and sweet I almost started to cry.

Gran clucked her tongue and gestured for me to lean forward. Supporting me with one hand against my shoulder, she used the other to straighten my pillow. She was as smooth and efficient as a nurse.

"What happened?" This time, I got out both words. I was encouraged enough to push. "Where's David?"

"You've been sleeping, dear. David had to go to Sedona last night, so he asked me to sit with you."

She'd been here all night? But what about my nightmares? Why had I dreamed about David comforting me, if Gran had been watching over me? And what was David doing in Arizona anyway?

Gran took the cup from my hands. "Perfect, dear. Now, maybe just a bite of something light. Melissa dropped off some Bunny Bites, but I think the frosting is a little too rich for your first meal back."

Dropped off? Wait. "What day is it?" I croaked.

"Sunday, dear. Don't you remember? You've been awake several times."

Sunday. We'd attempted our Lughnasadh working on the first of August, on Thursday. I must have dreamed about the ospreys that night. And woken from more nightmares the next day, Friday. And David had bathed me that night. So, two days later, I managed to return to the world of the living.

As I worked through the miracle of the Gregorian calendar, Gran wrestled open a package of peanut butter granola bars. She wrapped one in a paper napkin, as if I were a five-year-old child who might muss her dress with a snack.

Even as I wondered how Gran had smuggled the processed treat past Raven's whole foods vigilance, I nibbled on a corner. The sweetness bloomed across my tongue like pure sugar, and I had to fight not to gulp down the entire bar without chewing. In between tiny bites, I asked, "When will David be back?"

"I'm not sure, dear. Your mother needs him for a working tonight. He's helping her prepare things today."

Shakespeare said jealousy was a green-eyed monster. Melissa would know the play—Othello—and she'd have no problem knowing that Iago spoke the famous line. But Iago was wrong. Iago and Shakespeare and Melissa herself, if she'd ever believed the Bard's words. Jealousy was bright red, scarlet, the color of blood streaming from a newly opened vein.

I blinked, hard. David was bound to Clara by a warder's sworn obligation, just as he was bound to Gran and to me. Nothing had changed that—not the disastrous working by the lake, and certainly not the weeks we'd spent separated before Lughnasadh.

Still angry, but embarrassed by my visceral flash of emotion, I took another bite of the granola bar. I forced myself to focus on chewing and swallowing before I asked, "Did he tell you? About what happened here?"

She nodded solemnly. "I know you pushed yourself too hard. You wanted to impress your students, and you tried to do too much too soon, with too little support from the other witches."

I shook my head. "That's not what happened."

"Why don't you tell me, dear?"

And so I did. I admitted that I'd lost control of the Lughnasadh ritual on the beach. I told her about fighting with David on the Fourth of July, even though I didn't say what we'd argued about. I told her about how much I hated changing the magicarium's curriculum, how much I missed the communal magic I'd always planned to teach.

I didn't notice when Gran handed me the second granola bar. Or when she supplemented my "meal" with a smooth-skinned nectarine. Or when she passed me the cup of water and, finally, a small plate with two perfect Bunny Bites.

"So I'm trapped in a house that isn't even mine," I concluded. "I can't walk down the hall without running into Raven or Emma. The living room is a film editing studio, and I'm cross-examined on every bite of food I put in my mouth. Rick Hanson is here so often, I might as well be living at the fire station. What am I going to do?"

Gran nodded, a pillar of wise, silent support.

"No," I said. "Seriously. I want an answer. What am I going to do?"

"Bring the familiars into the house."

"What!" I guess my improvised meal had restored my energy. That was certainly the loudest exclamation I'd made since awakening. "I just said the house is too crowded."

"There's nothing wrong with my hearing," Gran said sharply. "You're having trouble finding the right balance with your students, right? That was the basic problem with your Lughnasadh working?"

I nodded.

"You need to know them better. You need to understand them. What better way to learn about a witch than to watch her interact with her magical partner? Your students came into their own powers when they awakened their familiars. If you want to know Emma and Raven, you have to know Kopek and Hani."

I tried to imagine the familiars crammed into the house with the rest of us. Beyond the challenge of simply finding beds for two more people, there'd be more bodies to slide past in the hallways. More rationing of hot water for morning showers. More dishes in the kitchen sink.

Gran nodded as if her idea was brilliant. "And your students will get to know you better. When they see how well you and Neko get along, they'll be better prepared to join you in your next working."

"Oh, no," I said, realizing the full import of Gran's scheme. "I lived with Neko for three years, and he nearly ate me out of house and home! Do you have any idea how much cheese he can tuck away? And ice cream? I won't even mention the liquor…"

Gran looked serene. "Am I going to have to ask for a promise?"

Gran and her promises. She always insisted she wasn't asking for anything major, that her demands were merely common sense. But I knew better.

Nevertheless, my grandmother had seen me through my tempestuous years of high school. She understood me better than I understood myself. If she insisted…

"No, Gran," I said meekly. "I'll move the familiars into the house."

"Excellent!" she said, and she actually clapped her hands with glee. "Now, dear. Get back in bed. It's time to get more rest."

"I'm fine!" I protested. But even as I said the words, a wave of weariness threatened to topple me.

"Don't make me cast a spell on you," Gran warned. But I was already yielding to the mere power of suggestion. Bed. Rest. My eyes were getting heavy. I barely managed not to dislocate my jaw with a yawn.

I scrunched the pillow into a more comfortable position. At the same time, Gran pulled the covers up to my shoulders. She smoothed them gently, and then her dry palm brushed against my forehead. I was catapulted back to all the times she'd checked my brow for fever, nursing me through childhood illnesses. I sighed deeply, and then I fell asleep.

Poke.

I moved away from the edge of the bed, trying to protect my side from whatever was digging into it.

Poke, poke.

I pulled my knees up, putting a barrier between me and the annoying thing.

Sniff. Sniff, sniff, sniff.

I opened my eyes. Neko's nose was millimeters from my own. His hand was poised above me, fingers stiff, ready to deliver another decisive poke.

"Don't even think about it," I said.

"Oh! You're awake!"

I grimaced and pushed myself upright as Neko bounced up and down on the edge of my bed. "What day is it?" I groaned.

"Sunday." His tone suggested I was an idiot for asking. But then he conceded, "It's almost midnight."

"Where's Gran?"

"David took her home. He thought I could keep an eye on you now."

"David's back?"

I pushed off the bedcovers, almost sending my familiar flying. He only recovered by bracing one foot against the floor, and then he tried to look as if he'd intended to assume that position all along.

"Is that any way to treat your loyal, devoted familiar? The man who watched over you, hour after hour, while you slept away the one decent weekend we've had all summer long? I refused to leave your door, even when David wouldn't let me in. I didn't go, even when your grandmother ordered me to take a shower and a nap!"

I narrowed my eyes. Neko was being his usual histrionic self. But beneath his declarations of fidelity, I could sense a true ripple of concern. "What's going on?"

"Nothing!"

I resumed the process of getting out of bed. "Fine, then. Thanks for your help. Goodbye."

He looked up at me through his eyelashes. "Well, there might be one little thing..."

"Such as?"

He actually dug his toe into the rug beside my bed. If he'd been physically capable of it, he might have shrunk a foot or two. "It was all my fault." He whispered the words to his knotted knuckles, not daring to meet my eyes.

"What was?"

"The Lughnasadh working." He sighed, and his entire body quivered in misery. "I never should have let you start the ritual when I was so unfocused. I was thinking about

Tony, worried he was going to move back to the barn. I didn't pay enough attention to you, and I twisted the energy you raised, and instead of feeding it back properly, I ruined everything. Jane, I'm so, so sorry. I understand if you want to banish me. Offer me up to the Washington Coven. Strip me back to a statue. Go ahead. I deserve it."

Almost three and a half years, and I'd never seen Neko grovel before. Sure, he'd made some apologies. Even begged my forgiveness. But he'd never truly believed he was at fault.

This was different. This was a confession that went to the very root of his being my familiar.

"Neko, I…" I trailed off. There were so many things I wanted to say. Needed to say. The words all jumbled in my mind, and I wondered if I might have been more coherent if someone hadn't just poked me awake.

Neko's shoulders collapsed, and he caught a breath that might have been a sob. He turned toward the door. With his hand on the knob, he whispered, "David can find you another familiar. And this time, make sure not to wake it on a full moon."

"I'm not awakening anyone!"

Neko whirled back, faster than I'd ever seen him move.

"Lughnasadh wasn't your fault," I said. "Yes, you were distracted. But so was Emma. And Raven didn't help matters, going skyclad and pulling all that power." I took a deep breath. "And I wasn't focused, either. I kept thinking about…"

David. Of course Neko knew I'd been thinking about David. Even if he hadn't been attuned to my every witchy sensation during the ritual, he knew I'd been sleeping alone for a month.

"He's down in his office right now," Neko said helpfully.

My belly tightened as I remembered the feel of David's arms around me on the beach. I flashed on his steady command as he ordered me to look into his eyes, as he guided me back to myself. I was halfway to the door before I realized I'd moved.

"Not so fast!"

I ground to a halt.

"You may have forgotten, but you've spent four days in that T-shirt. It's more than a little ripe."

I tried to steal a surreptitious sniff at my own armpit, but Neko only sighed like I was breaking his heart. "Trust me. Take a shower. And for once, don't go straight for the shorts and T-shirts when you get dressed. And one more word of advice? A little lipstick never killed anyone. "

I stuck my tongue out as I headed toward the shower. I was already closing the bathroom door when he called out, "Jane?"

I glared at him. "What now?"

"Thank you." He finally met my eyes. "I won't let it happen again."

"No," I said. "I don't think any of us will make the same mistakes."

My heart pounded as I stood at the bottom of the basement stairs, wiping my palms against my sides. After trying on three outfits, I'd settled on my sea-green sundress, the one with the halter straps. I'd worn it the first time David and I had ever slept together.

Come to think of it, that encounter hadn't gone very well. We'd had a number of misunderstandings, crossed wires that took months to straighten out. It was too late to go upstairs and change, though. He had to know I was hovering on the edge of darkness.

I watched as he scribbled a note in the corner of a document, underlining his words twice. He picked up the page and held it up to the light, as if seeking some secret message. Obviously not finding anything of interest, he shook his head and added it to a pile on the far corner of his desk. I could make out the array of ribbons and flash of grommets that marked the documents as belonging to the Court.

I stepped over the threshold into his office. "Having trouble?"

He put down his fountain pen with the precision of a surgeon returning a scalpel to a tray. "The connections are there. I'm just not seeing them."

"Maybe you should let this go. There are more important things than stopping one petty bureaucrat."

"He's not petty, and the bureaucracy gives him far too much power over hundreds of innocent witches. I'm a warder. I *have* to stop him."

"You sound obsessed." The words were out my mouth before I could help myself. I watched him shut down, pull away from me without ever moving an inch.

But this wasn't why I'd come downstairs. I didn't want to fight about the Court. Or anything else. "Hey," I said, purposely pitching my voice low to counter his tension. "Thank you."

He sucked air through his teeth as if I'd splashed acid on him. "I'm sorry."

I hadn't been fishing for an apology. "What are you talking about? I needed you, and you were there."

"You needed me because I screwed up."

"I'm the one who lost control of the storm!"

"And I didn't protect you!" He slammed his fist down on his desk. My first instinct was to recoil from the violence that trembled through his forearm. But I knew his fury wasn't directed at me. It would *never* be directed at me. I settled my palm on his shoulder.

"You found me," I insisted, even when he flinched. "You called me back. You held me when I needed that, and you chased away the nightmares." I leaned forward to kiss him. I felt the moment he started to give in, started to settle his hands on my waist to pull me closer. But then his fingers slid up to my biceps, and he eased me back to the desk.

"We can't do this, Jane. I'm your warder. I was only acting as your warder."

"Stop punishing me!" I lashed out before I'd even thought my way through the words. "I said I was sorry!"

"I'm not punishing you!" He whipped out his denial before I'd finished speaking. Then he leaned back in his chair, putting greater distance between us. He took a deep breath and exhaled slowly. "Okay. I *was* punishing you. But I'm not anymore. I'm trying to be practical. Your entire magicarium is on the line. We both know it. Your Major Working is more important than me, than *us*. At least for now."

My cheeks prickled with embarrassment; I felt like a schoolgirl rejected by her first crush. David hadn't rebuffed me since the first weeks we'd worked together, the very first time we'd kissed. "If our work is so important, then why did you leave me? Why did you go to Arizona before I even got out of bed?"

"I had to. Your mother called me."

"What did Clara need that was so important?"

His face tightened. "Ask your mother, Jane."

"I'm asking you."

He shook his head. "Call her."

"Fine," I said. "I will." I turned on my heel, frustration and lingering chagrin speeding my retreat. I stopped, though, when I got to the doorway. "I don't know if it matters for your *warder* responsibilities, but the greenhouse and the garage will both be vacant by the end of this week."

"Why?"

"I'm moving the familiars into the house."

"I don't think—"

"But I do. I think it's best for the magicarium. And I'm the witch in charge."

My skirt caught on a nail as I flounced up the stairs. I yanked it free, not even caring when the fabric ripped. It was a stupid sundress anyway. Time to cut it into rags.

But first things first.

I stomped across the kitchen and grabbed the telephone. Clara was on speed dial, number three after Gran and Melissa. I glanced at my watch. It was late in Arizona, but she should still be awake. In fact, she answered on the first ring.

"Jeanette!" That's all I needed to know this conversation was not going to go well. "You caught me just as I was walking out the door."

Great. I didn't have to bother with formalities then. "What are you working on?"

"We're going to the Bell Rock Vortex to harvest juniper berries at the stroke of midnight. The stronger the vortex energy, you know, the greater the axial twist in the branches.

It's early in the season for anything to be ripe, but we don't want the birds taking all the berries from perfect spirals."

I shook my head, feeling like I was spinning into a vortex of my own. "What are you working on with David?"

"David? He isn't here. I thought he was back with you. Maybe if you check with your grandmother?"

"No," I said. "What were you working on last night? Why did you make him go to Sedona?"

"*Just a second!*" my mother called, loud enough that I had to hold the phone away from my ear. "Jeanette, my ride is here. I have to run—we can't chance letting the feminine side of the Vortex fall out of sync with the masculine."

"Clara—I started, but she was talking to someone else. "Mother!"

"Bye, dear! I'll send you some juniper berries!"

And she was gone.

I swore as I set the phone back into its cradle. Not only had I failed to get a straight answer to my question, but I hadn't reminded Clara to send her belated tuition payments for Emma and Raven. I'd rather have cold, hard cash, than a fresh harvest of axial twisted juniper berries.

But I'd be a fool to actually make plans based on any promise from my mother. I sighed and headed upstairs. The morning was going to come all too soon—and I suspected the familiars wouldn't be thrilled when I told them they had to move.

Chapter 11

"WOULDN'T BE THRILLED" was an understatement.

Actually, Hani was fine with his new living quarters. The cocky little familiar made it a practice not to complain about anything. Instead, he took first claim on the best corner of the basement, making sure he was the farthest from the creaky stairs.

It was hard to measure whether Kopek's hangdog expression was generated by shifting out of the greenhouse, or if he was merely exercising his usual pessimism. He tucked his cot close to a collection of little-used books on the construction of labyrinths, and he shoved his footlocker next to the water heater. I decided not to comment when he placed a few personal items on the shelves above his head.

Neko, though, threw a fit.

"You can't make me live down *there!*" From his scandalized tone of voice, I might have suggested that he start wearing Croc sandals and socks. Black socks. Calf-high. With sagging elastic.

"You make it sound like I'm sentencing you to a prison

cell." I was unimpressed with his dramatics. "You lived in the basement of my Peabridge cottage for three years. This is exactly the same."

"Except for my roommates, you mean."

He had a point. But... "It's just for this semester. Until we finish the Major Working."

"That's practically *forever!*"

"My hands are tied. If I show you any favoritism, Hani and Kopek will be upset."

"They'll be a lot more upset when they have to share our *dormitory* with Tony."

"Don't go there," I warned.

"Where?"

"If your romantic relationships start having a negative impact on the magicarium, then I'll have to draw some lines. No fraternization with students' team members is a great place to start."

"Spoken like a woman who isn't getting any."

"Neko!" I flushed, but I wasn't sure if my response was triggered by anger or embarrassment.

"I'm just saying you shouldn't take out your own frustration on innocent bystanders."

"For your information, Mr. Brilliant Familiar, I have perfectly good reasons to make this change."

"Such as?"

Well, it wouldn't be fair to throw my poor, elderly grandmother under a bus driven by my strong-willed, motivated familiar. I stood fast and set myself up to take a direct hit. "We've got a lot of work to do, and not a lot of time to do it in. The only way we can possibly make our Samhain ritual a success is if we all work together as a team. And that requires getting to know each other better. We have to *trust* each other."

"Can't we do a ropes course instead? Maybe stand on a stepstool and fall back into each other's arms?"

I laughed at the plaintive note in his voice. "Seriously, Neko. This is important." I hadn't thought it was, when I promised Gran I'd make the change. But now I realized it could be the fuse I'd been seeking, the missing spark to ignite our elusive magical success.

Neko wasn't giving up yet. "Maybe Caleb can put up a few walls down there?"

I thought about the cost, quickly weighing lumber and drywall against my familiar's continued sulking. "You can ask him—*once*. But if he says he doesn't want to or it can't be done, that's it. End of discussion."

Neko nodded, transforming his sulk to a beatific expression. "May I borrow your credit card?"

"Absolutely not!" My shout was a visceral reaction. "What do you want it for?" I asked reluctantly.

"I need to buy some baseball tickets. Fast."

I shook my head. "Finance your own bribes. And no asking David for a handout, either!"

Neko was still grumbling as I walked away.

With the house in chaos and the familiars unavailable for magical work, I decided to play hooky for the afternoon. I headed down to DC to visit Melissa. I wasn't sure when I'd next be able to break away, not with the full court press we were about to mount to save the Madison Academy.

For once, there was a parking space just a few doors away from Cake Walk. I slipped inside as a family of tourists was leaving, laughing with Texas drawls as they exclaimed about the size of the Monster Mouthfuls they'd just consumed. I shut the door quickly to keep the air-conditioner from working any harder than necessary.

"I'm meeeelting," I said in my best Wicked Witch imitation, as I staggered dramatically toward the counter.

Melissa laughed and poured some Boardwalk Blackberry over ice. A pair of crisp Ginger Sequins were the perfect complement.

"All right," I conceded after administering emergency food and drink. "I might live."

Melissa responded with, "Rock, paper, scissors."

"What?"

"Come on! Rock, paper, scissors." She tapped her right fist against her empty palm. "One." By reflex, I mirrored her actions. "Two. Three."

I cast paper. She threw scissors.

"I win!" she crowed.

"Win what?"

"You're going to help me select a watercolor artist."

"Why do you need a watercolor artist?" I looked around the shop, with its sunny yellow and orange walls. It really wasn't a watercolor kind of place.

Melissa sighed. "Jane, Jane, Jane. You have to keep up! We've become too addicted to computerized images in our daily, electronics-laden life. We have to get in touch with the emotions behind the things we see. We need to reach out to the people we truly love in new and unique ways. We should have an artist paint our wedding reception—a collage of watercolor scenes, plus special portraits of the groom, the bride, and the bride's second cousin, once removed."

"Ah," I said, finally clued in by that last self-centered bit of information. "So this is another relative's idea?"

"Cousin Genevieve. On my father's side."

"What do I have to pay, to make sure the artist doesn't paint the maid of honor?"

"You've got a bad attitude!"

I shook my head. "Is there any way to have a good attitude about this? Seriously, Melissa. Watercolors?"

"Believe me. This is the lesser of a million evils."

"What else could anyone possibly be pushing?"

"Cousin Marty thinks we should have a cigar roller, to create personalized smokes for everyone. Aunt Laura wants a special lighting feature, with Rob's and my entwined initials projected onto the walls. Great-aunt Terry can't imagine anything more hilarious than a pair of granny panties, size 34, for Rob to display after he goes for my garter. Ha. Ha. Ha."

Poor Melissa. This wedding insanity was enough to make me grateful I had a tiny family. Even if that limited pool included Clara. "Fine," I said. "I'll go with you. But I don't know the first thing about evaluating watercolors."

"You're a librarian," Melissa said loyally. "And you have three weeks to do your research. We're meeting artists on the 23rd. I'm sure you'll be an expert by then."

When she put it that way... I tried a wry smile. "It'll be a good excuse to get away from the farm."

"Things aren't any better?"

"If anything, it's worse." I filled her in on the past few days, concluding with: "So now, I've wasted a month of classes, David's living in the barn, five people I *don't* want as roommates are living in the house—six if I count Tony—

and we have less than three months to figure it all out and complete a Major Working. I don't remember the last time I felt this lost."

"I do," she said helpfully. "It was when you started at the Peabridge."

Before she could elaborate on my past sense of failure (what else are best friends for?), the bakery door opened to admit a customer. A tattooed and pierced guitar player leaned his instrument case against the counter and started to quiz Melissa about her selection of vegan and gluten-free treats. I wondered if I should invite the guy back to the farm. It sounded like he and Raven would get along brilliantly.

As Melissa ran through her options, I thought about what she'd said. My struggle with the magicarium *wasn't* all that different from my fight to get settled at the Peabridge. Sure, as magistrix I didn't have to worry about wearing a colonial costume. I didn't have to greet neighborhood matrons or babysit local kids or brew coffee by the gallon.

But both jobs represented major turning points in my professional life. With the Peabridge, I'd finally left behind the world of academics, of collecting university degrees for the sheer joy of learning, without paying any attention to things like paying the rent and buying groceries. For the first time in my life, I had to come to work on time and stay all day long. I had to meet the very specific job requirements of a very demanding boss. I'd needed to find ways to work with others, even when I disagreed with them about the finer points of my profession. I'd become a grown-up.

With the Academy, I was carrying all that training one step further. I was the one responsible for setting the schedule. I determined the scope of our study, and I was the very demanding teacher. I forged the paths to communicate with my students, even when one insisted on sounding like an extra from *Downton Abbey* and the other gave pin-up girls a run for their money. I was responsible for all of it.

But this time through, I had the tools to make it all work. I'd earned them, fair and square, at the Peabridge reference desk.

Guitar Guy left, and Melissa turned her bright gaze on me. "What? You obviously had some epiphanic breakthrough while I was wrapping up Belly Laughs."

"I need to be a librarian."

"What? You're going back to the Peabridge?"

I shook my head. "No. Not literally. I need to take the skills I learned as a librarian and apply them to the magicarium."

Melissa's doubtful shrug was cut off by the arrival of two young lawyers. Despite the summer heat, both wore button-down shirts and ties, and they were spiritedly debating the merits of res ipsa loquitur with regard to medical malpractice cases. Those words meant less than nothing to me, and I let their chatter become white noise as I thought about my discovery.

I'd reached out to my students when they first arrived, finding out who they were and what they wanted from the Academy. I'd done that by applying the technique of a reference interview—a tried and true library tool. I made them focus, made *me* focus on what was really important.

Relying on familiar methods had given me the backbone to put a stop to Raven's cinematic aspirations. The reference interview had helped me understand the unique aspects of my students' power, why they had come to *me* instead of any run-of-the-mill coven magicarium. It had carried me through my first crisis of faith about the Academy.

Only when Melissa refilled my glass did I realize the lawyers were long gone, and I'd been completely lost in thought.

"Okay," she said. "So you're going to open a library, instead of a school for witches?"

"No." I shook my head. "I'm going to apply what I learned in the library to make my school a better place."

"How are you going to do that?" She honestly sounded curious.

Well, that was the tricky part, wasn't it? My fingers opened and closed, as if I could almost…just…grasp an answer. "Budget," I finally said.

"What?"

"As a librarian, I had to learn how to manage an institutional budget." I thought about some of my spectacular failures on that front, especially seeking grant funding that had been as difficult to track down as Clara's tuition payments. "I'm going to tell David to sell the southern point. That money will remove a lot of pressure—our day-to-day concerns about food, and supplies, and Neko's shopping sprees."

"David has enough land to cover *Neko's* bills?" Melissa and Neko had not always been on the best of terms. I made a face.

"I hate to do it. But we'll need the funds for future semesters, even if we scrape by now. Even if Clara *does* finally send a check."

"And he *did* offer," Melissa reminded me.

Of course that was before the Fourth of July. Before everything had changed. But I knew David would say the money was a warder thing. It was part of his protecting the

Academy. I hated the necessity, but I'd ask him to complete the sale.

"What else?" Melissa asked.

"Education. Librarians are always learning about new developments, applying new technologies."

Certainly, I'd read the basics about magical education; that had all been part of my summer procrastination. I'd focused on how the Rota worked, how most covens structured their classes. That sort of basic background had been mandatory, because I'd never completed a traditional education on my own. Under David's tutelage, I'd avoided the standard steps.

But I hadn't done anything like a complete literature review on magical educations. I hadn't thought I needed to—the Madison Academy was supposed to be so thoroughly different from any other school for witches out there.

That oversight was easily rectified. I would survey my collection as soon as I got home, focusing on footnotes and indexes, on references to other materials. Neko would be invaluable—he could reach out to the familiars' silent communication network. With his help, I could identify additional materials in no time. After that, it was a relatively simple matter of obtaining them. I'd borrow what I could, and buy what I had to.

Melissa nodded, as if I'd spoken my self-education plans out loud. "And?" she urged.

"Selling new ideas."

"What do you mean? Three ideas for a dollar? An extra if they're day-old?"

"You should stick to running a bakery," I said, wrinkling my nose. "No. I mean getting buy-in. When I worked at the

Peabridge, I realized I needed an assistant. I couldn't begin to complete my daily duties, much less work on the big projects, the ones that made the job fun. Evelyn rejected the idea immediately, of course, because we didn't have any money. But I convinced her to bring in an intern. For the summer only, at first, but then during the academic year. I just had to make her understand that increasing our manpower was a benefit for the entire library, not just for me. I had to sell the new idea."

"I think it'd be easier to price them three for a dollar."

I was spared the need to come up with a real retort when the bell jangled and another family of tourists surged into the shop. As they started debating the relative merits of Mocha Mud Bars and Triple Chocolate Madness, I sipped my Boardwalk Blackberry and plumbed my library skills for further inspiration.

"Where were we?" Melissa asked, after she'd boxed up both chocolate desserts, with a handful of Lime Stars on the side.

"Organization skills."

"We were?"

"Close enough. As a librarian, I put books where my patrons needed them to be. Sometimes, I ignored the classification system and grouped items by specialized collections. I need to do the same thing with magic. Forget about individual items from specific disciplines—herblore, crystal work, runes. We need to approach things from the end-point. From the overall segments of the actual ritual."

Melissa laughed. "I'm sure that makes sense to you. To me, it sounds like gibberish."

It *did* make sense. It was like a specialized form of communal magic, similar to the theory I'd had when I first launched the Academy. I never should have panicked when Norville Pitt showed up and ruined everything. I never should have retreated to the limits of an ordinary education. The bell above the door rang again, and I didn't even turn around to see what customers entered. Instead, I asked Melissa, "Do you have a piece of paper and a pen?"

She thrust a legal pad at me, along with one of the pens she kept by the register. As she dished up baked goods, I started scribbling notes to myself. I began with broad topics—Purification, Centering, Calling the Elementals, all the building blocks for our ritual. Beneath each general category, I started to list individual items—specific crystals and herbs and witchcraft tools. I added entries for individual books in my collection, actual texts that spoke to precise magical points.

I started to flip back and forth between my scribbled pages, adding details to one category, taking them from another. Some topics—Weather-working, for instance—were gigantic. I had to break that down, into Rain-making and Preparing the Earth, and Protecting the Innocent.

But in the end, it all made sense. In the end, it all held together. I had reduced our Major Working to a giant outline with roman numerals and capital letters and numbers and periods and parentheses.

And when I read through the list, I was nearly overwhelmed. There was so much to do. So much to explore. How had I ever thought my students could handle any of this in our Lughnasadh working? We'd be pushing to get it all done by Samhain.

I looked up to find Melissa drying a stack of plates.

"What are you doing?" I asked. "I mean, when did you wash those?"

"Somewhere between that page," she gestured toward one of my scribbled documents, "and that one. It's good to see you fired up about what you're doing. And before you panic about how late it is, here's dessert for tonight."

She handed me a pasteboard box as I looked at the clock. How had it gotten to be 5:00? I handed back her pen with a grateful smile. "Is everything in here organic?"

"Nope. But you can tell Raven it is."

"Or maybe I won't," I said with an evil chuckle. "Then there'll be more for the rest of us to enjoy." I folded my papers and clutched them close. "Hey," I said, sinking back in my chair. "Thank you."

She laughed. "Glad I could help. At least I won't be totally in your debt on the 23rd."

The 23rd? Oh. Watercolor day. I was actually looking forward to using my librarian skills to find out more about wedding watercolorists. It was the least I could do to help my best friend in the world.

Chapter 12

IT SEEMED LIKE such a simple thing, my discovery at Melissa's. And yet, it opened completely new horizons.

On Tuesday morning, I summoned the entire magicarium into the living room. It took us a couple of minutes to find seats for everyone—several chairs were filled with boxes from the familiars' not-entirely-completed move.

Fortunately, Rick was on duty at the firehouse, so there was no need to excuse Emma's boyfriend from our conversation. Mundane companions might accept the existence of magic in the world around them, but this conversation was going to get into the specifics of a new approach to witchcraft. It was going to be a challenge for everyone concerned, and I didn't want outsiders muddying the waters.

Everyone stared at me expectantly. I'm sure they thought I was going to change the living arrangements yet again. Maybe I'd have the warders take over the house, and the rest of us could live out of the minivan... I forced myself back to the challenging topic at hand.

Swallowing hard, I said, "I realized something important

yesterday, something I'd forgotten for far too long. It affects all of you, and I'm sorry I didn't think it through before now."

That got their attention—a magistrix apologizing. I hurried on. "I've been coming at this all wrong. I've been focusing on the individual elements of our working, pushing us to perfect each component part of our magic. Over and over again, I've invested our efforts in mastering the tiny details."

Emma nodded and Raven shrugged. Of course I'd focused on perfection of form. That's what witches *did*. I held up a hand to forestall their questioning.

"But you know I planned on something different for the Academy. I told you that, your first day here. We were going to find communal balance, work together with mingled powers as we relied on the reflective nature of our familiars. But we failed the first time we tried that, and then I changed our focus. We never found our new paradigm."

This was it. Time to launch the Jane Madison Academy 2.0.

"Okay," I said. "Starting today, we're doing something completely different. We're tearing down the old classification schemes—herb magic, separate from crystals, separate from runes. Instead, we'll do them all at once, all combined." Oops. From the blank looks on their faces, I'd lost them completely. Frustrated, I paced two steps away, then whirled back to face them. "We want to purify an altar cloth. What do we need?"

They stared at me like I was speaking in tongues. "No," I said. "I'm really asking you. What do we need? Emma?"

She shook her head, obviously not understanding where I was going. She glanced at Caleb, then at Kopek, but both men offered confused shrugs.

"Don't think about it!" I said. "You walk into the basement, and you collect the supplies for the ritual. What do you grab? Emma!"

I shouted her name, jolting her out of her hesitation. "A silver bowl!"

"Raven, what else?"

"Rainwater collected under a full moon."

"Exactly. And what else?"

Emma answered. "A branch of rosemary, to sprinkle the water."

"Or?"

"Sage," Raven said. "And a source of fire."

"Exactly!" I almost clapped my hands, but they might think I was mocking them, treating them as if they were preschoolers. And that was not my intent, not at all.

"It's all about classifying the information," I urged. "Instead of thinking about rituals as individual bits, as solitary elements where we succeed or fail on our absolute understanding of each tiny piece of magic, we're going to focus on the whole. How does the silver reflect the power of the rosemary? What happens when the fire kindles the sage? When the droplets of water turn to steam, what effect does that have on the bowl, on the rosemary, on the sage? It's all connected. It's all a system. We're all parts of the whole."

Raven shook her head. "But every witch has an innate bond to a single practice. We're best at herbs *or* spells *or* crystals. Emma and I work well together because I can manage herblore, and she can balance the elements."

"You *have* worked well together," I agreed. "But you've never grown beyond your basic skills. You haven't moved past the magic you could work when you were children." I rounded on Emma. "You know what I'm talking about. You felt it when we cleaned the kitchen."

She nodded slowly. "But washing up was such a wee thing. I could grasp it all at once. The energy it would take to hold onto everything in a Major Working..." She trailed off.

"It *will* require energy. But we'll structure a system for that. A new balance. Throughout the working, we'll each give where we have strength. Then we can take where we have need."

I could tell they wanted to believe me. They wanted to understand. They wanted the time they had spent at the magicarium to mean something.

I held out my hands to them, pushing the last drop of my enthusiasm into my explanation. "We'll all be working together, so we can share the tricky parts. We'll help each other past the truly tough sections. Three witches. Three familiars. Three warders watching over us. We'll have more than enough power to do it all."

David cut through my excitement with a chainsaw. "It's too dangerous."

I whirled to face him. I had expected resistance from my students—I was asking them to rethink the essential way they used their powers. I wasn't surprised by the skepticism on Kopek's face either, or even Hani's. My proposal would require them to find new methods to bolster our powers.

But David? Splashing cold water on my proposal when I'd barely finished presenting it? Belatedly, I realized I should have brought him into the loop before I shared this plan with everyone. But I hadn't, and now I had to live with the consequences. What was it I told Melissa yesterday? *I had to sell the idea.* And that sale began with letting him express his objections.

"Why is it too dangerous?" I asked.

"You'll raise too much energy before you have enough control to manage it."

"You've seen me do it before! This is exactly how I work with Clara and Gran."

He shook his head. "Your students here have more raw ability than your mother and grandmother. Your method multiplies forces, creates greater energy than any of its component parts. Until you learn how to manage that, it will be Lughnasadh, all over again. In a worst-case scenario—"

"What about a best case?" I couldn't keep from cutting him off.

He shrugged. "I'm a warder. I don't spend time on best cases."

I *knew* he was a warder. We'd both made that abundantly clear, ever since the Fourth of July.

But I wouldn't get anywhere by losing my temper. I needed allies. "Caleb? Tony? What do you think?"

I'd purposely addressed the guys in that order. Caleb was sitting opposite Emma, taking his cues from her. I'd only known the man for a month and a half, but I'd learned that he built things. He crafted solutions—whether that meant picking up a hammer or adjusting to a witch with a new man in her life. He was my best bet for structuring a resolution that would work for everyone.

We all looked at the tall, blond warder expectantly. He leaned forward in his chair and dangled his hands between his knees. "I guess I see it this way. It's the bottom of the ninth, and we're down by two runs. The bases are loaded. Two outs; the count is three and two. You bring in your best pinch hitter, and he swings for the fences. Everyone goes wild. But if the ball doesn't get out of the park, you've got to have a coach you can trust at third base. If he makes a mistake, waves home the guy from first, and the runner gets tagged at the plate, you're into extra innings. You might lose it all. But if he holds up the runner, your game is tied, and you're still batting."

I stared at him. He might have been speaking Urdu, for all I understood. But if I asked him to explain, was I going to get another extended metaphor about table saws and nail guns and ball peen hammers? Or could it be worse than that? Did Caleb have other hobbies I didn't even know about?

"Sorry," I said. "I didn't quite follow that."

Tony cut in. "He's saying it's a dangerous situation, and you have to manage the risk. Will you trust your warders if we say you've gone too far? Will you break off a working if your warder says to?"

I heard the old belligerent Tony in the questions—the man who had challenged David at swordpoint, the fighter who had punched a car in mindless anger. But the aggressive Tony was the same man who had waded into battle to protect his witch from an unknown enemy with unknown skills on unknown territory. He could be hot-tempered and short-sighted, but he was also fiercely devoted to Raven.

Caleb nodded, accepting Tony's translation. "If you let us have the final say on what is and isn't safe, then I'm in."

Tony shrugged. "Me too."

I could see David wasn't happy. He was the only one of

the three warders who had witnessed communal magic of any real complexity. He understood the multiplier effect; he had watched Gran and Clara and me become more than the sum of our parts.

But he also knew how much this mattered to me. If I couldn't pursue a new method of teaching, the magicarium would never complete a Major Working by Samhain. David's veto would effectively terminate the Madison Academy.

And then Norville Pitt would win.

I saw David reach the same conclusion, at nearly the same instant in time. His jaw tightened, and he raised his chin. "All right," he said. "But only if you promise. If any warder says a working is too dangerous, will you stop immediately?"

"I will," I said and waited for him to nod his acquiescence.

I looked at my witches. "Any questions?" When there weren't any, I squared my shoulders. "All right. Let's eat a light lunch, and then we'll get to work. By the end of today, I want to complete a purification ritual."

Chalk one up for the librarian team. I'd successfully sold an idea.

Alas, I'd always been an optimist.

By the end of Tuesday, we were nowhere near completing a purification ritual. With David taking first shift as warder (or babysitter or third base coach, whatever *that* really meant), we witches had gathered all our supplies and moved out to the stretch of sun-dried lawn between the house and the cornfield.

We'd discussed the various steps for the rite and defined

how we were going to proceed. We'd attempted to balance the energies inherent in mugwort tea, in fresh-needled rosemary sprigs, in rainwater and silver and sage and spells.

And we'd failed miserably, spectacularly, each and every time we tried to work the rite.

There were simply too many things to keep in balance. There were the four literal elements—earth and air, fire and water. And there were the component tools—herbs and water and a silver bowl. And there were the words of a spell, along with its undefinable arcane power.

Mostly, though, there were the jagged edges of our personalities. If I tasked Raven with taking the lead, she could rapidly build a bridge to Emma's strengths. But as soon as she brought me into the loop, that span twisted, torquing under my unfamiliar weight and collapsing into nothingness.

If Emma started, she could bond with me or with Raven. But the instant she brought the third person into the meld, our was overwhelmed, toppled by distractions.

And if I started, we got absolutely nowhere. I was diverted by the flicker of power between the sisters. My attention snagged on Emma's British facade, by the foreign rhythm of her speech. I lost my concentration when Raven ran her fingers through her hair, highlighting the violet stripe at her temple. There was always something that kept me on edge, something that kept our work from flowing.

Once, just once, I found the proper balance. It was late afternoon. Despite numerous applications of sunblock, we were all turning pink from the sun. We had consumed gallons of water to fight dehydration. We were sweaty and tired and ready to give up for the day.

But I took energy from Emma. I fed it to Raven. I felt the

swirl of our collective forces growing, swelling, as if it were a new-birthed animal breathing on its own.

The potential astonished me. Even I had never expected to find so much pure energy available. I gasped in surprise, and the bond broke. The energy washed over us, as shifting and shapeless and impossible to grasp as water pouring from a broken balloon. I came back to full awareness of the mundane world, of David's hovering form.

I was actually shaken by that last effort. Maybe we *were* attempting too much. Maybe I *was* stretching the definition of witchcraft too far.

But I shoved my doubts down as deep as I could. "Excellent," I said, faking the confidence of a proper magistrix. "We'll pick up from here tomorrow morning."

My witches lost no time stepping away from our circle. They were both steady on their feet, but I could see fatigue in their sloping shoulders. Kopek tagged along beside Emma as she made her way to the porch, to the farmhouse and its air-conditioned rooms. The familiar looked like a weary puppy who didn't have anywhere else to go. Hani might have given Raven the same sort of support, but she shook her head irritably, telling him to take a break before she headed indoors alone. I suspected her fingers were itching for her phone. Maybe she wanted to play spare-time cinematographer without his intervention. In any case, Hani took offense and stalked off into the forest.

I looked at Neko. "Well? I'm sure you have plans, too."

He actually blushed. "Tony and I had talked about going out tonight."

"To a party?" I tried to picture Tony in a costume—*any* costume—and I came up totally empty.

Neko shook his head. "To dinner. We were thinking about trying the new steakhouse in Frederick."

The new steakhouse. I couldn't imagine that red meat had been Neko's first choice. Maybe his relationship with the warder actually *was* something deeper than I'd believed.

"Go ahead," I said. "Thanks for all your hard work."

As he scampered off, I was surprised to find myself stifling a yawn. David's raised eyebrows might have been an off-hand question. How was I doing? Tough day at the office? How about that ninth inning?

But he wasn't making any casual inquiry. He was gathering evidence about our new model of working. And I had promised I would accept his evaluation of our safety, safety that included my health. "Okay," I conceded. "Working this way *does* involve a lot of power. You were right, and I was wrong."

"I don't want you to be wrong," he said, and his voice was gentle enough to bring tears to my eyes. I must be even more exhausted than I'd thought.

I rubbed hard at the back of my neck, trying to release some of my tension. "You just want to be right?" I asked.

He rewarded me with a smile as he eased behind me. I leaned into his touch, letting his strong fingers find the pressure points along my spine. "That feels like heaven," I said.

"Just another footnote in the warder's handbook." He kept his tone light, but I heard the subtext as if it were shouted through a bullhorn. *Warder. Witch. And nothing more.*

I braced myself for the conversation I'd been avoiding. "About the southern point," I started.

"Jonathan's drawing up the papers. He's got three buyers, already interested."

"How did you know I would agree to the sale?"

He shrugged. "We'll need the money for the future. Even if your mother comes through with funds for this semester." Those were practically the identical words I'd said to Melissa. Of course they were. David and I both wanted the magicarium to succeed.

"Thank you," I said. The two words weren't nearly enough.

He smiled and urged me toward the house with a gentle push. "Eat," he said. "I'll call Jonathan."

In the kitchen, I barely managed to stand in front of the refrigerator long enough to find a piece of fruit. I stumbled upstairs to my bedroom and fell asleep in my sweaty clothes, too spent to pull on pajamas.

Wednesday dawned, and I immediately headed for the shower. Alas, my housemates had shared the same idea before I did; we were out of hot water. In the kitchen, I had to rinse a bowl for my cereal. Even then, my breakfast was interrupted by the acrid stink of coffee baking dry on the heating element.

I hadn't thought it would make a huge difference, having the familiars living in the basement. After all, they'd been around the house constantly before they moved in. But I'd underestimated the impact of their twenty-four-hour-a-day presence. I was seriously regretting my promise to Gran.

At least I didn't feel as penned in when I met my students on the lawn outside the house. Hot, yes. Sweaty, yes. But there were no walls to feel like they were closing in.

Caleb watched over us while we worked. We didn't make any progress, but we did succeed in exhausting ourselves to the point of punch-drunk silliness. At one point, Emma fum-

bled the words of our spell, and we all collapsed into hysteri-
cal giggles.

Thursday wasn't any better. On the household front, I
went to the linen closet for a hand towel, only to find that
the cupboard was bare. Literally, bare. There wasn't a towel
or sheet to be found. Down in the basement, I solved the
mystery—half a dozen loads of laundry were piled in front of
the washing machine.

My exasperated cry startled Kopek, who acknowledged
the pile with a sheepish expression. Hani started in with an
explanation that involved an abortive attempt to hang sheets
as temporary dividers between rooms, pending the comple-
tion of Caleb's renovation work. I stormed upstairs, trying
not to think about rusty nail holes ruining all of Neko's recent expensive purchases.

Under Tony's gaze, we tried our working again, but we
never came close to succeeding. That evening, I tried to find
a quiet corner to figure out what we were doing wrong. But
Hani and Raven were bickering in the living room, and
Emma was cooking dinner for Rick in the kitchen. I retreated to the basement to collect a few books, working on the
literature review I'd promised myself back in the bakery.
Before I could find the most recent arrivals, Neko's loud
throat clearing alerted me to the fact that the room was occupied. I grabbed the closest book in the room and fled.

I literally stumbled over Kopek in the upstairs hallway.
"Sorry," he said, pulling in his legs, so I could get by. "I was
just looking for a place to read." He held up a battered paperback. I sighed and closed my bedroom door behind me.
For the rest of the night, I felt like I was hiding in my own
home. That feeling of claustrophobia wasn't helped by my

being awakened at least half a dozen times. It seemed like there was always someone going up the stairs, down the stairs, in or out of a room and slamming doors.

And that brought us around to David's watch again. And we repeated the entire cycle. For two entire weeks.

All right, not fourteen straight days. I gave everyone time off on Saturdays and Sundays. Otherwise, we might have killed each other. Even with those breaks, the sniping got pretty bad in the house. By the end of each weekend, everyone felt the need for a little alone time. There just weren't enough rooms, nowhere near enough spaces to escape the constant pressure of witchcraft relationships, and family relationships, and romantic relationships, and every other possible interaction.

By our third Friday, I decided we were only going to work until noon. All three of us witches were drained. The familiars were showing stress as well—I'd caught Neko snarking at Hani twice, rolling his eyes at the gelled ridge of the redhead's hair and mocking the turned-up collar of Hani's polo shirt.

David was warding us, with his usual perfect attention to detail. In an effort to focus more deeply, I'd skipped breakfast that morning, allowing myself only a single cup of chamomile tea.

Now, flanked by my students, I stared at the equipment between us, at all the accoutrements displayed in perfect balance. Silver bowl. Flask of rainwater. Mugwort leaves. Rowan wand. Rosemary sprig. Closing my eyes, I allowed myself to envision each item against a velvet backdrop in my head. I knew these tools completely. My palms knew their weight to within a fraction of an ounce. My fingertips understood the cool touch of silver, the prickle of rosemary, the smooth warmth of my wand.

I held that knowledge inside me and let it swell with a dozen steady breaths. I settled the fingertips of my right hand on Emma's palm. I reached out to Raven, on my left. I glanced at our familiars, carefully placed across the circle from each partner witch in a hopeless, helpless effort to bolster our strength.

My students were ready. I breathed with them, another dozen breaths. Deep. Even. Centering.

I opened myself to Neko, to his familiar energy emanating from his seat at Emma's side. He leaned against her, curving easily against her flank. Hani was next to me, doing the exact same thing. At some point I had become accustomed to the bantam familiar's psychic presence; I now knew the balance of his energy without giving it a conscious thought. The same was true of Kopek—I didn't need to *think* about how he mirrored Raven's strengths for this working.

"Power of silver, gathering light…"

Part of my mind was aware there was danger in speaking the first line of our incantation aloud. We were supposed to say it together; it was supposed to add to our joined power, creating more energy through a sort of feedback loop. Too many times, the spoken word had shattered our rapport. All too often, the spell had torn us all apart.

But not this time.

"Fresh cut greenery, bitter and bright…"

Energy grew inside us, between us. The power was set alight by a tiny thrum of surprise—we'd never completed the second line of the spell before. We'd never reached that level of bonding.

"Purest rainwater, collected at night,
Wand of pure rowan, commanding all might.
Make strong, keep clean,
Save this witch from threat unseen."

In another world, in another lifetime, I would have laughed aloud. The magic was spinning around us, gathering us in a circle and whirling us about as if we played an arcane game of crack-the-whip. As in that children's game, the motion only brought us closer, only bonded us each more tightly to the other, and I could not laugh because I was drawn in by the wonder.

I pulled from Hani, and I felt an answering tug from Neko, from Kopek. I offered my power to Raven, to Emma, and I felt each of the witches accept my gift, making a present of her own distinct force. I didn't have to think about their energy; it was simply *there*. My students' power had become an extension of my own.

I'd kept my eyes closed as I chanted the spell, but now it did not matter if I opened them. Now, the power between us was strong enough that nothing as ordinary as vision could ever tear it apart.

I reached toward the rainwater flask, but it was Emma's fingers that closed around the bottle. I started to steady the silver bowl, but it was Raven's palm that kept the vessel even. Water poured out, and I was the liquid, swirling against the cold silver, taking on the heat of a witch's hand.

Emma was the one who understood that water. Her powers were innately linked to it. The element spoke to her; it *was* her. Through my link with Emma, I became one with the water.

Together, all three of us added mugwort. The herb be-

gan to infuse the second the fresh green leaves slipped beneath the liquid's surface. My physical eyes could not measure the change, but my arcane senses filled with a tingling
force.

Raven was the one attuned to mugwort. With every cell
of her being, she sensed the bitter flavor leaching into the
collected rain. She tracked the acerbic strength of the ancient herb.

I was the one who actually reached for the rowan wand.
My palm closed around the smooth wood. My fingers tightened so I could stir the mixture—once, twice, three times.
With each pass, the mugwort offered up more of its protective strength.

Nestling the wand on a snow-white cloth, I filled my
lungs with the invisible power of our solution. The energy
sparked inside me, clean and safe. Closing my eyes, I gathered together the thrumming force. I collected strength from
Hani, bolstered it with reflections from Neko and Kopek.

My action bound all of us closer together, witches and
familiars. An invisible web tightened around the six of us.
Each twitch of power from the elements of our working
ratcheted the bonds closer, uniting us until we shimmered
with a single, indomitable light.

One of us, all of us, reached for the rosemary. All of us,
one of us, dipped the spiked branch into the water. I, we,
offered the rosemary to the east, to the elemental home of
air. We, I, shook the branch three times, shedding a cascade
of drops, releasing a lyrical glissando.

South was next, then west, then north. Each time the
rosemary dipped into the water, it harvested the perfect
power of the mugwort, the flawless force of rain. Those

drops were shed in an unbroken span of cleansing, of virtue, of purity. Wherever the water passed, an arc of light remained. Gold, violet, silver—all merged into a single metallic glory. I caught my breath at the beauty, and I laughed at the ozone tang that sizzled against the back of my throat.

Emma was laughing too, and Raven. Our familiars looked on, willing partners, silenced by our ongoing draw of their energy. Beyond the circle, beyond the pure working, I was aware of David, conscious of his warding strength, his watchful gaze.

If we had been completing a real working, it would be time to move to the next step. We would have prepared the earth for the gift of rain. We would have proceeded to build the next module of our next spell, merging our powers on an even deeper level, finding the true apex of our joined strength.

But we needed more practice before we could do that. We needed to build our endurance. Even now, my fingers tingled so hard that I could not truly tell where my flesh ended, where the outside world began. I drew a breath, and I could not fill my lungs, could not truly sate my body's need for air.

I pulled back on my bond with Hani. I felt him shift, just a little, but enough that I lost the mirrored link to Neko. Kopek fell away, too, and I was bound only to the witches. Raven rolled her shoulders, twisting the link between us, and Emma sighed deeply, like a woman emerging from deepest sleep.

I dropped my arms to my sides, and the magic faded away.

"That was incredible," Emma whispered.

Raven nodded. "What made it different this time?"

I forced a smile, trying to act as if I'd always known we would succeed. "Practice makes perfect."

They laughed, but I saw Emma catch a yawn against the back of her throat. I hazarded a quick glance toward David. He looked attentive, but not worried. I'd managed our strength well. We were all fatigued, exhausted even, but none of us had pushed ourselves anywhere near a point of danger.

He raised his ceremonial sword and sliced through the circle he had cast for our protection. Chanting together, we witches dispersed the final remnants of our arcane energy. We matched our words, spoke at the same time, but there was none of the wild power left.

As soon as we were through, David said, "Let's go. Lunch for all of you. And *no* magic for the rest of the day."

I let him bully us into the kitchen, and I accepted the cheese and crackers he placed before me. The familiars talked quietly among themselves, with long pauses between spoken words. I suspected they were commenting on the experience in their own magical way, with the silent communication of their kind.

Under David's watchful eye, I made small talk with Raven and Emma. For the first time ever, I saw traces of their twin language. No words; they no longer verbalized with their private, unique tongue. But there were tiny gestures. Hints sent through glances. A constant exchange of information, attunement, *focus*.

I couldn't translate all of it. I couldn't know how it felt to be them, to be tied that closely to any other human being. But I could see ways to use the bond between them. I could strengthen it, splice it to include a third witchy power. I could rewrite the organization they had used all their lives and classify their secrets to make all of us stronger, better witches.

The next time. When we advanced to the next stage of our working.

When I sat back in my chair, Spot came over for a pat on the head. (All right, he probably came over for one of my crackers, but I wasn't that much of a sucker.) He rested his chin on my lap and sighed deeply when I found the perfect scritching spot behind his right ear. I missed having the lumbering beast up here at the house. The kitchen looked bare without his bed in the corner. But I could hardly take the Lab back from David. That wouldn't be fair.

I sipped my lemonade and started to daydream about my next working with Raven and Emma. We could move beyond purification to a working that actually changed a state. Kindling candles, maybe, or even summoning rainclouds. I closed my eyes and tried to imagine how it would feel to be suspended in the element of air.

Which made it all the more jarring to hear a knock at the back door. I looked at David, and he looked at me, but neither of us was expecting any visitors. He shrugged and worked the deadbolt before opening the door.

"Ah," came a voice I never wanted to hear again in my life. Spot stiffened by my side, and I felt the growl deep in his throat, more than heard it. "I would have come earlier, if I'd known you were serving lunch."

As my stomach tightened, David said something impossible: "Please. Come in."

And Norville Pitt strode into the kitchen.

Chapter 13

MY PULSE SKYROCKETED. Why had David let Norville Pitt into our house? We were surrounded by magical protections—every door and window was guarded against astral and mundane intruders. Without an explicit invitation, Pitt could never have stepped over the threshold.

Even now, Spot interposed himself between me and the door. His hackles were raised, and his lips curled back from his teeth. David issued a curt hand gesture, but it took a repetition before Spot slunk to the floor.

The Head Clerk seemed oblivious to the canine threat. He still looked like a refugee from a television show: *What Not to Wear: Coven Edition*. This time, his slacks were blue serge, worn thin across his ample thighs. His yellow short-sleeve shirt was dingy, and his pocket protector was askew. His right shoelace was knotted multiple times.

"Ah," Pitt exclaimed, in that voice that reminded me of light crude oil spreading over a peaceful bay. "Don't mind if I do." He collected a plate from the center island and started to fill it with remnants from our recuperative meal—a bunch of grapes, a handful of Triscuits, a fistful of Marcona almonds.

I cast a frantic look at David. What was he thinking of, letting his enemy stride into our midst? Was blood going to be shed on our kitchen floor?

David's face was utterly opaque, though. A casual observer might even think he just *happened* to cross the room on that particular line, just *happened* to to take up a watchful position that kept him an identical distance between Pitt and me. If David had a plan, he wasn't sharing it with me.

And that meant I had to take the lead. I had to pretend like this visit was absolutely ordinary. I cleared my throat and said by way of greeting, "Mr. Pitt." I prayed he wouldn't notice the slight quaver in my voice.

In fact, the wheezing clerk scarcely acknowledged my greeting at all. Instead, he oozed over to the kitchen table and extended a sweaty hand toward Raven. "Norville Pitt," he said, using his free hand to smooth back his greasy hair. "No relation to Brad."

Did the guy only have the one pick-up line? My student, to her credit, merely shook the offered hand. "Raven Willowsong," she said. But for the first time since I'd met her, she didn't accompany her words with a single seductive gesture—no roll of the hips, no toss of the hair, not even a smile.

Emma submitted to the social nicety as well, offering up her own name in a flat midwestern accent. All three familiars stared in watchful silence, obviously aware—perhaps even grateful—that the Court did not consider them worth speaking to.

David poured a glass of lemonade and passed it to Pitt. I

didn't get it. David hated this guy. He was obsessed with bringing him down. Why was he acting like this visit was a present from Hecate herself? "What brings you here, Norville? We weren't expecting you until Samhain."

Pitt drank down half the glass before responding. "Mabon," he said, with a toothy smile.

"Excuse me?" I injected myself back into the conversation. I knew what Mabon was, of course—the next sabbat in the witch's calendar, less than a month away. Mabon continued the celebration of the autumn harvest that we had launched with Lughnasadh.

"Congratulations, Miss Madison." Pitt put his glass down on the center island so he could pump my hand.

"For what?" I barely resisted the urge to wipe my palm clean against my shorts.

"The Madison Academy is now a Class Two institution."

"A Class Two…" I trailed off, uncertain of the significance of Pitt's words.

But David figured things out before I did. "The Court is getting involved again?" He chose his words carefully, but I could practically hear him shout "interfering" instead of the far more mild "getting involved."

Pitt's smile turned my stomach. "The Court has a *very* special interest in the Jane Madison Academy. We couldn't help but notice that you completed a working this morning that registered thirteen point two."

I understood the individual words, but I had no idea what he was talking about. "Thirteen point two?"

Pitt nodded eagerly. "On the Circe scale."

I glanced at Neko, who offered the slightest of shrugs. David didn't recognize the phrase either, from his narrowed eyes.

"I'm sorry," I said. "I don't know the Circe scale."

Pitt tutted quietly. "Now, you won't want to say *that* when your magicarium is being evaluated officially."

Yeah. There were a whole lot of things I wouldn't want to say under those circumstances.

David spared me the need to push for a clarification. "What has the Court devised this time, Norville?" His tone walked the narrowest of lines between curiosity and contempt.

"Why, the Circe scale is the latest metric for magicaria. It allows us to measure the combined power of all magic workers—students, instructors, and Affiliated Institutions—in a given magicarium. Your initial Circe rating, the one calculated before you signed your charter, was one point seven five."

"One point seven five," I echoed. "But we hadn't completed any workings when I signed the charter."

"Precisely," Pitt agreed.

"Then how could you complete a rating?"

"Our initial assessment was based on your personal accomplishments, Miss Madison. You should be quite flattered to be included in this pilot program."

"How many schools are in the pilot program?" David asked.

Pitt met his narrowed eyes with a slimy smile. I wasn't surprised when the clerk said, "One."

David's fingers curled into fists. I took a step forward, silently reminding him that he had to keep a grip on his temper. "What changed, then?" I asked. "Between the initial rating and today?"

"The working you completed this morning, of course. With this morning's score of thirteen point two, the Madison Academy is now a Class Two institution."

"That's ridiculous!" I protested. "There were only two students added to the mix! We don't have any *Affiliated Institutions*. Your metric can't have changed that much, just from the addition of two witches!"

Pitt clicked his tongue and shook his head. "The Court isn't concerned with the absolute number of witches, Miss Madison. We focus on *power*."

They certainly did. The brunt of their *power* was goading me more with every second that passed. I tried another tack. "We completed our working this morning in preparation for your inspection on Samhain. You can't penalize us just because we're getting better."

"Oh, Miss Madison." Pitt pushed his Coke-bottle glasses up his shiny nose. "It has never been our intent to penalize *you*." There was just enough emphasis on the last word to expose Pitt's ongoing conflict with David. If he regretted showing his cards so blatantly, though, he recovered quickly. "It's certainly not a penalty to be ranked a Class Two."

"What do we get out of it, then?" I snapped.

Pitt twisted his wrist and somehow produced a familiar sheaf of papers. It was the charter for the Madison Academy, the document I'd first seen down on the dock. Now, though, a copper grommet attached a puffy gold ribbon to the first page. The festoon looked like it belonged to a kindergarten student who was voted "Most Improved" at Field Day. It bore the words "Class Two" in a flowery script.

Pitt cleared his throat and turned to a page at the back of the charter. "Class Two institutions shall have all the rights and appurtenances pertaining to the foregoing Class One institution, including any right, title, and interest of the Magistrix in and to adjacent territories, magicaria, and unaffiliated bands of students."

The legalese made my head spin. "Doesn't that mean a Class Two is the same as a Class One?"

"But you get a *ribbon*. And specially trained Class Two examiners, of course. It's such a shame—not *one* of our Class Two Watchers is available on your previously scheduled date of Samhain."

What a coincidence. "And I can't hold off and test later in the year? After Samhain? Yule, maybe?"

Pitt laugh sounded like a leaf blower. "With a new program like this, the Court has to insist on completing all testing as early as possible. And we'l have a full complement of reviewers. Eight, in fact. That's best for everyone, you know."

Best, how? How, exactly, was anything about this ridiculous situation best for me? But I could already imagine the made-up, jargon-filled explanation Pitt would throw my way if I protested. I was actually surprised when he said, "You *could* file an appeal."

"How do I do that?"

His smile revealed a row of shark-like teeth. "You simply complete a Notice of Appeal of Charter Review, and file it with the Court. Along with mandatory character references, of course."

"Character references?"

"Seven people who can testify to your magic abilities and your good standing within the community."

Gran and Clara. David and Neko. Raven. Emma. Who

would I use as a seventh?

Pitt cleared his throat. "That's seven people, of course, for each discipline you're testing for." He flipped through the charter. "For the Madison Academy, that will include herblore and crystals. Runes. Spellcraft. General magical principles. Academic inquiry. Am I forgetting anything?" He pawed the paperwork. "Oh, of course, elemental magic, and advanced craft. So, fifty-six references. Of course, none can be related to you, or a current student of yours."

With anyone else, I'd assume they were joking. But I was pretty sure Norville Pitt wouldn't recognize a joke if it rose from the center island and kissed him on his pursed, liver-colored lips. And he still wasn't done grinding my dreams to dust. "Your appeal will have to be notarized and filed in triplicate one month before your scheduled test."

"One month before—"

He looked at his cheap Timex, as if it had some special calendaring function. "Ah, yes. That would be yesterday."

"That's not fair!"

"I wouldn't be too upset, Miss Madison. Appeals take at least three months to get on the Court's docket. Of course, you'd need to pursue certification in the meantime. We can't fall behind on our testing schedule, now can we?"

I could rant. I could rave. I could tell Pitt to take his bureaucratic claptrap, fold it three ways, and...

But I was the magistrix of the Madison Academy. I had a reputation to uphold. Besides, I had to make sure David didn't do anything foolish. He'd been suspiciously silent as I explored the parameters of the Court's trap, and I didn't completely trust him not to extract some sort of revenge on Pitt, right there in the middle of our kitchen.

Determined to avert *that* disaster, I threw back my shoulders and extended a hand, as if I'd just concluded a successful business meeting. I looked Pitt in his piggy little eyes and said, "Thank you very much for taking the time to look in on our operations."

"No trouble." He pumped my hand and flushed with obvious pleasure. "No trouble at all. Always glad to be of service."

"David?" I asked pointedly. "Could you show Mr. Pitt out?"

My warder nodded, as if the departure had been his own idea. But first, he extended his hand. "I'll take the charter."

Pitt showed his teeth and passed the document to me. "Keep an eye on that, Miss Madison. You wouldn't want it to get *misfiled*, would you?"

I took the scroll, with its gaudy yellow ribbon. If David were insulted by Pitt's remonstrance, he gave no visible indication.

Pitt turned to my students. He bowed first toward Emma, then made a deeper obeisance toward Raven. As if by reflex, she crossed her arms over her low-cut blouse. "Ladies," Pitt said, and the simple word somehow sounded obscene slipping off his lips.

"Norville," David said, bristling. He set a firm hand on Pitt's elbow and escorted the Clerk to the back door. Pitt started to reach for another clump of grapes, but Spot rose from the floor with a possessive snarl, apparently tested beyond his even Labrador retriever temper. I dropped the charter and clutched at the dog's collar, while David hustled the intruder out the door. I didn't release Spot until the deadbolt was thrown home.

Raven and Emma looked appalled. Emma pushed her plate away, as if she'd lost all appetite for any restorative meal. Raven plucked at her blouse, attempting to hide more completely behind its limited offerings. I unlocked my knees and reached blindly for the chair Neko nudged toward me.

Astonishingly, though, David seemed unaffected. In fact, he was smiling as he turned back to all of us. He patted Spot on the head and affirmed that the Lab was a good dog. For the first time in days, David's shoulders seemed relaxed, and he actually laughed as he picked up the charter from the floor.

"Am I missing something?" I asked. "Why did you let him in the house?"

"I knew he couldn't resist leaving something behind. That's why I offered him lemonade," he nodded to the half-empty glass on the center island, "but this is even better." He gestured to me with the charter, making the yellow ribbon tremble.

"Better for what?"

"I'm going to scan for Pitt's aura."

That sounded like Clara's kind of crazy talk. "You're kidding. Right?"

"Not at all. Oh, it's not what you're thinking. To a warder, 'aura' has a very specific meaning."

"And that is?"

"The after-image, when a person has worked magic."

Once again, I had to admit, "I don't understand." And if I was lost, I could only imagine how my students must feel. They had no idea that David and Pitt were longtime antagonists.

"An aura's like an astral fingerprint. Pitt produced this

document out of thin air. I can trace his power on it."

And David could compare that trace to the documents down in the basement. He could identify which Court papers Pitt had manipulated with magic. But wouldn't the Head Clerk have handled the vast majority of the materials that David had pilfered?

I wanted to ask more questions, but I couldn't. Not with my students listening. Not with Neko paying far too much attention.

I hated the entire idea of David working with those stolen documents. I worried they were only going to bring him grief. But I wasn't ready to be the one who blew his cover. Yet.

"If you'll excuse me?" David asked. I nodded acquiescence, and he crossed to the basement stairs. Before he headed down to his office, though, he turned back to look at all three of us witches. "I wasn't joking before. No more magic, for the rest of the day. You all need a break after your working this morning." He looked down at the charter he held lightly in his fingertips. "Your *Class Two* working."

I shook my head as he disappeared down the stairs.

Up in my bedroom, I wondered if David would count a little fatigue-banishing spell as magic. I had to drive down to DC to help Melissa review watercolor artists that evening.

Yeah. Right. Who was I kidding? David would go *ballistic* if I used magic to prepare for the trip.

Better to leave early and take my time on the drive. And if I ended up with extra time in DC I could swing by Gran's apartment. Which was why I knocked on her door halfway through the afternoon.

"What's wrong, dear?" she asked, as soon as she saw me.
Wow. Maybe I *should* have used the fatigue spell. "Do I
look that bad?"

"Not at all sweetheart. I just can't remember the last time
you showed up unannounced on a Friday afternoon." Well,
she had a point there. "Would you like some tea dear?"

"Anything with caffeine."

She tsked and led the way into the kitchen. In minutes, I
was soothed by my grandmother's routine. She put the water on to boil while I took down two of her delicate teacups.
Matching saucers, a sugar bowl, spoons—Gran did things
properly, or she didn't do them at all. It wasn't long before
she was spooning enough sugar into her Earl Grey to knock
out a Clydesdale, and I was sipping pure, caffeinated heav-
en.

"How are things going at the school, dear?" she asked.

And that was all I needed. I told her about our weeks of
frustrations, our attempts to work with my new model. I outlined our great success of the morning. And I filled her in on
Pitt's ominous visit.

Frowning, she put down her teacup. "That man sounds
like a menace."

I barely stifled a yawn as I agreed. "I'm sorry," I said. "I
haven't been sleeping all that well."

"Why not?"

Her concern warmed me more than any hot drink ever
had. "I've been worried about the magicarium, of course."

She correctly read my tone. "But that's not all?"

"You have to release me from my promise, Gran! Let me
send the familiars back to the greenhouse!" I really *was* tired.
I hadn't planned on bringing that up at all. As long as the

proverbial cat was out of the bag, though… "Gran, you have no idea how crowded the house is. Whatever room I go into, there's already somebody there. Half the time, there isn't any hot water, and I can't find anything in the refrigerator or the pantry. You've got to help!"

She nodded wisely. "Bring the warders into the house."

"Gran!"

"You told me yourself, your ritual worked this morning because you recognized the familiars' power. You've finally gotten to know your students and their assistants. So you need to work even more efficiently to meet the Court's new challenge? Bring the warders into the house."

"We'll kill each other!"

Even as I protested, though, I started to think things through. Tony already spent a lot of time in the house, in Neko's corner of the basement. Surely, we could find *some* place for Caleb. We were talking about less than a month.

Tony. Caleb. That left David.

If all the warders moved back from the barn, then David would live in the house again. We'd have to work things out—everything—and return to how we'd lived before the Fourth of July.

The thought excited me. I couldn't deny that.

But it frightened me, too. David's obsession with Pitt was only growing stronger. At least if David stayed in the barn, he'd be forced to keep some distance between himself and the stolen materials. He'd have to *think* about them before he used them, before he slipped deeper into their sway. If he moved back into our bedroom, the temptation in the basement would be that much closer, that much easier to embrace.

"Gran, I really don't think that's going to—"

She cut me off. "Do we have to talk about promises *again*, Jane?"

She was serious. And I'd spent thirty-one years caving every single time Gran asked for a promise. I wasn't going to change now.

Even if the thought of more bodies in the house drove me mad. Even if I had to complete a Major Working in less than a month. Even if Gran was insisting that David move back into my bedroom, into the life we'd been building together.

Actually, that last point made the hassle all worthwhile.

"Fine, Gran," I conceded. "I'll move the warders into the house."

She smiled and dusted her hands, as if she'd just completed a Major Working of her own. "Excellent, dear. Now, would you like another cup of tea?"

My fingers were actually trembling from caffeine overload as I made my way up the street to Cake Walk. Ordinarily, I imagined Melissa's bakery treats before I even opened the door. Now, though, I craved protein—a nice, lean chicken breast or a turkey sandwich would absolutely hit the spot.

I stopped short as I got to the bakery. The sign said *Walk On By*.

I looked at my watch. It was barely 4:00. Usually, Friday afternoons were Melissa's busiest time. People cut out of work early and stopped to buy a cookie for the road. They headed home for weekend celebrations, cupcakes in hand. Office warriors gave themselves a treat just for surviving another work week. I don't think Melissa had *ever* closed the store early on a Friday.

I took out my phone and punched her number, but the call shifted immediately to voicemail. "Hey," I said. "I thought we were meeting up with watercolor artists tonight. Call me when you pick this up."

I shrugged and walked around the side of the building. The gate hung open, and the air was heavy with the scent of basil, rosemary, and mint. A quick glance at the plants confirmed that someone had been stealing herbs from the garden—there were fresh gashes on the stems. The hum of bees seemed ominous as I closed the gate behind me, taking care to fasten the latch.

I fed some of my nerves into my stride, taking the steps two at a time. When I knocked on the door, there wasn't any answer. I tried to lean over the railing, to peer into the living room window, but the curtains were pulled.

Adrenaline danced in my veins. Melissa kept a key under one of the flowerpots up here. Was it the geraniums? The begonias? In between pots, I shook my fingers, barely remembering not to wipe them on my skirt.

No key.

I ran over our plans in my head. It was Friday. We had definitely intended to meet with watercolor artists on Friday.

Should I call the police? What could I tell them? My best friend shut up shop early on a summer afternoon, and someone has been cutting herbs in her garden? Yeah, I'm sure DC's finest would speed to the scene of *that* crime.

Melissa had been frustrated when I'd spoken to her in the middle of the week. She'd been putting on hated makeup, getting ready for dinner with Rob's parents and a gaggle of his aunts, uncles, and countless cousins. What if things hadn't gone well? What if she'd finally put her foot down over one more ridiculous wedding request? Maybe Rob had told her that *he* couldn't take it any more? I could see Melissa ripping off her engagement ring, throwing it in his face as she fought back tears. Now she could be standing in her kitchen, surrounded by sharp knives, by the tools of the trade she'd practically ignored for months as her wedding spun further and further out of control.

"Melissa!" I shouted, knocking hard on her door. "Melissa! Open up! We can talk about it! Whatever it is! Melissa!"

I stopped pounding and scrabbled for my phone. The fire department could break in, couldn't they? What did it matter? 911 would send everyone.

I steadied myself against the door, fighting down panic as I punched the nine and the first one. I was just starting to hit the one again when the door flew open, and I collapsed onto the floor in Melissa's living room.

I blinked, staring up into my best friend's face. She was wrapped in a gigantic towel, and her hair was piled on top of her head in a terry turban. "What the hell?" she asked, as I scrambled to my feet.

"I thought you were dead!"

"That's why you were screaming my name?"

I brushed off my skirt. "Well, I thought you weren't dead yet." I cleared the two digits from my phone before I accidentally summoned the city's emergency response team.

"Get in here," Melissa said, laughing. "All the cold air is getting out."

I slipped inside. Her window unit air conditioner was roaring, loud enough that I could barely hear myself think. "What were you doing?" I asked.

"Um, taking a shower?"

"Someone raided your garden!"

She gestured toward the kitchen counter. "Let me guess. They were going to make pesto? And rosemary foccacio? A pitcher full of mojitos?"

"But you didn't answer when I knocked!"

"Hello!" she said, gesturing to her towel. "I was taking a shower!"

Okay, so I felt a little foolish. A lot foolish. I said defensively, "You never shut the bakery early in the summer. It never gets too hot for you."

"I needed a mental health day. Mental health afternoon, anyway. It was either close Cake Walk, or take a chance on murdering the next innocent customer who walked in the door."

I winced. "What happened now?"

"Rob's mother called this morning. His Great-Aunt Deanna decided we should release a pair of matched white doves the instant we complete our vows. The whole time I was on the phone hearing about the Marvelous Symbol Of Our Eternal Love, I just kept thinking about how that poor bird's heart would feel, fluttering against my fingers. That, and how it would probably crap all over me as it flew away to freedom."

"Did you tell her no?"

Melissa shook her head. "She didn't give me a chance. Another call came in, something about the menu for the rehearsal dinner. When she called back fifteen minutes later, I pretended not to be there. She'll call tomorrow, I'm sure. With some other lunatic idea from a relative I've never met."

I made sympathetic noises, but I was laughing at the

same time. I nodded toward her towel-wrapped head. "Shouldn't you get ready?"

"For what?"

"The watercolor artists? I thought we were supposed to be at the gallery by seven."

"Oh!" Melissa swore. "I'm so sorry! Mom canceled the watercolor artists last night."

I stared in disbelief. "Wait a second. You had a chance to 'get in touch with the emotions behind the things we see' and to 'reach out to the people we truly love in new and unique ways' and she canceled?"

Melissa nodded. "We're hiring a silhouette artist instead."

"You've got to be kidding."

"Nope. Cousin Caroline's idea. Black paper, sharp scissors, and silhouette portraits for two hundred."

"How the hell are you going to tell apart two hundred silhouettes?"

"Write the names on the back in chalk?" Melissa shrugged. "It turns out silhouette artists are a lot more rare than watercolorists. There's only one available for our wedding date, so there's no need to make an artistic decision." She sighed and shook her head. "I'm really sorry. I totally spaced on calling you."

And that admission, more than any of the other wedding insanity, made me realize how crazy Melissa's life had truly become. She didn't forget things. Not rock, paper, scissors victories that had committed me to a trip to DC.

I shrugged. "Well, I'm here now. You can cook me dinner before I head back home."

"Why don't you stay over? It looks like you could use a

little Mojito Therapy yourself."

My best friend always was perceptive. But I couldn't take her up on the offer. Not with warders moving into the house, and a suddenly escalated training schedule for a Mabon working.

"Sorry," I said. "I have to get back to the farm tonight."

Melissa accepted my verdict with equanimity. "Fair enough," she said. "Make yourself comfortable while I get dressed." She gestured toward the overstuffed couch and its accompanying coffee table. "Oh, you can look at paint chips while you're waiting!"

"Paint chips?"

"Rob's grandmother decided our rented chairs should match the flower arrangements. We're going to paint them all the morning of the wedding and paint them back after."

"That sounds like a recipe for disaster. What if the paint doesn't dry in time for the reception?"

Melissa rolled her eyes. "Maybe that's her underlying plan. Make the *guests* match the flower arrangements. Can you imagine the cleaning bills?"

She was still able to laugh as she headed back to her bedroom, but I couldn't see the humor. Was she planning a wedding or a Broadway play? Or a military operation more complicated than D-Day?

Maybe I'd have a single mojito after all. It was going to be a long evening, deciding between paint chips ranging from Constant Rose to Gracious Coral. The Great Warder Relocation Project could wait until the morning.

Chapter 14

IN THE END, I skipped the mojito, and I drove home immediately after dinner. I was truly exhausted—a combination
of my previously interrupted sleep, my successful working
with my students, and my ever-present worry about Norville
Pitt. Melissa, of course, was perfectly understanding—and
happy to drink more than her share of cocktails to drown
her wedding tribulations.

When I got home, most of the group was hanging out in
the living room. Caleb and Tony sprawled in the oversized
armchairs, watching the Diamondbacks beat the Nationals.
Neko sat on the floor, leaning against Tony's legs. I was pretty sure he knew that the game on TV was baseball, but I was
certain he didn't have the first clue about the rules. He was
much more engrossed in the casual pressure of Tony's fingers against his nape. I could practically hear him purr from
across the room.

Kopek was dozing on the couch. Raven and Hani
crouched over the coffee table, debating the merits of two
different fonts for their epic documentary. Neither Emma

nor David was in sight.

I dropped my purse by the door and dragged a chair in from the dining room. Strategically, I waited for a commercial break before asking, "Where's everyone else?"

Raven jutted her thumb toward the ceiling. "Emma's upstairs." *With Rick*, that meant. His next shift wasn't until Sunday; he'd be around for most of the weekend. I was a little bemused that I knew the fireman's schedule.

Neko stretched lazily, before settling back in the exact same position. "David's in Sedona."

Great. What a perfect night for Clara to summon him. He had to be drained after watching over our morning working. With Pitt's mid-day visit and the charter's aura, he surely spent the afternoon obsessing over the Court's documents. On second thought, maybe it *was* a good thing my mother was keeping David occupied. I liked anything that separated him from those damn papers.

But that left me alone to deliver my bad news. Because I had no delusions about how Gran's edict was going to be received. At least the Diamondbacks were ahead. That would make everyone a little more kindly disposed toward my announcement.

The commercial break ended, and the game came back on. I watched in dismay as the pitcher gave up back to back home runs, putting the Nationals on top. (And when had I become such a baseball aficionado? I could thank Caleb for that. Caleb, and near-constant exposure to the sport for the summer.)

An ad for an airlines came on—*Need to get away?*—and I cleared my throat. "Starting tomorrow, we have another change in living arrangements." Tension condensed in the

room like fog in a swamp. I hurried on before anyone could
protest out loud. "All of the warders are moving into the
house."

Neko let out a squeak of surprise. Kopek opened one eye
and stared at me with bleary skepticism. "You've got to be—
" That was from Raven, but she cut herself off before finishing.

I forced myself to focus on the two men most directly affected by my announcement. "Caleb?" I asked. "Tony?"

Tony's lips twisted into a dyspeptic frown, but he offered
up a shrug. Caleb said, "You're the boss."

I could have hugged him. Instead, I showed my gratitude
by settling back in my chair to watch the next inning. When
the Diamondbacks were down by three runs, though, I took
the hint from all the fates and headed upstairs. Whispered
complaints about the new housing arrangements began before my foot was on the first tread of the steps.

In my bedroom, I glanced at my alarm clock and saw
that it was just after nine o'clock. With the time difference, I
might be able to catch David before my mother began
whatever ritual she had planned for the night. I took out my
phone and pressed his number. Four rings. Voicemail. I
started to leave a message, but there wasn't anything specific
to say. Not that I wanted to leave in a message, anyway.

I hung up and went to sleep.

The following morning began with a bang, followed by
countless whimpers.

Before breakfast, Tony volunteered to bunk with Caleb
in one of the upstairs guest rooms. Neko launched into pre-
dictable orbit. I spent a full hour convincing him Tony

wasn't rejecting their relationship. If anything, the warder wanted to preserve some sliver of privacy; in pursuit of sexy times, it was easier to get rid of one warder roommate than two familiars. Neko pounced on the opportunity to have Caleb finish putting up walls in the basement, but I told him there simply wasn't time. We needed all magical hands on the astral deck to prepare for our Mabon working.

I should have been able to predict the resolution of Neko's crisis. I handed over my credit card, and my familiar and Tony took the rest of the day on a restorative field trip far away from the farm. I wondered if I could forward the receipts to Gran. After all, *she* was responsible for creating this mess.

I went back to wrestling accommodations. Kopek whined about people walking across the kitchen floor. He insisted he could hear every step when he lay on his cot, and he moaned that things would only be worse with three new residents in the house. I promised we'd make the kitchen off limits from midnight till six in the morning.

Hani was up next, announcing that the basement was starting to stink. Kopek was predictably offended. I refereed by lugging two huge box fans downstairs. After a liberal application of Febreze, I turned on the fans to literally clear the air. Another crisis averted.

Emma and Raven balked at sharing a bedroom. I barely resisted pointing out that they'd lived together for years; by their own admission they'd been inseparable as children. Of course, when they were children, Emma hadn't been involved with Rick Hanson. They only stopped sniping at each other when I threatened to draw up a formal schedule for who could be in the bedroom when. I'm sure neither of them really believed me when I said I'd make them sign in blood.

Caleb spent half the morning programming the television to record every important baseball game for the next six weeks. He spent the other half reorganizing the refrigerator, determined to find room for a full case of some rare Czech beer he'd just bought. In the end, he left a gallon of Raven's organic oat milk on the counter, and I could hear her screeched protest from behind my closed bedroom door.

On and on it went, until I felt more like a Cub Scout den mother than the magistrix of a Class Two magicarium.

And David was missing all the fun. I'd called him when I woke up, but I still got his voicemail. I tried Clara then, too, and ended up leaving her a message, asking her to give me a call.

I reminded myself that David *was* her warder. She was allowed to work her own magic, even when I was caught in the midst of turning our house upside down, trying to meet an impossible deadline for a Mabon ritual.

When I hadn't heard from either of them by the middle of the afternoon, I decided to do some sleuthing. While witches, warders, and familiars completed settling into their new rooms, I ventured into David's office, determined to glean some information about Clara's secret rituals.

I hadn't been down there for days, and the space had been transformed. Once, it had contained a handful of filing cabinets and one large desk. It had been a working man's refuge—as spare and efficient as its owner.

Now, the room was filled with dozens of neatly stacked cardboard boxes. Each was labeled in David's strong handwriting. Expense Reports—one box for every year from

1985 to the present. Contracts—at least twenty boxes. Charters—half a dozen more. On and on it went, with some containers stacked so high I would need a step ladder to reach them.

There were maps, too, precisely pinned to the wall with brushed steel thumbtacks. Pushpins bristled from the surface. Red seemed to indicate covens, and blue marked magicaria. I wasn't sure what the green and yellow pins meant.

Reference books lined the shelves. There were directories and rule books, along with several dozen leather-bound ledgers. A cache of scrolls was organized in a series of cubbyholes that looked like they belonged in an old post office.

The Madison Academy charter occupied the center of David's desk. Its numbered pages were laid out on a field of white linen, and David's familiar fountain pen sat nearby, its sleek lines reflecting the overhead light. The yellow ribbon proclaiming our Class Two status curled over the edge of the desk.

I crossed the room to look at the document that was causing us all so much grief. The fluorescents tinged the rosette with a sickly glint of chartreuse. Its lettering was flaking off. I fingered the edge of the silk, wondering if it had yielded any secrets to David, if it had given him the forensic clues he'd hoped to find.

Nothing out of the ordinary was visible, not with mundane sight. I extended my hand over document, taking care not to touch it directly, and I closed my eyes to take a deep, centering breath.

"From the chaos upstairs, I can see you've been busy."

I shrieked and leaped back from the desk, holding my fingers to my chest as if they'd been burned. Even as I moved, though, I recognized David's voice.

I tried to slow my thundering heart as I took in the appearance of my prodigal warder. His shoulders slumped, and his face was drawn. Fine lines fanned beside his eyes, as if he'd aged a decade since I'd seen him last. His lips were chapped, and he looked like he was ready to sleep for a century.

But he took the time to measure the charter. From the intensity of his gaze, I could tell he was scanning it with his warder's senses, making sure I hadn't touched it, hadn't ruined whatever he was trying to do. I gestured toward everything around us—the boxes, the maps, the collected books and scrolls—and I finally responded to his words. "I could say the same to you."

He eased past me and collapsed into the chair behind the desk. "I don't want to fight, Jane."

"This isn't a fight."

His bitter smile was fleeting. "It will be."

"What are you doing with all these things? Does the Court know you have them?"

He shook his head.

"How could you do something so dangerous? If the Court found out, they'd send a Termination Team in a heartbeat!"

He had to know that. He had to understand. And the fact that he didn't care scared me more than Norville Pitt, more than the possibility of closing the magicarium after Mabon. David was ignoring a lifetime of warder's training to pursue this momentary passion. And I could only imagine how deeply he would regret things, if it all went wrong.

"You've got to let this go," I said. "It's hurting you more

than it could ever possibly benefit the Court. Or me. You have to stop."

He met my eyes. "Is that an order?"

I could do it. I could seal my demand with a witch's compulsion, and that would be the end.

The end of David's investigation. But the end of more. My witch's command would terminate, forever, the trust we had between us.

When I'd commanded him on Independence Day, I'd spoken out of frustration. My order had been impulsive. I had never dreamed of the damage I would do to our relationship as lovers, as *partners*.

If I commanded him now—with full consideration before taking the action—I would sever those bonds forever. I would consciously end any life we had outside our magical connection.

But I would spare him the terrible cost of his obsession. I would protect the Madison Academy. All it would take was destroying his free will.

I shook my head. "It's not an order. It's a plea. I am *begging* you to stop."

His lips thinned into a nearly-invisible line. "Anything else?" he asked, as if I'd given him a list of chores to do around the house.

He'd heard me. He'd even *listened*. But he was choosing not to change.

I shook my head. "Have Caleb help you move your things back from the barn. All warders sleep beneath this roof, starting tonight."

He nodded. He'd already seen everyone shifting rooms upstairs.

When I didn't say anything else, he picked up his quill pen, obviously intending to work. I wanted to tell him to put it down. I wanted to say he looked like hell. I wanted to tell him to take a shower and get some rest.

Instead, I left the room, closing the door softly behind me. I told myself that the tears filling my eyes were only a product of stress and fatigue. But I knew I was lying. And I didn't have any idea what to do about that.

Chapter 15

GRAN WAS RIGHT. I got to know the warders better, by having them live in the house.

I learned that Caleb used Dial soap and Suave shampoo. Tony was a Head and Shoulders man. And neither of them picked up their towels from the bathroom floor.

As for David, he made it to bed on Saturday night. He even leaned over and gave me a chaste kiss on the cheek before he turned out the light on his nightstand. But for all the passion between us, we might have been siblings sharing a tent on a summer camping trip.

Maybe that had something to do with my evil mood on Sunday morning. With our new Mabon deadline, we no longer had the luxury of taking weekends off. So, seven o'clock. Maxwell House coffee and Lipton's tea, both brewed double-strength. Boot camp was in session.

"Here's the problem," I said, without preamble. "Friday's purification ritual took almost everything we had to give. That would be fine, if all we wanted to accomplish was a bit of magical housekeeping. But it's going to take a hell of a lot more than clean living to win over the Court."

Neko snorted at the phrase "clean living."

"Did you have something to say?" I whirled on him. I had to keep everyone focused. I had to get them to understand how little time we had. He shook his head promptly, but he wasn't fast enough to hide the sardonic twist of his lips. I wondered exactly what he and Tony had gotten up to yesterday afternoon. But then I remembered I really didn't want to know.

"Laugh if you want. But if I were a familiar, I'd save my energy. Because you're going to need every last bit of it to bolster our spells. We'll start with raising the wind."

I turned on my heel and led the way out of the cool, air-conditioned living room. When Emma realized we were going outside, she wiped her palms against her jeans and glanced toward the stairs. Too bad. She could change into shorts when we broke for lunch. *If* we broke for lunch.

I ordered Tony to mark off a safe circle for our work. We were going to retreat deep into our powers, and I didn't want anyone—not Emma's beau, not some innocent Parkersville civilian coming to collect for March of Dimes, no one—to interrupt us.

And so it began.

Our Major Working would build on elemental magic. We were trying to restore a balance between air and earth, fire and water, to correct the chaos of climate change. It made sense for us to start our expedited studies with Air. The element was associated with the East, with the first quarter we called on in all our workings.

I already owned everything we needed. Agrimony and senna leaf, butcher's broom and lavender—all herbs that were traditionally associated with Air. Quartz in all its shades—clear and rose and blue and smoke. Hematite. The rune kenaz, carved in jade and wood and clay.

By combining all those tools, my witches would learn the true properties of the element. We would feel its power with every fiber of our astral beings. Balancing herbs and crystals, runes and spells, we would become a part of Air, balanced on it, melded with it.

That was the theory, anyway.

And that was how we spent our Sunday. We harnessed every item at our command, using the tools to raise up wind, to strengthen a slight breeze, to calm a gale. We focused on changing direction, on creating sudden downdrafts, on letting everything fall so still we could scarcely fill our lungs.

I pushed everyone to work through lunch and to skip dinner. Such hard labor was actually a calculated part of the training. By measuring how our bodies reacted to stress, we learned how to rebalance ourselves with the tools at our disposal.

With every exercise, I felt my magic solidify a little more. I understood my arcane self, comprehended the roots of my ability better than I ever had before. I drew power from Neko and the other familiars, let them reflect my strength back to me like the shimmer of heat haze above an asphalt road.

By nightfall, Emma and Raven were more spent than I'd ever seen them before. When I nodded to Tony to release his protective circle, he rushed toward his witch, catching her as she started to collapse. I chose to ignore the filthy glare he shot at me.

Caleb wasn't much better. He waited on the porch, pacing like an expectant father. As soon as he was allowed, he bounded down the steps to help Emma. He actually cursed when Kopek sank to his knees in the sere grass.

I hardened my heart. My students and I had accomplished our goal. We'd pushed ourselves to our limits. We had mastered Air and all the magic that was bound to it.

I asked Neko to make sure everyone ate a grounding supper, and I carried a plate up to my bedroom. My students needed a chance to recover, and the crowded house gave them little chance to air their grievances if I haunted the downstairs. I was asleep before David came to bed.

Monday was Water. Barberry and comfrey and frankincense. Amethyst and turquoise. The rune laguz. Through those tools, we found the individual molecules in the grass beneath our feet. We studied how our blood flowed in our veins, thickening it, thinning it. We unraveled the blanket of humidity that oppressed us, reveling in the pure water we extracted from the atmosphere.

Caleb guarded us, but Tony stayed by his side the entire day, only leaving when darkness settled over the yard. Even then, he was gone just long enough to collect a simple meal of bread and cheese, of refrigerated water untouched by magic. As the late summer sun set, we all chewed in silence, lost in memories of the power we had raised.

Tuesday was Fire. Garlic, thistle, cinnamon. Obsidian and tigerseye. The kauno rune. We concentrated heat out of the air, focused it like a magnifying glass to kindle controlled flames on the grass. We made lightning fork above our palms, the jagged bolts crackling against the protective dome above us.

David cast our circle that morning. I felt the familiar

surge of his warder's power every time we tested the boundary with flame. I could relax into that safety; I could draw
from it. And there was a part of me that reveled in the
knowledge that I was keeping David from his secret study.
Every minute David spent protecting us was one I denied
him from spending with the Court's papers.

That reality wasn't lost on him. At the end of the day,
David saw us witches back to the house. He handed Raven
and Emma over to their attentive warders, and he checked
on the welfare of all the familiars. Then, he excused himself
from our supper, and he headed downstairs. Once again, I
was asleep before he came to bed.

In the morning, I realized I'd actually seen more of David when he lived in the barn. That didn't matter, though. I
couldn't cut back on our schedule now. The magicarium
and the Mabon working had to come before everything else.

Wednesday was the last of the elements: Earth. Barley
and Corn. Amber. Garnet. Inguz. We witches eased our
bodies between individual grains of dirt. With the mid-day
sun beating down upon us, we buried ourselves up to our
knees. It took all our concentration to shake ourselves free,
siphoning off our carefully invested power so we released our
bodies without destroying the rattling stalks in the nearby
cornfield, without undermining the porch where Caleb once
again kept anxious watch as Tony guarded us.

And then we took four more days to repeat all those lessons—Air, Water, Fire, Earth. Practice, practice, practice,
drumming our knowledge indelibly into our minds and
hearts.

The following Monday, we rested. Not because I discovered any sense of mercy. Not because the Academy's need

was any less urgent. Rather, because Emma came scratching against my bedroom door in the grey light before dawn. Her voice quavered like an old 78 record.

"Raven needs to sleep."

"We're all tired," I said as I heard David roll over in bed behind me.

"This is more than feeling manky! She was sleep-walking last night. She got to the front door twice before Tony stopped her!"

That got my attention. "Where was she going?"

"How do I know?" Emma was anguished. "She did this when we were children. Before we understood our powers. Before we learned to manage them."

I was still calculating my reply when Tony loomed out of the darkness. "Raven will *not* work today."

David smothered a curse as he pulled himself out of bed. He came to stand behind me, his chest bare against my back. He rested one hand on the doorframe, automatically staking a claim in the conversation.

By then, Caleb had stumbled out of his bedroom. His Diamondbacks T-shirt was rumpled, as if he he'd slept in it for months. He scratched at his rough beard, and I was surprised to realize he'd stopped shaving at some point in the past week. He planted his feet and said, "Emma needs rest, too."

It had been two months since my students had arrived at the farmhouse. Two months since David had faced Tony at swordpoint, and I'd used the Word of Power to protect everyone. To *control* everyone. I'd learned from that experience and from the intervening time. I could yield on this relatively little thing and still maintain power over the magicarium.

Perhaps we'd all be better off in the long run.

"Fine," I said. "But we'll be back at it tomorrow morning."

I closed the door and leaned against it. I could hear a whispered conversation between Caleb and Emma before both bedroom doors closed. My students and their warders were going to catch up on desperately needed sleep, and that seemed like a brilliant plan to me.

But David was pulling on his pants.

"Where are you going?"

"I was supposed to help your mother in Sedona tomorrow. With the shifted schedule, you'll need me here. I'll go out there today."

"What does Clara have you doing?"

He just looked at me. I already knew the answer: *Ask Clara.*

"Fine," I said. "I'll call her now." I'd wake her up. And she'd be even less coherent about her magical plans than usual. So first I tried, "This can't wait till after Mabon?"

He shook his head. "Sorry." He cupped my jaw with his hand, and I heard honest regret in his voice.

"Come back to bed." I closed my fingers around his wrist. "For just a while."

He broke my hold by moving his hand to the back of my neck. "I can't."

"Can't?" I asked as he stepped away. "Or won't?" My heart pounded as I waited for his answer.

"I need to go. I'll be back before tomorrow morning." He didn't even try a perfunctory kiss.

I grabbed the phone before our bedroom door had closed. My first call went to Clara's voicemail. I hung up, waited for the line to disconnect, and tried again. Voicemail. On the third try, she picked up.

"What sort of ritual are you working out there?"

"Jeanette," she mumbled. "I was dreaming about you."

"Why do you need David to ward you?"

"In my dream, you stood by the road with a sign. It said, 'Will cast spells for cake.' Are you that hungry, Jeanette?"

"*Jane,*" I said, trying to correct her. "Wake up, Clara. I really need to know this. What are you working on with David?"

"Cake…" She sounded like she was half-way back to dreamland. "In Rocher's *Dream Quests*, cake means sharing your workload. You can't do everything yourself, Jeanette."

I was *trying* to share my workload with my students. And my warder. I had a copy of Rocher's *Dream Quests* somewhere in the basement. It was part of a set that included *Animal Divination* and *Cloud Scrying*. I put about as much stock in *Rocher* as I did in the Vortex.

"Clara!" I put real steel into my voice, trying to force my mother to wake up. "Can't your working wait until after Mabon?"

"No, Jeanette. The cake will be stale by then."

"What are you talking about? Clara? Mother?"

But I heard a doorbell ring in the background. "I have to go, Jeanette. Someone's at the door. Sweet dreams."

And she hung up before I could tell her it was *David* at the door, that he'd used his warder's magic to leave me and travel to her. I glared at the phone long after she was gone.

After that frustrating phone call, it was impossible to get back to sleep. I finally gave in to the inevitable and stumbled down to the kitchen. Of course, the only thing that sounded good to me was cake. Preferably chocolate. With lots of extra frosting. I settled for almond meal biscuits, left over from Raven's cleanse. No amount of butter could transform them into something edible.

The next day, we were back in the academic saddle. David warded our working as if he'd never gone to Sedona. I shifted our arcane focus from the four elements to the specific building blocks of our ritual.

As we had done for our disastrous Lughnasadh ceremony, each of us witches would commence our Major Working with lighting a candle. For Mabon, they would be traditional autumn colors—gold and brown, yellow and orange. I procured the beeswax candles from my extensive stash, and we spent four entire days working with them, learning to sense their power with our astral forces, without the least resort to mundane senses like vision and touch.

Once again, this was more than a simple study of witchy tools. I urged my students to focus on the wholeness of candles in the magical process—how they interacted with our warders' protective walls, how they drew from the elements, how they fed back heat and light and power, drying out nearby herbs, scorching crystals.

Over and over, we lit the wicks, separately and then together. We joined our powers, Raven and Emma, then Raven and me, then Emma and me. Finally, at the end of our fourth day, we found the perfect balance, all three of us witches braiding our power together, pouring it into a quartet of flames.

Power spun between us like a web, joining us together, supporting us. I took strength from the violet of Raven's astral force; I smoothed it with the silver power that Emma poured into the working. I poured my own golden energy into the mix, and I basked in the accompanying leap of heat and light.

This was what I'd imagined when I created the Academy. The unity, the harmony—everything I'd found lacking in the Washington Coven's traditional workings. I saw wonder spread across my students' faces.

Tony and Caleb leaped forward the instant David let his warding circle die down. For the first time, though, since we'd begun to work in earnest, my students didn't collapse against their warders. Rather, they stood tall and strong, proud of what they'd done. What *we* had done. Hani and Kopek basked in the warders' praise. We all ate dinner together that night, nine of us, gathered around the dining room table.

Alas, that was the last time we were gathered in relaxed household harmony.

With one successful communal working under our belts, I doubled our training efforts. I was pushing my students harder than I ever had before. I was pushing *myself* harder than I ever had before. I had never come close to a sustained outpouring of energy like the one I now demanded.

Every third day, David watched over us. Otherwise, I scarcely saw him. He spent hours in the basement; his office light was on whenever I went downstairs to collect tools, to check books for half-remembered details about rare herbs, to compare the relative strengths of various crystals.

And he was traveling back and forth to Sedona. I caught whiffs of smudged sage from his clothes, along with the tang of juniper. He carried back desert dust on his shoes. I could smell the sharp scent of creosote on his pillow, even when he wasn't there.

I gave up trying to reach my mother. This was the woman who had ignored me for twenty-eight years. I could hardly command her attention now. Better to stop trying, and to invest my limited energy in my Mabon working.

So, my students and I took two days to explore Preparing the Earth, finding the most effective ways to channel the energy we raised. We wanted to make sure our power went to actual *healing* instead of dissipating into nothingness. We invested three full days on Protecting the Innocents, making sure no blameless bystanders—human or animal—suffered from a backlash of our working. I had trouble sleeping those nights, and my dreams were haunted by the cries of ospreys.

We finally got to Rainmaking, to the delicate process of harvesting water from air, by way of all our witchy tools. For two straight days, we witches stood beneath a magical cordon, generating mist and drizzle and a steady, driving rain. Our fingers and toes were shriveled every time we took a break for sustenance.

"All right," I said, after we had built and dissipated a particularly vigorous thunderstorm. "Let's take a quick break for dinner, then reconvene."

I waved my hand for Caleb to remove his protective warding, and his sword sliced through the circle he'd cast hours before. I ignored the taut lines on his face as he handed out towels.

"Neko," I said, as the others dragged themselves toward the porch, dry clothes, and the promise of supper. The autumn nights were already growing shorter. My familiar's face was in shadow as the sun sank below the treeline. "I want to get started on incense as soon as everyone's eaten.

Could you make sure we have enough rosemary?"

"No."

I was already concentrating on the other elements we needed—sandalwood and pine, dried oak leaves and cinnamon. I blinked. "What?"

"I said, no."

"You *can't* say no. We've only got nine days left."

Before he could answer, there was the sound of tires crunching on gravel. I looked to the driveway and could just make out Rick Hanson's F-150 behind the glare of headlights. Suddenly, I understood how Gran had felt when I begged her to let me have some elementary school girlfriend spend the night, with said friend standing right in the middle of our living room. I shook my head and started over to tell Rick it wasn't a good night, that he had to leave.

Neko put his hand on my arm. "Emma needs this. We *all* need a break."

Before I could argue, Rick called out a friendly greeting. Neko immediately looped his arm through the fireman's.

"Aren't *you* a sight for sore eyes! Emma's in the kitchen. Come right in." Neko kept the burly man between us as he crossed the lawn. I barely resisted the urge to buffet him with an arcane slap. Traitor. Neko didn't give a damn about Emma's love life. He was only focused on his own, on getting Tony to a remotely private corner of the crowded house.

I gritted my teeth and started to collect the discarded tools from our hard day's labor. Crystals and runes and wands were strewn about the waterlogged grass. My legs felt unbearably heavy, as if I'd run a marathon, or somehow given in to Melissa's pressure to spend an entire day doing yoga in some overheated studio.

Melissa. I'd been a bad friend for the past couple of weeks. I'd listened to her wedding complaints on voicemail, responded to her texts when I could spare a few seconds, but I owed her a trip into town, a long night of Mojito Therapy, and countless maid of honor consultations.

After Mabon. After the Madison Academy had completed its Major Working. After, after, after...

I dragged myself up the porch steps. Spot whined from his place on the glider. Poor dog. I'd barely spent any time with him during the past month. I absently patted his head before I reached for the door. With the familiarity of frequent use, I turned the knob and leaned in at the same time, letting the weight of my body push my way inside.

Except, I didn't move.

Plucked out of my fatigued haze, I looked down. No, I'd turned the knob all the way to the right. The door just wouldn't budge. I pushed a little harder. Nothing. I swore and put my shoulder into it. Nada.

I folded my fingers into a fist and pounded with the meat of my hand. My gesture was met with an explosion of laughter on the other side, and the door finally burst open.

Emma's cheeks were as bright as an Empire apple. Rick was roaring, apparently oblivious to her embarrassment. He seemed rather proud, in fact, of her bee-stung lips. Emma clutched her blouse closed, and I realized she and her boyfriend had managed to cruise past first base in the short time since he'd entered the house. Their bodies had blocked the door.

"Get a room!" Hani shouted to the happy couple from the living room.

"You're letting in all the mosquitoes," Kopek added in a mournful voice.

I muttered a retort as I pushed my way into the foyer. Of course I'd let in all the mosquitoes. And every last one would find me. That's what mosquitoes were born to do.

Amid a chorus of good-natured teasing, Emma and Rick disappeared upstairs. Hani crowed toward the kitchen, "Hope you don't need anything from your room, Raven! You're stuck with us rejects out here!"

A quick glance confirmed that Neko and Tony were nowhere in sight. They must have commandeered the familiars' dormitory, forcing everyone else into the confines of the dining room. Maybe that's why I felt like I was caught in a frat house on a Saturday night.

As if to make that point, Caleb leaned forward and cranked up the volume on the television set. I wondered if his warder services included a guarantee that no one would ever overhear his witch in a compromising situation. According to the 200-decibel bellowing that echoed through the living room, some Diamondback had just made the third out in the bottom of the first inning, leaving the bases loaded.

As the TV roared to commercial, Caleb swore and snatched up a beer, one of those fancy Czech things that had caused so much grief when the warders moved in. The bottle had a complicated swing-top clasp, and by the time he managed to release the wire brace an arc of beer was splashed across David's antique coffee table.

Caleb hollered for Raven to bring him a rag. She shouted back, then sauntered into the room with a sponge. She was filming as she walked, clearly working on some artsy angle for the picture.

With no magic at play, I could hardly censure her for the camera. Instead, I plowed through the wall of sound toward the kitchen. A glass of ice water, that's what I needed. Maybe an apple. A handful of walnuts.

I fixed a small plate and carried my supper upstairs. But I could still hear the ball game; it echoed through the floorboards. Alas, that noise wasn't actually enough to drown out the sounds from the bedroom next door. Emma's headboard was hitting the wall with frightening regularity. From the accompanying exclamations, my student definitely did not believe in the Victorian admonition to "lie back and think of England."

I snarled and picked up my plate and glass. There was one place in this house where I could steal a single, silent moment to eat my long-overdue meal. One place no one else would dare to venture. I stomped down the steps and through the living room. I threw myself down the basement stairs, moving fast enough to be sure I wouldn't confront Neko and Tony. I tumbled into David's office.

And I came up short.

Because David wasn't actually in Sedona that night.

His back was to the door as I charged in. He was standing in front of the gigantic map, the one dotted with precise pushpin markers of covens and magicaria.

But now, the map was scattered with photographs as well. Images of Norville Pitt were sprayed across the surface—Pitt with women in golden robes, with men in formal attire. Pitt with gatherings of witches and warders. Pitt with a collection of carved wooden creatures, familiars who had not yet been awakened.

Court documents hung behind some of the photos—ribbons and grommets gleaming in the harsh overhead light. String stretched between the compositions—red and blue and green and yellow, linking image to image, paper to paper. Across it all was jagged writing, a disjointed scrawl. Some of the letters had been scratched into the map, over and over and over again. Words were slashed through, underlined with ink that had run down the wall.

I was looking at the obsessive creation of a serial killer from a thousand bad movies and television shows.

And my warder completed the image. David's hair stood on end. He had one shirtsleeve rolled up, but the other was ragged and torn. His hands trembled as he tried to shove a pushpin through a massive stack of papers. Even from the doorway, I could hear him muttering, a terrifying word salad about Pitt and money and witches and time.

My fingers turned to sand. My glass crashed to the floor, splashing water from one end of the office to the other. My plate followed, shattering into jagged shards.

David whirled to face me, his hand automatically dipping for the leather sheath he kept strapped to his ankle. When he straightened, he held a silver dagger pointed directly at my heart.

The knife clattered to the ground as I turned and fled. I took the steps to the bedroom two at a time, ignoring David's frantic cries for me to stop.

Chapter 16

I CROUCHED ON the edge of the king-size bed, folding my arms around my belly and reminding myself to breathe, breathe, breathe.

"Open the door, Jane." David's voice was low, urgent.

"Leave me alone."

"We need to talk."

"There isn't anything to say."

"Dammit, Jane!" His fist thudded against the door. He wasn't trying to break it down; he could have done that easily enough if he'd wanted to.

"Go away!"

Another door opened. Emma's. "Hey, buddy." That was Rick, wrapping an audible smile around the voice of a professional hero.

"We're fine here," David said.

"Of course you are." I could picture Rick's easy-going manner as he slid himself between David and the door. "If she doesn't want to talk, buddy, leave her alone."

"Jane—"

"Come on, man." I could picture Rick settling a hand on David's arm, and David pulling away. Angry footsteps faded down the hallway.

There was a trio of quick knocks, Rick's knuckles against the door. "You okay in there?"

I tried to keep my voice steady. "I'm fine."

A long pause, while I imagined Rick weighing his obligations to me, to David, to the witch who undoubtedly awaited his return to her bed. Ultimately, Emma won, and he stepped away. Her door clicked closed.

I went back to reminding myself to breathe.

The TV suddenly clicked off in the living room. A door slammed. I heard low voices, then nothing at all.

I fumbled for my phone, ready to spill out all my angst to Melissa. As if she had anticipated my call, there was a text waiting. "New plan. Aunt Martha. Leaving reception in hot air balloon."

There were a million things wrong with those words. Melissa was afraid of heights. A hot air balloon couldn't fly safely at night. And what were the guests supposed to do, stand around waving like all the Munchkins in Oz, seeing off Dorothy and the Wizard?

I knew I was supposed to call Melissa, to commiserate with her on this latest example of horrifically bad taste. But what could I possibly say? She had a man who loved her. A normal man. A sane man. A man who wasn't an obsessed warder with a silver dagger strapped to his ankle in the supposed safety of his own home.

I couldn't call Melissa.

But there was someone else I'd cried to when things went wrong—in elementary school, in high school, in college.

Someone who understood me, who always listened. I punched in the number and waited while the phone rang three times.

"Gran!" I exclaimed as soon as she picked up.

"What's wrong, dear?" She never was one to beat around the bush.

"David..." I started. But what could I tell her? My warder had gone crazy in the basement? I tried another tack. "Norville Pitt..." But I couldn't tell her that, either. Even now, even when I'd seen what David had done with the documents, I didn't want anyone to know that he had stolen from the Court. I shifted to a third thing, a safe thing, a thing no one could blame me for saying. "Everyone's in the house! It's too crowded. And loud. It's crazy." I babbled on, trying to explain about the television and the beer on the coffee table and Raven filming again and Emma's bed banging against the wall, and there was water all over the floor, and I'd broken my plate, and Clara wouldn't tell me what was happening in Sedona and David, and David, and David, and Mabon was only nine days away, and everything was falling apart around me.

And when I finally wound down, gasping for breath, I heard silence. No grandmaternal words of wisdom. No wry comments on the morals of youth today. No shrewd observations about the expectations of institutions of higher learning when she was a girl.

"Gran?" I finally asked, my voice barely more than a whisper.

"Send them all out of the house."

"What?" I practically shouted my question.

"Put your students back above the garage. Send the familiars to the greenhouse and the warders to the barn."

"What are you talking about? We only have nine days until the Major Working!"

"Perfect, dear. Take the weekend to get everyone settled, and you'll still have a full week to practice." She waited, while I gulped in disbelief. What had happened to my promise? To all her words of advice? Why was she telling me to do exactly the opposite of everything she'd required in the past?

"Was there anything else, dear? Uncle George and I were just getting ready for bed."

"No," I said. "Um, good night."

Because, really? What else was there to say?

I thought about going downstairs and telling everyone the new plan, right then and there. But I couldn't face the chaos. Couldn't face David. Morning would be soon enough to break the news.

Of course, I couldn't fall asleep. Around two in the morning, I gave up any pretense of a restful night, and I crept downstairs, making my way past a snoring Kopek on the living room couch. I wrote a note and taped it to the refrigerator door: "Effective tomorrow, please return to your original assigned quarters at the Madison Academy. I apologize in advance for any inconvenience."

I climbed back upstairs and settled into bed, finally falling asleep as the sky blushed pink. I must have been exhausted, because I barely heard the commotion as everyone complied with my note. There were occasional bumps and a few loud curses, but each time I woke I was able to turn over, pull the sheet up to my shoulder, and submerge back into sleep.

☙ ⚬⚬ ❧

When I finally came back to full consciousness, the house's silence felt like a quilt, heavy and soft and comforting. I opened the bedroom door and looked down the hallway.

Both guest room doors stood open wide. The beds inside were neatly made. The nightstands were empty; in fact, every horizontal surface was bare. The bathroom was clean as well—no extra towels or shampoo, soap or a forest of toothbrushes.

I moved down to the living room. The armchairs were back to their usual places. The television remote was centered on the dry, unstained coffee table. The dining room was immaculate as well, and the kitchen looked like it had never been used. If not for my note glaring from the refrigerator door, I might believe the magicarium had never existed.

I took a deep breath and headed for the basement.

The framing for unfinished bedrooms remained, but each of the familiars had removed his cot from his alcove. Personal belongings were absent from my shelves of magical paraphernalia. A snowbank of laundry billowed beside the washing machine, but there was no other sign of human habitation.

I forced myself to cross to David's office. I knew the light was on; I'd seen it leaking from beneath the closed door the moment I came down the stairs. I caught my breath and raised my hand to knock.

And I couldn't do it.

I knew he was in there. I could sense it, with every strand of my witchy being. And I knew he wouldn't hurt me. I'd known that when he was pounding on the bedroom door the night before. A tiny part of me had known it, the first second I'd seen the dagger glinting in his hand. I'd startled him. His reaction had been sheer instinct, a warder's reflexes responding to the crash of my plate and drinking glass.

My horror wasn't from his weapon. It was from the madness—the map and the photos and the terrifying umbilical cords of string. I had recoiled from the life-size portrait of insanity.

The door opened.

David had slept and showered, probably eaten a square meal or two as well. As if to convince me he was a level-headed professional, he wore an open-necked white dress shirt tucked into neatly pressed trousers. I wondered fleetingly if he'd retrieved the charcoal suit from Sedona, or if he'd actually gone clothes shopping on a Saturday morning. His black wingtips were polished.

The instant I saw him, my heart launched into overdrive. Adrenaline kicked my kidneys, and I caught my breath against the punch. I glanced from him to the wall, hoping, praying that the map would be gone.

It wasn't, though. If anything, there were more pictures, more documents. Additional lines of strings linked ideas, ran from the dripping ink of words to images.

David stepped aside, moving with the door to give me the maximum amount of space to enter the office. Spot rose from an impromptu bed in front of the desk, immediately crossing the room and pressing his broad head under my palm. He escorted me to one of the chairs before sitting at my side like a guardian statue.

David waited until I was safely seated before he moved behind his desk. He walked slowly, gracefully, twisting just enough to be certain I could see both his hands the entire time.

"May I explain?" he asked. His voice was quiet. Calm. The tone I'd heard a thousand times, as he deferred to my power as his witch.

I nodded.

He only betrayed his nerves with a quick hitch in his breath, and then he nodded toward the wall behind him. "It's all there. Pitt's job, since he first took the title of Clerk." David pointed to a red pin in the center of the country, in Kansas City. "He was a warder for an elderly witch in the Kansas City Coven. She died, and he went unclaimed, so he was transferred to the Court. His first responsibility was completing filings for his old coven. Over five years, he became responsible for the entire Central District."

My eyes scanned a scattering of pins. A couple of the photos were Polaroids. Others were printed on cardboard stock, the type with rounded corners that came from old film development labs.

"After that, he was detailed to the Western District," David continued, gesturing toward the southwest states. Oak Canyon Coven flashed its red pin. California, with its cluster of markers near Los Angeles and San Francisco. Oregon. Washington. There were more documents on that part of the board, charters and other contracts scattered among copious receipts.

David indicated the other half of the map. "He was promoted to the Eastern District, first to the Atlanta Region, then to Boston. He became Deputy Clerk of the Eastern District ten years ago."

Three years before David's run-in. The right side of the

map was thick with photos, with papers and string. Threads looped back and forth between coven markers, joining together magicaria and those yellow and green pins. There were dozens of photographs. Most of them seemed to be digital. Several were printed multiple times, in greater and greater detail until they disappeared in seas of pixellation.

I put my hand on Spot's head and asked, "What are the green pins?"

David looked so grateful, I almost cried. I was listening to him. I was trying to let this all make sense. "They're banks where he has accounts. A couple are under his own name, but most are aliases."

"And the yellow?"

"Caches of magical supplies." He pointed to one pin, somewhere near Milwaukee. "Crystals here." Another, near South Bend. "Runes." A third, just outside Washington, DC. "A collection of rowan wands—enough to corner the market."

"Then you figured it out?" I asked. "You've proven Pitt broke the law?"

David sighed. "Not yet. It's almost there. So close I can..." He trailed off. "I can track days when he met with prominent witches. Meals he ate with specific warders. And there are records of funds coming in and going out. But I can't trace a single transaction from start to finish. I can't prove anything."

I swallowed hard. It still sounded like a madman's nightmare. I couldn't believe that one file-pusher could be involved in so many transactions, that a single arcane bureaucrat could have his fingers in so many pies. Corruption on the scale David implied *had* to have been noticed by others.

I kept my voice even. "Show me an example. Show me what you have."

He leaped toward the map. I saw the instant he remembered to restrain himself, to pull back, to mimic absolute control. "Here," he said, and while he'd mastered the eagerness in his body, he could not siphon it from his voice. "The first record I could find. The Kansas City coven built a new safehold in 1995. They purchased a centerstone from an ancient coven in Romania, and Pitt handled the transaction. The coven paid $72,000 for the centerstone."

He pointed to a receipt. The total amount was underlined in dripping ink. Red string linked the document to a green pin in Wichita, Kansas.

"This bank account was opened in Pitt's name the day after Lughnasadh, with a deposit of $72,000. There are four separate withdrawals in equal amounts, following Mabon, Samhain, and Yule. The last was the day before Imbolc, the following year."

"A reasonable time period for the safehold to be built."

He nodded. "But there are other payments coming in to the account. One thousand here. Fifteen hundred there. A third payment of seven hundred dollars. Each time, they're listed as cash. They were transferred to a second account, one in Omaha, right before the final Imbolc installment." He pointed to a blue thread between the two green pins.

"Interest on the centerstone payments?"

He shook his head. "Too much money."

"You said the centerstone was coming from Romania. Was he gaming the exchange rate?"

"Again, that's too much cash."

I shook my head. I wasn't going to come up with any solution David hadn't already considered. He'd been at this for weeks. "Did my charter help? When you traced the aura?"

"Not much," he admitted, pointing toward the right side of the map. "All the documents have traces of Pitt." I could just glimpse my charter, hanging from its grommet on a blue push-pin. Its yellow ribbon was partially crushed by a photograph.

I peered at the snapshot. "Is that who I think it is?"

David nodded. "Teresa Alison Sidney, the Washington Coven Mother herself."

I suppressed a shudder of distaste. Teresa Alison Sidney was one of the strongest witches in the Eastern Empire. She had done her level best to get me to join her coven, but I'd rebelled against their cliquish ways. Their cliquish ways, and a hurtful prank that had been played on me by Teresa's sworn sister in witchcraft, Haylee James. The same Haylee James who had been responsible for sending David to the Court in the first place.

"Let me see that," I said.

David unpinned the photograph. I could see him tamping down his natural energy as he passed it over; he was still doing his best not to frighten me. The image in my hand, though, was as disturbing as anything David had ever done.

Teresa Alison Sidney was dressed in her usual flawless clothes—a sheath dress of scarlet silk. Her hair was sculpted in a perfect bob, and she wore her trademark string of pearls. Next to her, Norville Pitt looked like more of a troll than ever. His slacks sported a greasy stain, and his eyeglasses were askew.

"I don't get it," I said.

"What?"

"If Pitt has all these powerful friends, why does he still look like that? Even if he couldn't get anyone to work a glamour for him, he could dress better. Drop the pocket protector at least."

"It's camouflage. No one thinks the guy is capable of anything. No would ever suspect him of directing the most powerful witches in the world."

I studied the photograph more closely. His hand looked like a claw, where he and Teresa Alison Sidney both held a multiple-page document. "What are they doing with my charter?"

David shook his head. "That picture is from nine years ago, from the hundredth anniversary of the Washington Coven's magicarium. They had a huge celebration. The renewal had been in doubt, because the Court had shut down the three preceding schools that came up for re-certification."

I pointed at the document in the photo. "Look at the grommet. It's made out of copper. Just like mine."

David peered more closely. Then, he turned back to his map. "Yours *is* copper." He scanned the board. "I don't see another one like it." He pulled my charter from its pin, and then he passed me the paperwork that had lurked behind Teresa's photo.

As soon as the documents touched my hand, I felt *something*. I knew Teresa's magical signature; I had worked rituals within her coven. I wasn't surprised to find her presence in her own documents. But I was astonished to sense her magic in my charter.

No. Not in my *charter*. In its grommet.

"What?" David asked. "What do you see?"

I didn't have words, though. I couldn't explain the twists of magic. I could see them, *feel* them, but I wasn't certain what they meant. The more I tried to tell him, the more jumbled my thoughts became, until I couldn't be sure I was seeing anything at all. I didn't know what any of it meant, how any of it could be used.

David extended his hand to me.

His eyes were steady on my face. He knew I would remember that hand had held a dagger. That hand had shoved pins into the map, had stabbed at photographs and documents, had scribbled words and twisted threads and constructed a landscape of madness.

But he was asking me to balance years of trust against a single crazed moment.

My fingers were cold against the blazing heat of his palm. The instant our flesh connected, I felt the leap of his warder's magic. He pulled my tangled thoughts about the grommets, sensed them, *knew* them. And in the instant he read my tenuous understanding, he leaped to full comprehension on his own.

Teresa Alison Sidney had paid Norville Pitt two separate bribes. Cold cash, each time, wired to a secret account. The first had been to preserve the Washington magicarium, to secure its operation when other ancient schools were being shut down. The second had been to destroy *my* magicarium, to gain access to the Osgood collection once and for all.

The bribes had been sealed with magical agreements. Teresa and Pitt had each bound the other to perfect silence by way of arcane oaths, sworn over copper rings. Those copper rings had then been literally pressed into service as grommets, binding the charters of each institution.

David stepped away as soon as I had the image of the complete transactions. He whirled back to the map, no longer restraining his eagerness. He plucked a contract from a pin in Minneapolis. After hovering over the wall for a moment, his fingers twitched, landing on papers in Dallas. He used his arcane senses to double-check the connection, then stacked the documents on his desk before diving back into the mess.

I watched as he collected the materials. Now that he knew what he was looking for, the process was finally easy. Some of the threads he followed were invisible to me; others were clearly stretched string between pins on the map. In the end, there were dozens of stacks on the desk, neat groupings of contracts and receipts. Grommets and ribbons glinted through the piles, mute testimony to the crimes that bound them. Each documented transaction represented a bribe taken by Norville Pitt. Dozens of witches were implicated— Coven Mothers along with ordinary women. I wondered if some had been coerced, had acted out of a desperate fear they'd lose their magic, their covens, everything that made them true witches.

"There," David said as he collected the last pair. The word seemed too loud in the office, too strong after so long a stretch of silence.

"What do you do now?"

He sighed. "Pitt intercepted my documents about his expense account." The papers that David had forged. The lies that he had created years ago to catch the Clerk. "And he's far stronger now. We need to get the proof directly to the Court. But that's the entire reason they built the Clerk's office, to avoid direct contact with warders and witches."

"Not *all* direct contact," I said. "They'll attend my Major Working."

"So will Pitt. We can't just walk in with stolen documents and say, 'Your Head Clerk is a liar.' He has millions of dollars at stake here, hundreds of bribes over an entire career. And he has insurance against me." Those lies, again. The false documents David had created out of desperation.

I stared at the papers. Teresa Alison Sidney's photograph peeked out from the bottom of the closest stack.

When I'd joined the Washington Coven, I had hoped to find a magical home that would last me a lifetime. I'd brought a gift the first time I met the Coven Mother, a magical volume I'd bound with a prize citron from my collection. The present had been keyed for Teresa Alison Sidney alone; I had fashioned it so only she could open my offering.

"*The Illustrated History of Witches*," I said.

David understood immediately. After all, he was the one who had told me I was expected to reach out to the Coven Mother that way. "You can bind the documents in an offering."

"I'll seal it for the Court alone. Pitt said there would be eight Watchers for the Working."

"We can't do it there. These accusations will derail everything when we go public. You won't be able to complete the Major Working by Mabon, and your charter will be forfeit."

"Accusations or no, my students and I *will* complete the ritual." I smiled ruefully. "If the Watchers are too preoccupied to observe, we can always file an appeal."

I could tell he wanted to forbid me. He wanted to protect the magicarium. But more than that, he wanted to make the rest of this right, to remove Pitt's threat forever. I pushed a little harder. "We can place everything in the Allen Cask."

"You can't!" The alabaster Allen Cask was an ancient treasure, one of the most valuable artifacts in the Osgood collection.

"The Court has to be intrigued enough to open the gift then and there. They can't give Pitt a chance to escape."

David frowned, even as he nodded. "The cask will certainly do that."

"Get it for me. Let's bind it now."

He scarcely hesitated before striding out the office door. Spot whined until David returned, his arms stiff with the weight of the cask. Its stone sides were a creamy white, translucent beneath the overhead lights. The hinges were fashioned of gilded iron. The box was deceptively simple—six planes of unadorned alabaster.

The power of the cask came from the magical treasures it had held through the centuries. Witches from Asia, from Europe, from the colonies of the United States before they were free—each had passed the box from generation to generation. Every time a precious wand was stored in the container, or a book of great power, or a necklace of strength, a little of its energy seeped into the stone.

"Go ahead," I said to David. "Write up your explanation while I prepare the papers."

He wasted no time, collecting parchment from his desk. As this was the most formal of correspondence with the Court, he used a quill pen, dipping it in the crimson ink that marked a warder's priority communications. His hand flew from inkwell to scroll, and he formed his letters clearly, steadily, without a single hesitation. Light glinted off the warder's ring on his left hand as he wrote.

While he worked, I layered our findings in the box. Now that I understood what we had found, I felt the power in each clutch of documents. It shimmered from the grommets and rippled through ribbons. It echoed in metallic ink, in special blends Pitt had used to bind his earliest victims.

David finished his writing just as I completed filling the box. He read over the document carefully, then sanded it to dry the last of the ink. He placed it on top of the evidence, and we closed the cask together.

I worked my own magic then, gathering together strands of energy and weaving them into an intricate cloth. I complemented the magic of the Allen Cask, tailoring my creation to the specific container. I anchored the arcane fabric with double bonds of earth and air, fire and water. I tinted those eight strands with lessons from the heart of my magicarium, illustrating them with lush swirls that echoed the wild beauty of communal magic. The Court would have no doubt the cask and its contents came from me.

David's warder magic surged against my own as I lowered my arms and stepped back from the cask, an arcane brush of approval and gratitude and pride. "It's perfect," he said.

I studied him seriously. "Are you sure you want to do this? Pitt will fight back. He'll have to. He'll release the documents he's held over you for all these years."

"Let him. This has gone on long enough."

This. The lies. The fear of discovery. The rancid secret I'd pried out of David on Independence Day.

"I'll be there," I said. "No matter what happens."

"I know that." He swallowed hard. "I've always known

that."

And then his arms were around me. His mouth was hot on mine as his fingers tangled in my hair. There was a desperation in his touch, a plea and an apology.

He'd held back these weeks, these *months* because he wanted to protect me. He'd focused on his warder's duties so the Madison Academy would prevail. But the Academy was stronger than he'd thought. *I* was stronger. I'd faced my fears. Faced his madness.

Together, we'd figured out the secret of the documents that had haunted him for so long. The Allen Cask proved we could be witch and warder, man and woman. Partners in every sense of the word.

I laughed against the pulse point in his throat and fought to pull the shirttails from his slacks. The pearl buttons slipped under my fingers, and it took me three tries to work the top one. David leaned away from me then, laughing at my groan of frustration, but he only used the motion to pull the shirt over his head.

Spot suddenly wanted in on the game. The dog wagged his tail and crouched in a classic "play" position, snatching at one of David's sleeves. When he pinned the cotton between his teeth, David cursed and yielded the shirt. He took a precious moment to edge the victorious beast out of the office.

As the door clicked shut, I was already paying serious attention to the buttons at his waist. There were times when a little magic went a long, long way.

David and I spent the rest of the weekend reclaiming our home. We ate meals at the small table in the kitchen. We sat at opposite ends of the living room couch and read. We found classic movies on the television and watched them, back to back to back. And we spent an inordinate number of hours in bed.

It was heaven to have the house to ourselves.

And yet, I kept thinking of the others. Neko would have had a field day, snarking at my domestic bliss. I wondered if he was sleeping in the greenhouse with the familiars, or if he and Tony were bunking together in the barn. For all I knew, the guys could have gone away for the weekend. I could have checked, could have pulled on the astral thread that bound me to my familiar, but I had no cause. Neko deserved some time on his own.

As David and I watched *The 39 Steps*, I wondered if Raven had ever filmed in black and white. David read to me from an entertaining *New York Times* article about the cost of supporting the British monarchy, and I imagined Emma's spirited defense of the queen. The television announced a conflict between recording two of Caleb's baseball games, and I deleted both, hoping he was catching them out in the barn. I tiptoed as I crossed the kitchen floor, until I remembered Kopek wasn't trying to sleep in the basement.

Over and over again, I made the little adjustments that had become second nature in the crowded house, fully aware of them now because of the contrasting peace and quiet.

And by Monday morning, it was time to face the outside world. I had to push the Jane Madison Academy the last few steps toward its Major Working. And David was heading to Sedona. Again.

"I've *tried* to talk to Clara," I said as he finished knotting his tie. "The last time, she launched into a fifteen-minute discussion of how I needed to get in touch with my inner Aquarius."

He kissed away my pout. "Try again," he said. "Or just accept that she's not going to tell you what she's working on. I'll be back by Wednesday."

I might have resented his absence, if I hadn't had so much work to complete. Everyone was waiting for me on the porch. It was eight o'clock, sharp.

"Good morning," I said.

And it *was* a good morning. Everyone looked rested, if a little curious. We could spend a while talking about everything—my note on the refrigerator, how we'd regrouped over the weekend, whether we'd learned anything from living in such close proximity.

But we had more important things to do.

I looked from person to person as I said, "We're going to take the next five days to practice our Mabon ritual. We'll go from start to finish, combining all the individual parts we've practiced. Every time we get off track, we'll do our best to make a correction, but we won't stop. We'll fight for a new balance and do our best, just as if we were in the middle of the real test."

I waited for questions, for complaints, but there were none. I asked Tony to ward us, and we began our Major Working.

We practiced for five days. We worked and reworked the ritual until it was a ballet we could dance in our sleep. Each of use knew our roles; we all understood our parts.

Alas, no matter how hard we tried, we never had enough power to complete the entire working. Sometimes, we only got to Protecting the Innocent. Usually, we Prepared the Earth. One day, late in the week, when the air was particularly oppressive and we were exhausted by our earlier attempts, we barely managed to summon the elementals.

I'd tried everything I could think of to bolster our energy. I parceled it out stingily, skimping on the foundation of the working, only to have everything crash around our magical ears at the end. I poured energy into calling the quarters and lighting the candles, in fruitless hope that those building blocks would stabilize the final steps of our working.

Perhaps I truly expected the impossible—no magicarium, anywhere, in the entire history of witchcraft could have accomplished what I desired. Not with so few students. Not with so little time to build true rapport. Not with communal magic, instead of the Rota.

In the end, I was left with just one hope: Mabon itself was a gateway, a passage from summer to autumn. There was power in that transition. Maybe, just possibly, there was enough magical energy in the sabbat itself to boost us through the ritual we never mastered in our practice.

Because if we failed? I wasn't sure what would happen next. I couldn't say what would become of Emma and Rick, if their romance would survive her departure from a disbanded Madison Academy. I assumed Raven and Emma would return to Sedona, that they'd try to nurse their powers in the shadow of the coven that had already rejected them. Perhaps they'd lose their bonds to their familiars. Their warders could even be recalled by the Court.

The Allen Cask sat ready in the basement. The Osgood collection rested in the balance. And there was nothing more I could do to preserve the Madison Academy.

Chapter 17

THE ARCANE WORLD might be marking the occurrence of Mabon, but the natural world made no concession to the autumn sabbat. Sunday dawned hazy, hot, and humid, like every day for the preceding four months. The air conditioner wheezed like a two-pack-a-day smoker.

Mindful of our working that evening, David and I both avoided the spotless kitchen. Instead, I carried a pitcher of cool water up to the bedroom, pouring myself glass after lemon-steeped glass as I reviewed our working for the night. David kept to himself, giving me the psychic and physical space I needed.

I knew this ritual. I could recite its stages in my sleep. I could close my eyes and picture my students going through their paces, and I could feel the energy we would raise. The imagined scent of beeswax tickled my nose as I saw us lighting our column candles, and my toes twitched at the thought of walking on moist sand, scoping out the sacred circle of our working.

Nevertheless, a sponge of uncertainty filled inside my

chest. What if we couldn't complete the ceremony? What if our assembled power spun out of control, like the weather working that had destroyed the ospreys' nest? What if we didn't have enough strength to finish? What if the Court never let us attempt the Major Working, shutting us down completely after I offered up the Allen Cask?

Taking a soothing sip of water, I ordered myself not to dwell on things that were well beyond my ability to fix at this late date. Instead, I prepared myself, body and mind, for the ritual I was about to lead. And when the sun started to dip to the horizon, I stepped onto the front porch and greeted the full complement of the Madison Academy.

I wore a formal gown, one that Neko had found for me some time the previous year. Its gold-shot russet silk was smooth against my legs as I paused on the marble center-stone.

Raven and Emma stood together, close enough to clasp hands. Emma wore a deep burgundy gown, the shade of crimson leaves just before they faded to winter brown. The color was a classic choice for Mabon, but it only under-scored her delicate complexion. As if to counter her twin's fragility, Raven wore a tight-sashed robe of black. She clear-ly intended to work our ritual skyclad.

That was her right. In fact, our ritual might be stronger for Raven's nakedness—she would be true to herself, true to her powers. The Madison Academy was all about witches' journeys of self-discovery, and I had to trust that energy, had to have faith in my students' determination. That knowledge was part of the gift Gran had given me when she insisted I live with my witches. Raven and I might never be friends, but I understood her in a way I hadn't when she first appeared on this same porch, back in June.

Similarly, I had learned to depend on my students' entourages, their warders and familiars. I scarcely recognized Caleb and Tony. They'd set aside the robes of our abortive Lughnasadh working, choosing formal attire instead. Caleb had shaved, transforming himself from a shaggy bear back to the bluff, good-natured giant I had instinctively trusted upon his arrival to the farm.

Tony seemed to have taken a page out of Neko's fashion guidebook—I could swear he had *product* in his hair. His fists clenched and unclenched in a steady rhythm next to the satin stripe on his tuxedo pants, and his eyes darted about the porch as if he suspected attackers behind every post. I appreciated his appearance of constant watchfulness.

Hani stood beside Raven, his freckled face tilted toward her like a Gerbera daisy to the sun. Kopek held himself at a bit of a distance, closer to Emma than anyone else. His shoulders slumped, highlighting his eternal appearance of dejection, but his eyes were clear and focused.

Neko glided over to me. "Nice hair," he whispered, cupping his hand against my elbow as if to steady me as I stepped from the inset marble to the wooden porch. I resisted the urge to raise my fingertips to my scarcely tamed hair. I'd twisted it off my neck, pinning it into place with a single wand of ash. I waited for some sarcastic follow-up, but for once my familiar seemed truly to approve of my appearance. I allowed myself a fortifying breath, drawing from his store of reflective power.

"All right," I said to everyone. "David's waiting for us at the beach."

We walked together through the woods. I clutched at my

full-length skirt, pulling it high enough above my sandals that I didn't need to worry about tripping, about snagging the cloth on any of the desiccated vines that ran beside the forest path.

Our group flowed easily. Emma and Raven started out beside each other, but soon split up to walk with their familiars. Tony led the way, aggressively taking point, while Caleb watched from the rear. Neko ranged from the vanguard to my side. Although no one spoke a word, there was comfort in our community. We were bonded together, already working toward our common goal, even though we had yet to frame our first spell.

As we approached the lakeside edge of the woods, I paused and everyone gathered close around me. This was it. The moment I'd waited for since Raven and Emma appeared on the farmhouse steps. Whatever we had created together, however I had taught my students, now was the moment we'd all be tested.

My fingertips automatically ran to the pendant I wore on a narrow gold chain—a globe of polished amber. The fossilized resin added strength to other magic, enhancing all types of arcane workings. Taking a fortifying breath, I threw back my shoulders, lifted my chin, and led my magicarium onto the beach.

David waited by the dock, standing guard over the Allen Cask. His tuxedo was impeccable, and his sword gleamed in the light of the setting sun. This was the warder I had trusted with my entire magical being. This was the man who had followed me through the storm of our failed Lughnasadh working. This was the lover who had tried to protect me from his past, who had terrified me with his uncompromising search for justice.

This was my partner in all matters magical and mundane.

Holding my gaze without saying a word, David sank to one knee. He never took his eyes from me as he offered up his weapon. His hands were steady, and his face was utterly calm.

I crossed to the dock and settled my hands over his. The power of his warder's magic jolted against mine, surging into my physical body, stiffening my spine. Without having planned to, I lifted the golden chain from around my neck, capturing my amber pendant against the palm of my hand. When I brought it to my lips, it was warm, buzzing with an arcane force as if the soul of a thunderstorm was trapped inside its myriad of tiny bubbles.

David bowed his head, and I set the chain around his neck. The amber stood out against the pleats of his white shirt, blazing like a miniature sun. He closed his fist over its brilliance, brought the stone to his own lips, and sealed the new contract I had written between us.

He rose with the grace of a panther. I followed his motion and turned back to face my students, their own warders, and their familiars. And that was when I realized we were not alone. Our ritual was no longer a private gathering of the Madison Academy.

Hecate's Court had arrived.

There were four men and four women. Each was clad in cloth of gold—complicated robes for the men, with ornate sashes woven into intricate knots. The women wore shimmering gowns, as if they had stepped out of the pages of some medieval manuscript.

By all rights, they should have been overwhelmed by the heavy autumn air. They should have been assaulted by the heat and humidity, beaten down by the weight of their finery.

But the Court members vibrated with hidden power, with a collective energy. I could sense it without trying, an invisible charge like lightning about to strike. It was as if they spoke some unknown arcane language—the equivalent of high church Latin or ancient Greek—while I was mired in a common tongue.

I took a step closer, trying to read the face of the nearest woman, to gauge her disposition toward the Madison Academy and me. But that was another trick of the Watchers' magic—their features were obscured. The woman closest to me and all her sisters, all four of the men. No matter how hard I tried to focus, no matter how closely I peered, I could not make out their eyes, their lips. I could not reduce them to humanity.

I fought to quench a shiver of fear. If I could not see the people who judged me, how could I be sure I met their demands? How could I offer up the cask, with its indictment of Norville Pitt?

My incipient panic was shattered by the sound of a throat being cleared. As if summoned by my thoughts, the Head Clerk of Hecate's Court now stood upon the beach.

Apparently, he had missed the memo that Mabon was a major sabbat. His mud-colored trousers looked like he had slept in them for a week. His short-sleeve dress shirt was wrinkled, and his pocket protector had gone awry. One of his pens had left a dark blue stain on the approximate location of his left nipple.

Nevertheless, Pitt flicked his wrist with all the aplomb of a royal herald. A scroll manifested from the heavy air, its parchment curls cascading to the sand at his feet. Another twist, and his pudgy fingers were filled with an enormous quill pen. The feather trembled distractingly as he proclaimed, "We are gathered here today t—"

Really? I wanted to shout. Are you really going to use the form of a wedding service?

Before I could recover, David stepped forward and raised his right hand, exclaiming, "Hold!"

He couldn't speak a Word of Power as I had on the farmhouse porch so many months before; he was not a witch. But his single syllable had nearly the same effect as my Word had done. Pitt stopped his proclamation in mid-syllable. The eight Watchers seemed to lean closer, although not one had shifted on the sand.

I recognized my cue. "Noble ladies," I said, making obeisance to the Watchers. "Noble lords. I know it is not customary for a magistrix to interrupt a grand proceeding such as this. But I beg your humble indulgence."

My magicarium was taken off guard. Emma's face was pinched, and Raven clutched her robe closer about her. Their warders and familiars shifted uncertainly. Neko scrambled to my side, and I sensed his unspoken questions, the pressure of his thoughts, even as he brushed my arm with an offer of power. I regretted surprising all of them this way, but I had not wanted any chance for them to give Pitt an unintended warning.

The Watchers seemed as surprised as my magicarium; it was forever before a woman's voice proclaimed, "Proceed."

I could not see who had spoken; the obscuring magic

held. I continued to address all eight Watchers, speaking loudly enough for each to hear. "The Jane Madison Academy is indebted to the Court. We are grateful you saw fit to charter our operation, and we are eager to prove ourselves with our Major Working."

The first Major Working ever required of a magicarium, I longed to add, but I dared not challenge the Court's procedure. Instead, I raised one arm to indicate the Allen Cask, hoping my gesture conveyed sufficient grace and poise.

"Honored members, it is customary for a witch to offer up a gift to her Coven Mother upon first meeting. The Madison Academy stands before you today in something of the same position. We recognize your power over us, your authority to license us and bind us in Hecate's name. And as a gesture of that respect, we offer you the Allen Cask, and all the riches it contains."

"What are you doing?" Pitt spluttered. His oily glance slipped from David to me and back again. "What do you think you can accomplish by delay—"

"Peace," a Watcher interrupted. I could not be certain, but I thought this was a different woman than the one who had spoken before. Pitt choked off his words, but the fury in his bulging eyes was directed at David.

The Watchers seemed to conduct some silent conversation among themselves. I began to think I would have to continue. I would have to make some additional invitation. But the second Watcher finally said, "We will accept."

Pitt fussed and muttered as the Court members crossed the beach to the dock. Their golden robes left no impression on the sand; there was no physical evidence of their presence at all. They arrayed themselves around the cask, standing shoulder to shoulder, alternating men and women. The alabaster glinted, reflecting the brilliant cloth of their gowns. I could not see the Watchers' motions. Their hands remained obscured; their eyes stayed cloaked. But I felt their presence as they measured out the magical cloth I had used to wrap the cask. They tested the knot I had tied. They picked out the eight strands I had woven, the double bonds of earth and air, fire and water. Together, they tugged on the arcane wrapping. As one, they twisted it. And in a flash of gold, they cut it free.

I blinked, and the cask was open. David's missive lay on top of the evidence, the parchment explaining all the contents of the box. I could sense the energy of those documents, the charged grommets and ribbons, the magically bonded ink.

And Norville Pitt felt it, too. "What are you doing?" he thundered. As he slipped across the sand, tumbling toward the cask, he dropped his ornate scroll and his fancy quill pen. "Those are lies! Whatever they say, it's a lie!"

David took a single step forward, leveling his sword across the edge of the dock. In a heartbeat, Caleb and Tony were there as well, weapons drawn, feet planted in the aggressive stance of warriors.

Pitt scrambled for some sort of magic, some warder's power, but a golden flare froze him into place.

Unseen, the Watchers had moved again. Now, they were arrayed with their backs to the lake, standing in a semi-circle on the far side of the cask. David's parchment glowed, as if it had been invested with some arcane force. I felt the power of eight pairs of eyes bearing down upon me.

"Speak, magistrix." I thought that was the first woman.

"Explain."

I bowed my head. "These documents will speak for themselves, honored members. They'll show a record of evil done by one sworn to serve you in all things. They'll show greed, and lust for power, and disdain for fairness. They'll show that the Head Clerk of Hecate's Court has been forsworn, and he has served himself first and foremost."

"Slander!" Pitt shrieked. "Lies!"

But the documents that David and I had compiled had already grown stronger from their time in the Allen Cask. Their bonds were clearer, even at a cursory glance. Although I stood at a distance, I could feel the connections between charters and bank records, between binding contracts and petty receipts.

The Watchers' silence grew heavier, thicker in a way that I now understood meant they were conferring among themselves. Like falling barometric pressure, their will pressed down upon us, and after I blinked, they were arrayed in a circle around the snarling Head Clerk.

"Norville Pitt." This time it was a man who spoke, baritone and severe. "You will be bound over to the Court for the hearing of these charges at a date and place to be determined. You—"

"You can't *believe* them!" Pitt's face had turned a burgundy that matched Emma's gown.

The Watcher continued. "You will be be relieved—"

"That warder has betrayed Hecate before!" Spittle flew from Pitt's lips as he pointed at David. "He was stripped of his rank for three years!"

"You will be relieved of your duties immediately—"

"He tried to frame me years ago! He forged documents!

He's the liar! Not me! Montrose is the man you want!"

"—and you will be confined to—"

"It's *her* fault!" His finger pointed at me like a broken rowan wand. "She's only trying to delay her Working! That *bitch* is trying to distract you all!"

The flash of David's sword was blinding. Caleb and Tony were only a heartbeat behind. All three weapons were leveled at Pitt's throat, a handbreadth from severing his jugular.

"Stand down!" The shout came from another Watcher, a man with a bass rumble that shook the very beach.

David's arm trembled. Pitt's eyes grew large behind his glasses, and he caught his breath, half-snort, half-sob.

I started to reach for the link that bound me to David, gathering my will as his witch. I'd promised myself I would never wield that power again, but I needed to save him, needed to keep him from the Court's unbounded wrath. The link between us was there—gleaming and bright.

But David stepped back before I could use it. He lowered his blade, pointing it toward the sand. He inclined his head, patently accepting the authority of the Court. Out of the corner of my eye, I could see Caleb and Tony follow suit.

Pitt collapsed to his knees. His fleshy hands clutched at the sand. His breath came in short gasps, and his entire body trembled.

The baritone Watcher continued. "You will be confined to a chamber at Hecate's Court until such time as the Court shall hear this matter. So mote it be."

Seven other voices joined in. "So mote it be!"

There was a crack of thunder, louder than any my witches and I had ever raised as we practiced our weather working. A flash of golden light blinded me. I blinked hard, twice.

When my vision finally cleared, I could see that the dock was empty. There was no sign of the Allen Cask. Norville Pitt was gone as well, leaving behind only the smeared imprint of hands and knees in the sand. The eight Watchers remained at the top of the beach, still shrouded in their secrecy.

David looked to the left, then to the right, before he took his position beside me. Caleb and Tony returned to their witches. Raven and Emma looked stunned, utterly overwhelmed by all they had witnessed. Their familiars crouched nearby, equally aghast. Neko leaned in, sending a tendril of concerned energy.

"Now, magistrix of the Jane Madison Academy," a voice rang out, and I believed it was the first woman who had spoken. "You may begin your Major Working. Let all who bear witness judge you fairly and with mercy. In the name of Hecate, so mote it be!"

Chapter 18

MY HEART POUNDED. I longed for a break, for the opportunity to reassure my students. The Watchers had spoken, though. We had no choice but to begin.

I strode to the east and began the Mabon ritual for the first Major Working of the Madison Academy. The words were woven in the fabric of my heart. My body knew precisely how many steps to take. My fingers knew how to curl over the candle, how to summon the flame, how to greet the elementals of Air.

We all did our parts flawlessly. Emma summoned Fire. Raven shed her midnight robe and, skyclad, called on Water. Together, the three of us sealed the circle by drawing on the strength of Earth. Our familiars moved with us in our magic dance, catching our power, reflecting it back to us. I leaned most heavily on Neko, of course, but I did not hesitate to mix my strength, to pull from Hani and Kopek.

The warders followed along, tracing our magical circle with the fire of their swords. They did not close a cordon, though. They were watching over us, protecting us, keeping us safe, but they could not lock our magic under a charmed dome. Not for this working. Not tonight.

Watching Caleb and Tony, I felt honored and protected. Watching David, I felt cherished.

We worked quickly, building the basic framework of our ritual. We Protected the Innocent, confining our working to spare all unsuspecting creatures, human and animal both. We Prepared the Earth, priming the land beneath our dome. But this was the real Major Working, the actual ritual and not one of our endless preparatory studies. And so we expanded the Preparation, stretching our powers to include the lake we had sworn to repair.

Only after we'd set our boundaries—extended to include floating mats of duckweed, dead and blasted trees, the four dry streams that had once flowed with water—did I stride to the massive woven basket in the center of our circle. It was time to activate our eastern quadrant, to harness the power of Air.

We started with a fist-size chunk of coral. Its orange-red arms branched like a tree, gaining strength from the empty space that vibrated between the stretches of its solid substance. Coral was a classic protectant, a charm against evil. But most importantly for our purposes, coral was a bond against natural disasters, against storms that rose with too much power.

With Raven's help, I twined angelica flowers around its branches. The herb was highly protective, guarding against evil. It was particularly effective at the beginning of a ritual, when its awesome strength could spread over an entire working.

When we were satisfied with the twist of white flowers

around vermilion coral, Raven and I stepped back. In unison, we reached for Emma, ready to bring her into the circle of our magic.

Our powers merged—violet, gold, silver. Our hands hovered over the coral and angelica. The space between our palms shimmered, and the outlines of our fingers blurred. Together, we lifted a carefully selected rune, one of the jade plaques that I counted among my most valuable magical possessions. Eihwaz. The yew tree. The rune resonated with strength, with defense and protection.

We planted the plaque at the root of the coral, taking care to lean it against several fronds of angelica. Once all three of us were satisfied with the jade's placement, we chanted:

"Powers of the East, of Air,
Share with us your gifts so fair,
Wisdom, thought, perception shine,
Inspire us to be divine."

Our familiars fed the energy of our spell among themselves, bouncing it within the confines of our circle. I knew the moment the warders felt the power we raised—Caleb took a step back, and Tony pinned Raven with a fiercely protective glare. David was facing away from us, scanning the perimeter of the beach for any danger that approached by land. I could sense his attention, though, his raptor-sharp awareness of all that we were doing. The warder-witch bond between us tightened, and the tug on my belly stopped just short of pain.

The spell worked. Air rose in response to our summons. Not a whirlwind, nothing as dangerous as that, nothing like the storm we unleashed on Lughnasadh. Rather, a solid breeze rippled from the eastern quadrant of our circle, drying away some of the omnipresent humidity, carrying the fresh scent of pine trees on an autumn night.

Of course, the raising cost us strength. My muscles felt ropy and stretched, as if I had completed an entire day of yoga. I knew immediately that this ritual was demanding more than any other we had practiced. That was the cost of bringing in all the lake, all the territory we sought to heal.

The expense was worth it, though. We were forging a new type of magic, a new bond between the disparate parts of our working. Stone, herb, and rune together; we were reclassifying magic, making it something new, something unique to the Madison Academy.

Proud of our success, I led my students to the southern point of our circle. I'd chosen garnet for the Fire quadrant. The blood red crystal enhanced strength and endurance, offering up healing energy.

My prize stone was the size of a pigeon egg. Its facets caught the sparkle of the magic arrayed around it, fracturing the light, sending it back upon us a thousand fold. We teamed garnet with lovage, nestling the stone in the bright green of the plant's sharp-toothed leaves. Uruz was the rune for the southern point—a canted house sketched with three simple lines. Uruz was the symbol of strength.

As one, we chanted over our trio of symbols:
"Powers of the South, of Fire,
Wrap us in your magic gyre,
Energy and strength of will,
Passion with our hearts do fill."

Fire gathered around us—the dangerous flicker of electricity. The charge crackled against the silk of my gown.

Kopek flinched as the first bolt of lightning struck the ground. Emma reached out to him, comforting him, gentling him. Neko added to the wash of safety, confirming that the Fire was controlled, was ours to command.

Outside our circle, Caleb raised a hand. I recognized the lines of concern on his face, his worry about those he had sworn to protect. Emma raised her own palm to match his across the circle, across the coruscating bands of magic light. The warder settled back on his heels, accepting his witch's command, even as he tightened his grip on his sword.

We moved to the west, to Water. This time, it took more of my energy to walk away. I needed to spare more of my strength to control the Fire, to tame the lightning that wanted to reach out across the half-sphere of our ritual space. My fingertips tingled, and I recognized the danger of fatigue.

I steeled myself and concentrated on building our bond with Water. Sodalite for confidence, for wisdom and the calming of inner conflicts. The stone was the color of deepest, clearest water, echoing its quadrant's core. We added Solomon's seal, with its simple oval leaves and bells of white flowers. The plant radiated wisdom, the following of hunches, the achievement of dreams. We anchored the corner with Ansuz, the slanted F that resonated with the power of the oldest gods rising from primordial seas. Ansuz whispered of wisdom and harmony and truth, and we drew upon its strength as we spoke our spell.

"Powers of the West, of Water,
Reach out to your questing daughters,
Show us paths to joy, to pleasure,
Fill us in unstinted measure."

I stumbled over the opening rhyme, and it took Raven

and Emma's combined voices to bring me back on track. For a heartbeat, I thought we had failed, that we had neglected something, overlooked some vital part of our ritual.

But then I sensed the water hovering around us. It teased me, like a scent I could barely follow across a meadow, like the memory of a dream. There was no water in the ground, no water that flowed—that was the cost of four summers of drought. But water was layered in the air, in the humidity that pressed against our flesh.

We needed more power to extract that water for our spell. I reached for Neko, silently demanding his assistance. He braced himself against my pull, digging in his physical heels, as if to avoid the crumbling edge of a cliff. I pushed again, demanding more, reaching past my own familiar to Hani, to Kopek. After an endless moment, an epoch outside of time and space, Raven and Emma bolstered my claim. Their familiars responded to my need, reflecting power toward me. I collected it all—the energy of the familiars and the strength of my students, my sisters in this working.

Finally, we were able to pull Water into the ritual. It started like the finest of mists, the faintest haze. Encouraged by our success, I poured more of my core strength into our summoning. I repeated the last two lines of the spell like a child's incantation against monsters that lived beneath her bed, and the mist turned to drizzle, to a fine, steady rain.

And then it was time to drag myself to the last quadrant, to Earth. Each step felt like an epic journey. I realized I was clutching my students' hands; Emma stood on my right and Raven on my left. We supported each other as we moved, lending strength that none of us could remember possessing.

Moldavite was the last stone for our working, green and

glistening. The mineral was extracted from the core of the earth, from the dying breath of a meteorite that had plunged into our world eons before. Its crystals represented our higher selves, the heights to which we could aspire from our earth-bound base.

We added corn, that ancient gift of the gods, rich with its essence of healing. We anchored the corner with the Inguz rune, a stylized diamond, the archaic symbol of Earth.

It was hard to remember the words of the spell, almost impossible to recall the specific order of the rhymes. Raven stammered as we started, and all three of us stopped, blinking with stupid exhaustion. Emma took the lead, then, starting our incantation, and we finally joined in like a ragtag band of children reciting the Pledge of Allegiance.

"Powers of the north, of Earth,
Recognize our humble worth,
Bring us patience, strength, and wealth
That we might turn this lake to health."

I knew before we finished the words that we had not sparked the working. Earth was beneath us, of course. Our feet were anchored in the sand of the beach. Nothing we said, though, nothing we did, made anything come alive. Nothing turned the ordinary world to magic.

Pushing down a whisper of despair, I started to recite the spell again. I reached out for the combined strength of our familiars, tugging on Hani and Kopek, bringing them into a tighter circle with Neko. But as I reached the last words, I knew we had failed.

Raven and Emma understood the same. Raven was shivering; I could practically see her heart beating through the pale skin of her chest. Emma's face was drawn; the circles beneath her eyes looked bruised.

I looked through the dome, trying to measure what the Court members were making of our failure. Was there partial credit on this exam? The eight observers, though, were lost to me. I could not sense them directly.

For the first time since arriving at the beach, I started to panic.

Our careful balance over the elements we'd already summoned began to fray. A gust of wind swept toward us from our right, from the east, where we had confined the power of Air. The blow surprised me; I'd taken for granted our ability to maintain the control we'd already invested in our working.

As if to mock my over-confidence, a bolt of lightning broke free from the south. Fire branched from the apex of our ritual arch to the ground, flashing bright enough to blind us. The steady rain of the west surged with strength, pelting the ground beneath it, splashing us with energy that burned like acid.

Each magical surge ate away at the little power we still maintained. The summoned elements danced to a symphony we no longer controlled. They were out of balance, spinning without harmony. We needed Earth to settle them, to bind them, but Earth was the one thing we no longer possessed the strength to summon.

Raven and Emma tried. I felt them slip back into their age-old bonds, the twinned power they had shared as infants. They plumbed the depths of their familiars, swept through to include Neko in one final, desperate bid. I tried to offer up my own strength, tried to give them the raw force they needed, but I was too weak, too bound up in the spells we had already cast.

The storm began to slip away. Wind lashed the rain. Lightning sparked inside the tempest, tracing our limbs and framing our faces. I heard an osprey cry above the crash of thunder.

I dropped to my knees, as if I could better reach the Earth in my defeat. Nothing. No connection. No bond. Raising my eyes up to the sky above us, I longed to tell my students I was sorry I had failed them. If only I could release the familiars who had given us so much. There had to be some way to assure the warders that this failure was not theirs; they had kept us safe beyond anyone's expectation.

My vision was gone. My sight was filled with lightning, washed away by rain. The scream of the wind kept me from blinking, stunned me past any ability to see. I curled in upon myself, folding into a protective ball.

There was one bond left to me, though. One link to the world. I felt it, solid as iron. *David.* As I lay on the ground, silenced by despair, he stood before me like a door to safety. The amber pendant I had given him shone out like a newborn sun, illuminating the path I had to trod.

I staggered to my feet, taking steps like a baby. I stumbled and caught myself against the magical line drawn by our warders, the boundary that was meant to keep us safe. My hands were splayed across the field of energy, fingers stretched, palms flattened.

David matched me on the other side. His hands touched mine, pulsing across the barrier. We were bound as warder and witch. Awareness pumped from him to me, augmented by the amber drop we both had worn.

And that was when I felt it. A stir of energy. A whisper of witchy power.

It was a scent that veiled my vision. A flavor that scratched my fingertips. An image that flickered through my nose with every breath I gasped.

Energy. Pure, astral force.

I flattened my palms against David's, voicing my amazement with silent thought. We were far beyond the need for speech, past the puny limitations of letters and syllables and words. I imagined my query, and there it was, around us, within us. I lived the question of how I could harness this strange warder's magic, how I could transform it into something wild and witchy and wonderful.

And through the transparency, through the invisibility that was the core of David's strength, I understood the answer.

He was not offering me warder's power. He was channeling from another source. He was delivering magic from other witches.

From Clara.

Now that I understood, I could taste my mother's familiar strain of magic. I thought a question toward David, and he cast an answer back to me. This was why he had traveled to Arizona. Clara had primed him, building this channel so she and her sisters could pour power into our working. He was my warder, and he was Clara's warder, and he could bridge the gap between our workings. Clara's energy surrounded me, cradled me, sparking against the amber drop.

A bolt of lightning flared, blinding with pure electric fire, and I was back inside our circle. My russet gown whipped around me, shredding in the wind, in the brutal wall of rain.

My vision restored, I could see Raven once again, her vulnerable flesh striped red with welts from the storm. Emma hunched on the ground, her burgundy gown pooling around her like blood.

These were my students. These were the women who had trusted me, who had sworn to join me in a test greater than any of us had imagined. I had worked with them, studied with them, *lived* with them.

I reached out with new tenderness, gathering them close as if we had all shared a womb. I spread my strength above them, sheltering them, feeding them, nurturing them.

And then, I pulled down the full force that Clara offered through David. I inhaled magic, filling my lungs, suffusing my bloodstream. I poured my mother's offering into my limbs, letting it vibrate down my thighs, through my calves, into my feet. I collected the loaned strength my mother gave so freely, and I called Earth into our working. Atom by atom, molecule by molecule, I stabilized our spell, and then I balanced all the energies—Earth, Air, Fire, and Water.

Raven roused first. She understood what I was doing, even if she could scarcely glimpse the source of my new power. She anchored herself and drew on her oldest mastery, on the herbs we had worked into our ritual. She collected the magic of angelica and lovage, of Solomon's seal and corn. She magnified them inside the stony chasms of her magic, echoing them in the fractal channels of her ability.

Her determination brought Emma into our loop. As Raven and I tamed the storm, Emma plumbed the fathomless lake of her own powers. She excavated those depths, bringing up reserves she'd never dreamed of harvesting.

Stable now, balanced, we manipulated Air and Fire. We

managed Earth and Water. We moved our life-giving storm over the lake, and we fed the damaged world around us, weaving a new tapestry to replace the one that had been torn. We strengthened the fibers of animals, of plants, of the very earth that had been damaged. We healed the destruction of days, months, years of drought.

Together, we measured when we had accomplished our goal. Together, we recognized the success of our working. Together, we tucked in the last wild tendrils of our healing storm, freeing the wind, loosing the rain, releasing the final wild charge of fire into the earth.

Through David, I offered a grateful thought to my mother, to all who gathered with her in Sedona. I shivered as I finally broke that bond, shuddering down to the chambers of my heart. I joined hands with Raven and Emma. We let the candles flare one last time, then die away. We worked with our familiars and warders, dispersing the last stray energy of the dome that had sheltered our miracle.

We stood together on the beach.

The eight Watchers seemed stunned. There was a stillness about them, a silence of communion.

We could have waited for them to bestir themselves. Perhaps we *should* have waited. But Raven and Emma and I were still attuned to each other, still locked in the perfect balance of our communal magic. As one, we turned on our heels and strode to the end of the dock. We summoned our familiars to move beside us, and we gathered our warders to watch at our backs.

As we gazed out over the perfect lake, a shadow swept across the water. My heart recognized the osprey before my mind did. In the darkness, I could not tell if we watched a male or a female, but I could see the massive bird swoop down to the water. As it rose, I could make out its talons, closed around the silver curve of a fish. And I heard the raptor's cry of greeting as it settled in its new nest, high atop an oak tree on the western shore of the lake.

Chapter 19

AFTER THAT, THINGS BLURRED.

The Court members conferred among themselves, and the gravelly bass voice eventually made an announcement: "By order of Hecate's Court, this Major Working of the Jane Madison Academy is complete and acceptable to all who judged. From this day forward, the Academy shall enjoy all rights and privileges of a Class Two magicarium in the Eastern Empire."

And just like that, they were gone—disappeared in a golden cloud and a shimmer of magic. I might not have been able to follow their astral departure if I were at the height of my powers. Now, weary and weepy with our success, I did not make any effort to figure out the magic of their transport.

Instead, I yielded to David's increasingly insistent pressure. I led everyone back to the kitchen for yet another shared meal.

While we witches shed our waterlogged garments in favor of sweatshirts and pajama bottoms, Neko took over in the kitchen. He moved with authority, as if he'd been born to the job (which, as a familiar, he had been). In short order, he had Caleb firing up the grill. Tony was tasked with providing beverages. Hani and Kopek were pressed into service as porters, ferrying the entire contents of the pantry and the refrigerator to the dining room table.

Emma and Raven watched, looking as dazed as I felt. I'd taken care to congratulate them as we walked back from the lake, but now words seemed superfluous. They leaned their heads close together, and Raven whispered something that made her sister laugh.

I smiled and headed toward my bedroom, but David intercepted me at the stairs. "You need to eat."

I tried to edge past him. "I need to phone Clara."

"She can wait."

"I need to thank her!"

"She'll be grounding herself. Feeding her own witches. You can talk to her tomorrow."

Clara must be as exhausted as I was. She had poured her strength across miles. It wasn't fair she should be left to recover alone. She should have a warder to protect her, to stabilize her. "Go," I said. "Make sure she's all right."

"She's fine," David said. "There were two dozen women there, pooling their strength. They were warded by others."

How? I started to ask. *Why? When?*

But there would be plenty of time for questions in the morning. For now, I let my warder take me back to the table. I took the plate he settled in my hand, and I ate what he fed me. I was vaguely aware that Tony was serving Raven in a similar fashion, that Caleb was looking out for Emma.

At last, I stood beside David on the porch, watching as

my magicarium dispersed into the night. Glancing toward the garage, I saw Rick Hanson's pick-up sitting on the driveway. Caleb shook hands with the fireman who was waiting for Emma in the shadows on the porch, and then the warder made his way toward the barn. Emma and Rick settled on the glider, his arm around her waist, her head resting on his shoulder.

Hani and Kopek shuffled toward the greenhouse. Tony escorted Raven to the garage. He opened the door to the apartment, and made as if he would lead her up the stairs, but she tossed her head and turned him about, sending him back into the night. As Raven shut the door, Neko edged up from the shadows and slipped his hand into Tony's. The men disappeared into the shadows, heading in the general direction of the renovated barn.

I could scarcely keep my eyes open. David closed and locked the front door, and he guided me up the stairs. His hands were gentle as he helped me out of my clothes. He slipped out of his own silently, seemingly without effort. His chest was warm against my back, and I sighed and settled close against him. "I love you," I whispered as he wrapped his arm around my belly.

"I love you, too," he murmured, and his kiss was soft against the tender hollow behind my ear.

He was gone in the morning.

The sun was high. A quick glance at the clock confirmed it was nearly noon. I struggled out of bed and shimmied into shorts and a T-shirt.

In a working nearly as great as the ritual we'd completed at the lake, the kitchen was somehow clean. Three fresh-baked blueberry muffins sat on a plate. I treated myself to one, spread thick with butter, then decided that a responsible witch kept her energy up. The second was even better than the first, and the third was best of all.

I collected the phone from the counter and went outside to sit on the porch glider.

Clara first. One ring. Two. A clatter and a breathless hello.

"Clara," I said.

"Jeanette!"

I grimaced at the name but remembered my priorities. "I want to thank you—"

"I can't hear you!" She was shouting, loud enough to wake the dead.

"Where are you?" I hollered back, feeling slightly ridiculous.

"By the waterfall, in Oak Canyon! We're restoring our energy by charging our auras!"

Charging auras. My mother and her crazy New Age dreams. She obviously was none the worse for wear after our shared ritual. I shouted back, "Good luck! And thanks!"

"I'll call you when we're through, Jeanette!"

She was gone before I could say anything else. Time for call number two, then. Gran answered on the first ring.

"So, I think I figured it out," I said, without preamble.

"Figured out what, dear?"

"Why you had me move everyone into the house."

"And?"

"I had to know them, inside and out. All their faults, but also the perfection of their power. Without barriers. Without walls."

Her laugh was amused. "The working went well, then?"

"Perfectly. Clara helped."

"So I gathered. She phoned me this morning, right be-fore she headed out to wash her hair in a waterfall, or some-thing like that."

"Something like that."

"She was quite excited. Said she'd been planning some-thing for months. She said, 'It was just like Jeanette's job at the Peabridge, lending books to other libraries. Witches lending power.'"

Interlibrary loan. My mother had compared her magical assistance to an age-old practice in the library world. I said to Gran, "I didn't think Clara paid any attention to the work I did at the Peabridge."

"You'd be surprised, dear. She's quite tickled with the notion of having an Affiliated Institution with your Acade-my."

And in that moment, basking in sunshine and content with the world, I suspected Clara would continue to surprise me, all for the good. Gran and I chatted for a few more minutes, and I promised to come down and see her some time during the next week.

When I hung up, I saw gleaming letters on the phone: Message Waiting. Who knew how long the message had been sitting there? I'd ignored the phone for ages. I dialed up voicemail, fully expecting to hear some telemarketer, some transparent plea for money. Instead, Melissa's voice danced over the line. "Okay, Jane. I've called three times, and you aren't picking up, but I can't wait any longer. You're fired as my maid of honor."

My heart thudded into my throat.

"Rob and I are at the DC courthouse, waiting for a justice of the peace. Next time we talk, I'll be a married woman."

I cut off the message and dialed Melissa's number, but it cut over to voicemail immediately. "You know what to do," said my best friend's laughing voice. "But don't hold your breath for a call back. I'm on my honeymoon. And if this is Mom, I'm sorry. No, I'm not. We'll talk when I get back."

Well, I wasn't going to interrupt her honeymoon with a phone call. I texted her a quick, "Congratulations!" and then I shook my head, thinking about how many contracts she and Rob had broken. Caterers, silhouette artists, hot air balloons... Oh well. He was a lawyer. He'd plow through the paperwork once they got home.

Paperwork. I suddenly flashed on the documents David had taken from the Court. I saw them stacked in the Allen Cask, the instant before the Watchers made them disappear. I heard Pitt's threats, his shouted accusations against David.

And suddenly, I couldn't wait one second longer to see David. I had to touch him, had to confirm that he was safe. I moved without conscious thought, across the lawn, through the woods, back to the lake where so much had happened the night before.

He was standing on the dock, as I'd known he would be. Spot whirled as I approached and came bounding down the planks. I scratched the dog's ears thoroughly before I went to look in the water.

David stepped aside as I approached, but his hand found mine without effort. His fingers laced between mine as I surveyed the results of our working. By daylight, the improvement was even more apparent than it had been the night before. The matted duckweed was gone, as if it had never clogged the surface. The sickly stench of rot was only a memory. Small fish kissed the uprights of the dock, and sunlight rippled over pebbles on the bottom.

"I don't believe it," I said.

"It hasn't been this clear in years."

"That doesn't make any sense. With all the rain, mud should be stirred up."

He squeezed my fingers. "It's magic."

"Like the clean kitchen this morning? I assume you're responsible for that?"

"I run a full service operation."

"You won't find me arguing, as long as blueberry muffins are included. I could eat those every morning for the rest of my life."

He grinned. "Speaking of which…"

He pulled his free hand from his pocket. On his palm was a diamond ring—an emerald cut, perfect in its simplicity. The platinum band gleamed in the sunlight.

"I wanted to do this months ago, on the Fourth of July. But then…" Before either of us could dwell on what had happened that night, he closed the distance between us. "Jane Madison, will you marry me?"

His eyes were laughing. The sun picked out the silver glints at his temples. His fingers were warm around mine, and I could feel the steady drumbeat of his heart. I caught my breath to prolong the perfect moment.

And then I pulled him close and kissed him. I was trembling, shivering with surprise, with happiness, with the aftermath of exhaustion from the night before. He pulled me close and anchored me, steadying me on my feet as I leaned into him. When we finally pulled apart, he said, "I take it that's a yes?"

"Yes," I said. "Yes, I'll marry you."

We both laughed as he slipped the ring onto my finger. But then, I caught his hands in both of mine. "Hecate's Court won't like this."

"Hecate's Court will have to manage."

I set my palm against the firm line of his jaw. "We shouldn't do anything to provoke them. Not with Pitt's accusations out there."

He held my concerned gaze. "We'll deal with Pitt together. If it comes to that."

He made it sound so simple. So easy. But he only spoke the truth. We *would* deal with Pitt together. We already had, solving the puzzle of the documents, binding them in the cask. We'd dealt with everything together—the best parts of launching the magicarium and the worst.

I leaned in and kissed him again, and now I was steady on my feet. He pulled me closer, reaching with his warder's magic to tug on the bond between us. Laughing, I answered with a flick of witchy power.

The sun was low on the horizon before we found our way back to the peace and quiet of the farmhouse.

ABOUT THE AUTHOR

MINDY KLASKY LEARNED to read when her parents shoved a book in her hands and told her she could travel anywhere in the world through stories. She never forgot that advice.

Mindy's travels took her through multiple careers – from litigator to librarian to full-time writer. Mindy's travels have also taken her through various literary genres for readers of all ages – from traditional fantasy to paranormal chick-lit to category romance, from middle-grade to young adult to adult. She is a *USA Today* bestselling author.

In her spare time, Mindy knits, quilts, and tries to tame her endless to-be-read shelf. Her husband and cats do their best to fill the left-over minutes. You can correspond with Mindy at her website: www.mindyklasky.com.

ABOUT BOOK VIEW CAFÉ

BOOK VIEW CAFÉ is a professional authors' publishing cooperative offering books in multiple formats to readers around the world. With authors in a variety of genres including fantasy, romance, mystery, and science fiction, Book View Café has something for everyone.

Book View Café is good for readers because you can enjoy high-quality books from your favorite authors at reasonable prices.

Book View Café is good for writers because 95% of the profits goes directly to the book's author.

Book View Café authors include New York Times and USA Today bestsellers; Nebula, Hugo, Lambda, and Philip K. Dick Award winners; World Fantasy and Rita Award nominees; and winners and nominees of many other publishing awards.

www.bookviewcafe.com

Made in the USA
Coppell, TX
08 April 2020